Avidaura:
War of Wizards

Katlin Murray

For Alex, a true adventurer.

ACKNOWLEDGMENTS

Thank you to all of the usual suspects, the ones that brought this book to life; Alan, my perpetual cover designer, Sarah, the early reader, and everyone in between. From first drafts to final edits my team never fails to inspire me. And as always a very special thank you to the readers, though perhaps I should be apologizing for what is about to come...

WARNING

They watched as the Dragon swooped, circling their village for a second time. It was a moment later that it finally dove in for a landing, right in the center of the main clearing.

Its wingspan was massive, enough to touch the trees and the ocean at the same time. Its scales gleamed in the morning light, casting a sparkle of light over the sand.

Dragons had never ventured into these parts before, they were ill prepared to face a creature of such magnitude.

Gatlin stepped forward, hand on the hilt of his sword; watching as the Dragon turned to face him, ready to face its wrath. His villagers were behind him, swords at the ready.

They would fight if they had to.

Dark beady eyes stared him down, but he did not back up. There was something strange about the way the Dragon stood, so still, not wavering. It sent a chill up his spine.

The great beast could easily take them out with a single blast of its fire. And yet it stood calmly, watching them, waiting for something.

From behind the wing a figure appeared, that of a man stepping forward, the Dragon at his command.

"What a lovely village." He commented lazily, stepping around his Dragon towards Gatlin.

Gatlin kept his hand on the hilt of the sword at his waist, his hooves pawing at the ground impatiently.

"Not even going to welcome me?" The figure stepped closer still, "I suppose that is fine, I have only come to give you and your kind a warning, a courtesy really…" He trailed off, looking over Gatlin's shoulders at the rest of the Centaurs, standing ready.

"A warning?" Gatlin's voice boomed across the quiet clearing.

"Well, yes. A warning." The man had stopped walking, he stood before Gatlin, his robes billowing beside him in the ocean breeze.

Gatlin waited, he would hear the Human out. But the only warning would be a message from him, not to disturb the Centaurs with vague threats.

The man looked amused.

"You and your kind will stand down." He declared, "Avidaura is mine, and I intend you and your kind no harm….as long as you do not stand in my way." His voice rose, allowing the crowd to hear his demands.

"Stand in your way?" Gatlin gripped his hilt.

"I will have this land, and you will not oppose me." The man declared, quite sure of himself.

Gatlin drew his sword, slowly, showing the man the extent of his blade. "This land is ours, you would be best to leave it that way." He stomped his rear hooves, his men followed suit and sending a rumbling across the sand.

"Soon it will all be mine." The man flicked his hand towards Gatlin, the sword flew from his hand. "And there is nothing you can do about it." He smiled sinisterly.

"A Wizard?" Gatlin breathed, his eyes growing wide, "But how?"

"You have been warned." The wizard turned his back and began to walk to his Dragon leaving Gatlin staring after him.

Mavera trotted up beside Gatlin, hand still on his hilt, ready to draw his weapon.

"Stand down." Gatlin, muttered, holding his hand out to stop his comrade from drawing his sword.

They stood no chance against a Wizard who could command Dragons, there were too few in their ranks to make a difference. That certainly didn't mean that they would go down, not without a fight. But it appeared that they would have to stand aside, at least for a while.

Gatlin watched as the Wizard mounted his Dragon. With one final nod of understanding to the Centaur, he was up and away, the down draft from the Dragon's wings causing a stir of sand to swirl around them.

Gatlin bowed his head.

A Wizard had taken Avidaura.

***

Felix walked the border of the camp, he had woken up well before dawn and there was nothing else to do but take a shift on patrol. He hadn't been sleeping well, not since he had become the King.

It wasn't a real title, he wasn't really a King; it was just a ruse to make the men in the woods feel like the world hadn't fallen apart.

He wasn't really sure what to do with the title yet, they expected him to lead them, they expected him to know what he was doing. Zarah had pulled him aside the evening before and given him an ultimatum, decide what they were going to do, or disband the army. They had been sitting in the woods for far too long, supplies were running low. They couldn't live like that, not forever.

So he had to make a decision, fight for Avidaura or learn to live like a commoner under the command of the Dark Wizard, the man who had killed his father and taken the throne.

He knew which choice he *wanted* to make, but it wasn't that simple. He needed to have a plan, and he was running out of time.

He had promised Zarah that he would make a decision by the end of the week, they had enough to live off of until then, after that they would have to find somewhere else to go.

Felix *wanted* to fight for Avidaura, he really did. The only problem was, he had no idea what he was supposed to do to make the world right again. Every time he tried to think of a solution his father drifted into his mind. He would have known exactly what to do to make things right, and he was gone.

Felix's breath caught in his throat as the memory surged back to him. Alone in the woods he could have a moment, but he couldn't show weakness before the army; Zarah had forbade it.

The forest was still and quiet as he walked the familiar border path letting his mind wander. Things in Avidaura had been *too* quiet since the siege, there hadn't been activity at the castle in a while, and it was making the knights nervous. It made Felix nervous too.

The woods however, had been chaotic since the siege on the castle. Many of the knights had been wounded, and those that had escaped captivity in the dungeons had needed extra care after their mistreatment at the castle by the Dark Wizard.

They had lost several men, and one true King, in the siege. Morale was low and everyone was on edge.

Felix knew that Zarah expected him to know what to do, but it was such a strange feeling, knowing that he had become King of the outcasts. It wasn't a real throne, that had been taken from him by the same man that had taken his father.

The Knights in the woods had taken to him like he was their true King, though he knew that he was far from worthy. They had fought at the castle siege and lost, retreating back into the woods like cowards, he had been among them.

Felix had been lucky to have returned to the woods at all, he had been having nightmares of his encounter with the Dark Wizard and that moment where he was sure it would been his last. If Piper and Ash hadn't come to find him, he wouldn't have made it out of the castle at all.

He replayed that scene in his head dozens of times a day, looking for a way to defeat the Wizard. It seemed such an impossible task, even with Piper and Ash on his side, they would need a fool proof plan.

Two Wizards against one, it seemed that the odds were in their favor, but the Dark Wizard had Dragons and an army, and Piper wasn't fully trained. Which left Felix scrambling to find a way to take the land back.

Piper had only just come into her powers, and though Ash had been working with her daily to teach her, she was still a long way from being a true Wizard. And they would need both sisters at full strength if they wanted to stand a chance against the Dark Wizard.

Each day that passed at the camp had become more routine, it was as though he had been exiled, a sentence that his father had once offered him when he was still foolish enough to believe that he deserved the world.

Some days he wondered if he would have been better off exiled instead of taking the quest to save Avidaura. He might have been there to stop the Wizard before he had gotten his claws into the throne. The Kingdom had fallen, despite his efforts to prevent it, it appeared that he had failed.

He knew though, that he still would have ended up in the woods, at least he had Ash and Piper at his side. He wasn't alone.

Zarah had left early that morning when the guard on the perimeter had spotted a Gwin approaching. News was coming, and still Felix hadn't decided how they were going to deal with the Wizard.

Supplies were running low, as Felix walked through the tents he could see that the Knights were feeling it. Their long faces staring up at him, searching for a glimmer of hope that he couldn't give them. It was a horrible feeling to know that they trusted him, and he had nothing to offer in return.

Piper approached, the same look on her tired face, "I heard Zarah found a Gwin. Is there any news?" She asked, quietly so the listening Knights wouldn't overhear.

"A Gwin…" Felix knew that it could only carry bad news, there was no other news to carry in Avidaura anymore.

"What did it say?" Piper whispered, her curiosity showing.

"I won't know until he returns. But I think it's time we called a meeting." Felix glanced around the clearing, "Can you find Ash and Finnigan, tell them to meet in the tent, we can't be sure what kind of news the Gwin has brought." He added.

"Absolutely." Piper nodded solemnly.

Felix watched as she walked away, not sure what exactly they would meet about. He hoped that Zarah had some news that would help them, he was tired of waiting around.

Felix walked to the perimeter to find the guard on duty.

"Send Zarah to the tent when he returns." He asked, watching the guards eyes grow large. "We will be waiting for him." Felix added, trying not to scare the guard into thinking they were in danger.

"Yes my King." He nodded, turning his watchful eyes back into the trees without hesitation.

Felix nodded and returned to the clearing. It would be a while before Zarah returned, and he still didn't know why he had even called a meeting. There was really nothing to discuss unless Zarah had some amazing news that the wizard had just given up.

Still, he paced, trying to look pensive as his mind filtered through all of the ideas that he knew wouldn't work. Trying to find any way to give his men a small sign of hope, a glimmer of victory.

It was time that they made a plan to take Avidaura back. It had been too long with an impostor at the throne, they needed to take a stand. And Felix knew that he couldn't do it alone.

He would need all the help he could find.

Felix had invited Finnigan to join their ranks, he had been fighting for Avidaura far longer than Felix, he knew what was out there, and the Knights trusted him. Plus he knew Felix, and he was one of the few that knew that Felix hadn't aged in the two years that he had been gone across to Piper's world. He was an asset that Felix trusted.

The whole camp had gone silent when Felix entered the tent, like they were trying to listen, or afraid of what might come to pass. Felix peeked out beyond the moss curtain while he waited for the rest of their group, watching the Knights staring.

He couldn't let them down.

Finnigan was quick to arrive, he slipped through the opening at the front of the tent and stopped, seeing Felix staring out at the clearing.

"Piper said you needed me." He whispered, trying not to interrupt Felix's staring.

Felix looked up, if Finnigan thought Felix had lost his mind, he was hiding it well.

"I think it's time for a meeting, a plan." Felix assured Finnigan that there was a real reason for calling him to the only tent. "I'm just waiting for the others to arrive." He added, peeking back out through the crack.

"Who are the others?" Finnigan asked, curious.

"Zarah, Piper and Ash." Felix answered plainly.

"Sounds about right." Finnigan answered, taking a seat on a stack of supplies while they waited.

Zarah was the last to slip past the moss curtain into the tent. They had been waiting for him on the edge of their seats.

Zarah was the leader of the men in the woods, the right hand man of the fallen true King. Felix knew that Zarah was more qualified to be the King than he, it ate away at him to think that he had somehow been given a title that someone else had truly earned. But Zarah didn't seem to mind.

"Are we ready?" Piper asked, pulling out a quill to take notes on a piece of bark.

"As ready as we will ever be." Felix smiled, standing to bow his head to Zarah.

"I call to order the second meeting of the fallen in the woods." Felix declared, returning to his seat on a log.

"We need a better name." Finnigan mused, smiling.

"We will have a better name when we have Avidaura restored." Felix shook his head sadly, "For now, that is all we deserve."

Zarah cut in, before the discussion of their name could continue. "Reports of the Wizard and his Dragon out in the High Village, delivered by a terrified Gwin this morning." He announced, causing the table to hush as they listened with rapt attention. "It appears that he has been visiting all of the villages, asking them to stand down. Ronan reports that he may have visited the Centaurs after his landing in the High Village."

"Centaurs?" Felix seemed surprised, "What would he want with the Centaurs?" He waited for Zarah to answer.

"We can't know for sure, they create the finest of weapons, it is possible that he has tasked them with outfitting his army." Zarah shook his head "It is also possible that he asked them to join him."

"There really is no way of knowing." Ash agreed.

"He has visited most of the villages now. If he hasn't already created an unstoppable army, then he is probably pretty close." Piper commented quietly, striking the Centaurs off of her list.

"Did the High Village join him?" Felix watched Zarah's face for a response.

Zarah shook his head, "The Gwin reported that Ronan stood down, but did not join."

"At least there is that…" Felix muttered, relieved that there hadn't been more deserters.

The Wizard had already amassed an army of men who had once been loyal to the King, his father. Felix couldn't bear to hear of any more men changing sides. They were already outnumbered.

"We need to do something." Felix stood, pacing at the head of the table. "There aren't enough of us to stop him, we need more."

"You are right Felix." Zarah paused. "There are not enough of us to stop him, the siege was proof enough."

Felix stopped pacing, staring at Zarah, he seemed defeated. Felix felt his stomach drop, if Zarah didn't think they could take Avidaura back then they were truly lost.

"What about the Low Village." Piper cut in.

"What about it?" Felix turned, resuming his pacing.

"How many do you think they could spare to join us?" She asked, a spark in her eye. "How many that are still true to the King?"

Felix smiled, turning to Finnigan.

"How many do you think would join us Finnigan?"

Finnigan looked up at the canopy overhead, thinking.

"About a hundred, if they were willing." He finally answered.

"And what about the High Village?" Felix continued, watching as Zarah lit up again, "How many do you think they would spare?"

"At least fifty…" Zarah answered, suddenly hopeful again.

"That's better than nothing." Felix smiled. "We could send a Gwin, ask them to send their best."

"I don't think the Gwin are willing to venture out, there are too many Dragons about…" Zarah noted, remembering how terrified the Gwin had been that morning, and how he had chosen to walk the forest path instead of flying.

"It's too dangerous for them." Ash agreed, "We would have to go ourselves."

"Would that even be enough Zarah? He has Dragons on his side…" Piper seemed concerned still.

"Who else could we count on to take Avidaura back?" Ash piped in.

"The Clurichaun." Piper exclaimed, bringing back memories of the small warriors who had taken out a Giant so effortlessly.

"The Dark Fairies." Felix added turning to Piper. "Make a list, we are going to have a lot to get done."

Piper began to write frantically, listing all of the creatures of Avidaura that may be willing to help them set the land straight again.

"We will need a proper camp to prepare, these woods are not suited for a crowd that large." Zarah noted when the tent had fallen silent again.

"Then we will have to move to the Low Village." Felix decided, "They are better equipped for the preparations that we will need to make. I am sure they will welcome us."

"Then we shall prepare to move the camp." Zarah agreed "We will send a messenger to let them know we are coming." Zarah decided putting an end to their meeting, there would be lots of work to be done. And they needed to move swiftly.

"We move at dusk." Felix declared.

Within the hour the camp had become a flurry of activity. Carts were filled, wood was chopped, they were preparing to move the camp.

Zarah had sent a scout ahead to inform the Village of the move, he was hopeful that they would open their gates to them. Felix had sent a letter to accompany the scout, it was the best that they could provide on such short notice.

Felix and Piper walked the perimeter on watch while the camp slowly disappeared around them. Ash had taken the other side of the camp, insisting that she was fine on her own, she seemed to have a lot on her mind after their discussion.

Felix preferred the company.

"Do you really think they will join us?" Felix asked after their second lap.

"I don't see why they wouldn't." Piper considered, "If you were given a choice between watching your world fall apart or taking a stand, which would you choose?"

"I would take a stand." Felix smiled, "But that doesn't mean they will be willing to stand with us..." He trailed off.

"You think they would stand on their own?"

"They might choose that..."

"It's worth trying anyway." Piper smiled, giving his hand a squeeze. "It's better than doing nothing."

"You're right." Felix mused, growing silent as they walked the perimeter again.

The Knights had nearly finished compacting the entirety of the camp. Six carts and a quiet crowd was all that was left of the once busy clearing.

Felix paused to watch, what had once been a bustling community had been packed up, there was nothing left for them in the woods.

It was time to move on.

Dusk would be approaching soon, and with the darkness the first cart would be moving on. They had agreed to separate for the journey. One cart at a time, to ease the tension.

Felix would be leaving with the first group, to guide the way to the Village and make way for the rest of the Fallen army in the Low Village.

He turned to Piper, "You're going with the second cart." He decided.

It would be difficult not knowing where Piper, Zarah and Ash were. But he couldn't bear to wait that long to know that Piper was safe.

"Sure." She smiled. "Should we finish the sweep before you leave?"

Felix nodded, following her as she walked the perimeter with him one last time.

It seemed so quiet, the calm had set Felix on edge. He couldn't help but feel like something was not right, as they swept the perimeter back to the camp he stopped again, afraid to ask the one question that was on the tip of his tongue.

Piper stopped when she realized that he wasn't walking anymore.

"What is it?" She asked, eying the trees, searching for danger.

"What if we don't win?" Felix asked quietly. It wasn't a question he had ever said out loud before, though it had been rattling around in his head for days.

Piper stared him dead in the eyes. "Then we go down fighting." Her face was serious, "Avidaura is worth fighting for." She added, turning away before Felix could respond.

In silence they continued their last walk towards the camp, Felix's mind was reeling. If a girl who had been raised in another world could feel so strongly about fighting for Avidaura, then they had to give it everything they had.

They would get Avidaura back, or he would die trying.

FALLEN

Ash was out patrolling the woods by the King's path, keeping to the brush to stay under cover and unseen. Normally it was a job that was done in pairs, but she had insisted that they would need the extra hands to pack up the camp.

She could see the turrets of the castle poking over the tops of the trees across the water on the other side of the path. Smoke billowed from the castle spiraling over the forest, dark and ominous. Something was happening at the castle, it distracted her from watching the pathway as carefully as she should have. She paused in the brush and stared across the waters wondering why it was suddenly busy with life. It had been days since they had seen any activity at the castle, clearly the Wizard had finally returned from his travels across the land.

Ash knew that she would have to inform Zarah of the activity, he would want to know that the Wizard had returned. It could only mean one thing, he had finally amassed his army and he was settling in as the King of Avidaura. They were running out of time to stop him.

It was about time Felix finally stepped up and made a decision, he had been their King for nearly a week, and the Knights were starting to doubt him. The entire Kingdom was crumbling and they had been reduced to living like savages in the woods. Most of the Knights had been there for years, some had only just escaped from the castle dungeon, it was clear that they expected their King to know what he was doing and have a plan already in place.

It was a lot to ask of Felix, only weeks had passed since he had left on his quest to stop the disturbance at the Field of Mirrors, but Avidaura had continued on without them. A lot had happened in their brief stay on the other side. He had come a long way from the unruly Prince to where he was now but it still wasn't enough to prepare him for what was expected of a King.

Ash found herself facing the same dilemma, she had only been a Wizard's apprentice two weeks ago. Then the world had flipped on its head and she was suddenly expected to know how to be the High Wizard.

Her first task hadn't been an easy one, the ritual of the King was a sacred spell, she hadn't even seen it done in her lifetime. Ash had only had her father's notes to guide her, and the look on Felix's face as she had laid his father to rest in the skies of the Idimmu Mountains had been pressure enough. She was expected to carry herself differently, know answers that she couldn't possibly know, and guide Piper as her apprentice when she had only just discovered they were sisters, and Piper had just learned of her power.

And it was all her fault.

If she hadn't been so determined to see her mother, if she hadn't taken off through the mirror, if she had only *asked* her father; he might have still been with them.

The guilt came in waves, thoughts of her father turning sour as she remembered that he was gone because of her. She had been so foolish, and now Avidaura sat in ruins. She didn't deserve to be the High Wizard, and Felix didn't seem ready to be King, but there was no one left to take their place.

There was no one left.

Ash let out a slow breath, calming herself as she walked the perimeter again. With the camp moving at dusk it was important that she watch the path, they couldn't afford to lose any more Knights.

Not a single person had passed by the woods on the path during her watch, it was unnerving. She began to wonder if there was something else happening that they should be worried about, it was too quiet for her liking and the castle seemed to be bustling with life. Usually there were Dark Knights patrolling the paths, she had memorized their schedule, they walked past at perfectly timed intervals, watching the woods.

They still hadn't discovered where the camp was, but she was willing to bet that they had narrowed it down. It was certainly a good idea that they were moving before they were captured, or worse.

Ash turned into the trees to check on the camp, it was still bustling with life, though she hadn't been able to hear it from the trees by the pathway. The Knights were making quick work of dismantling the camp, piece by piece it was coming apart.

Zarah approached, a wary look on his face.

"Is everything alright." He asked quietly, looking over his shoulder to be sure he wasn't overheard.

"The path is quiet." Ash whispered back, "Too quiet."

"The Dark Knights are still passing?"

"Not a single one, but there is smoke coming from the castle." Ash added.

"I think Felix was right," Zarah muttered, "It is time we moved camp. I will tell them to hurry." He added.

"Are we still going to stagger the carts?" Ash asked, curious.

"We will still stagger them, but I might ask them to take cover while they wait." Zarah seemed thoughtful.

The news of the silent path had set him on edge, much like it had for Ash. The Dark Wizard was up to something, and it couldn't be good.

"I will go guard the perimeter until dusk." Ash nodded a farewell to Zarah and turned back towards the path.

"Don't go alone." Zarah stared at Ash as though he already knew she would defy him.

"It is better if I go alone, you need all the hands you can get to prepare the move." Ash answered, much like Zarah had expected.

"Be safe." Zarah whispered after her. She was right, she could handle it alone, and he would need the knights to prepare.

"Always." She smiled, turning back to stare at the camp one last time before it disappeared into nothing.

When she returned to the cover by the path she could tell that something was wrong. It was silent, absolutely silent. Not a single bird chirping, not a breeze through the leaves.

Something was coming.

From a distance she could see a dark shape escape from the black smoke that plumed from the castle towers. A Dragon had taken to the sky.

She considered turning back to alert the others, but the Dragon was near enough to see her if she moved. She would draw too much attention trying to alert them.

Ash ducked below the brush, looking overhead to see if she had enough coverage. She had heard that the Wizard had been making rounds to the Villages of Avidaura, but this was the first time she had seen a Dragon since the Badlands, it was clear that he had gained them as his allies.

Beneath the cover of the trees, Ash watched, wondering where the Dragon was off to, it was then that she noticed it circling.

It swooped overhead, scales glistening in the mid afternoon sun. The draft from its wings sent the foliage stirring around her and she had to move to take cover before she was seen.

She should have retreated, returned to camp and told them to take cover. But something about the Dragon enticed her to stay.

Ash stared as it looped around, lazily trailing its wing tips in the castle moat as it lowered, finally landing on the pathway right in front of the place that she was hidden.

She held her breath, watching as it sat down on its hind legs like a pet, staying still and silent. The Dragons in the Badlands hadn't behaved like this one, they had been wild, uncivilized. This Dragon seemed tamed, controlled.

From behind the wing a figure appeared, stepping past the Dragon towards the edge of the path, staring into the trees where Ash was hiding.

"Dear, there is no use hiding, I know that you are there." The Wizard seemed amused, waiting for Ash to show herself to him.

She hesitated for a moment, did he really know that she was there or was he just hoping that she was?

"Ash, I can see you." He smiled, his eyes turning towards her knowingly. "I am not here to hurt you." He added, though Ash didn't believe him.

She had been seen, the Dark Wizard and his Dragon were staring right at her. She was left with two choices, stand and face him alone, or lead him into the clearing and give up the army.

She had already made her choice, standing slowly, she tried to make herself look tall and proud. If she was going to die, then she would do it on her own terms. She wouldn't risk any more lives for hers, never again.

"Well, you have certainly grown well." He tipped his head to Ash, a small smile crossing his face.

Ash stood still and silent, she wouldn't engage in his conversation. She still wasn't sure where it was going, and she wasn't about to choose her last words, not yet at least.

The Dark Wizard stepped closer, "Do you not remember me?" He seemed slightly offended.

Ash stared at his face, his features coming into focus. She hadn't dared look directly at him in the castle, her concentration had taken too much of her energy to be bothered.

There was a look about him that seemed familiar, like a face from the past. He carried some of her father's features, the dark eyes, the tilted chin.

"Darius…" Ash whispered the name under her breath, the Wizard was clearly playing tricks on her.

"So you *do* remember me." He took another step forward. "It has been so long."

"Darius is dead." Ash's voice had grown cold at the cruel trick.

"Dead? No, I am afraid that is just what your father wanted you to think." His eyes flashed with anger, "He locked me away and took my place as High Wizard."

"No," Ash was certain, "Darius is dead."

Her body had grown ridged, she remembered well the day that her Uncle had been sent to the beyond, he had died and her father had become the Hight Wizard of Avidaura. She would never forget that day, it was the same week that her mother had left her.

"And yet," He smiled, "Here I am…it makes you wonder."

"No." Ash stared him down.

"I see that you have a younger sister," He continued on as though she were cooperating with his conversation, "are you certain that she will not take your place as my brother took mine?"

His eyes were knowing, and for a brief moment Ash considered what he was saying.

"Never." She tried to sound sure, but the Wizard heard the waver in her voice.

"She is quite close to your new *King*." He sounded amused for a moment, "Are you sure that she wouldn't be better suited as *his* High Wizard?" Darius stared at Ash and it felt like his eyes were seeing right through her.

"She wouldn't take my place." Ash defended her sister.

"That's what I thought about Fallon," Darius paused with a sigh, "Until the day he locked me away..." He trailed off thoughtfully.

Ash stared, waiting.

"You know..." He continued, "You *could* join me. I could use some company when the new realm is created. And what better company than family." He smiled.

Ash said nothing, she stared at him, waiting for him to reveal his plan.

"She wouldn't be able to stop you, you would be on the winning side. We would make an unstoppable team." He continued.

Darius leaned in, "And *I* wouldn't take your place...we would be equals." He hissed.

Ash had already made her decision, she had made it the day she had found her father charred in the front door of their home. She would stand for Avidaura and she would defeat the person who had killed him. Darius, the Dark Wizard who had taken Avidaura at its knees, was not an ally she wished to have.

And if it was the last thing she ever said, if this was her last moment in Avidaura, she would not stand down.

"I would never join you." She growled, her steely eyes boring down on the man before her. She had made her stand, her fists balled at her side and the magic flowing through her. She felt it pulsing from her, ready to ignite.

"That's too bad." Darius frowned, "Then you shall fall with your friends."

He turned away, mounting his dragon with a final nod.

Ash glowered at him, waiting for his beast to finish her. She would stand tall, she would make it known that she was not on his side, and never would be.

Instead his dragon leapt into the sky, beating its wings as they disappeared onto the horizon.

It seemed that she was frozen for a while, staring after the blank spot on the horizon where the Dark Wizard had disappeared. Finally she fell to her knees, the magic that had been radiating from her slowly dissipating as she took a long deep breath.

She could have died.

It felt foolish now, how she had dared stand against the Dark Wizard on her own, she *should have* died.

But he had let her live.

Her hands were shaking, nausea rushing through her, she was going to be sick. Turning to the side of the path she heaved what was left in her stomach, wiping her mouth with the sleeve of her cloak before collapsing to the ground.

***

"Are you okay?"

Ash turned, Piper was standing inside of the tree line, her face white with concern. Ash looked up at the sky, Dusk was not far off. She wasn't sure how long she had been sitting there, shaking, but time had passed quickly.

"Yeah." Ash brushed herself off and stood, following Piper through the trees, "Is it time?" She asked, changing the conversation before Piper could ask her any more questions.

Piper passed her a look of concern, "Yeah, the first cart is about to depart." She sounded worried.

"Is Felix leading?"

"Yes." Piper frowned.

"He'll be fine, Piper. And we will be following soon after." Ash rolled her eyes, Piper and Felix had certainly bonded, the Wizard had been right about that.

"You're coming with me?" Piper looked hopeful.

"Yes, second wave, that's us. We stick together." Ash smiled, nudging her sister in the side.

That was the one thing that the Wizard hadn't understood. Ash and Piper hadn't grown up together, but the moment that they had met they had instantly become friends. He couldn't break them apart, not with their bond. Piper would never do anything to hurt Ash, and she certainly wouldn't take her place as High Wizard, of that Ash was sure.

They broke through into the clearing to a stoic scene. The men were taking cover, up in the trees and down in the brush. All that remained were the first wave. Felix stood at the cart with his men, ready to lead them to the Village.

He waved at Ash and Piper, breaking away from the group to walk over to them.

"We're ready." He nodded, looking back at the cart waiting for him.

"We will follow." Ash nodded back to him.

"Wait for Zarah's signal, he will tell you when it is clear to go." Felix turned from Piper to look at Ash, "Are you okay?" He asked.

Ash brushed her hand through her hair, "I'm fine, we're ready." She shook her head.

"Okay." Felix stared at her for a moment longer, "We will see you at the Village." He pulled Piper in for a hug, and then turned to Ash, wrapping his arm around her as he leaned in, "Keep her safe…" He whispered.

Ash nodded as he pulled away, turning to join his men at the first cart.

***

The men were waiting when Felix returned to the cart, Zarah stood at the side, watching as Felix rounded up his troops.

"Stay close, stay quiet. Signal if you see anything." Felix kept it short and simple. Nodding to Zarah before he took one of the handles, heaving the front of the cart from the forest floor.

Finnigan had joined Felix for the first wave, he carried a map in his hand, leading them through the brush and the trees with ease. They had decided to avoid the pathway for as long as possible, even though it made dragging the cart more difficult.

There were five more carts that would be following behind them, they had to make sure that they were not spotted on the open path, or they would lose numbers, and Felix wasn't willing to take that risk.

Night fell quicker under the cover of the trees, but they dared not light any torches. Moving in the shadows they trailed through the forest winding around trees and leaving a path for the carts that would soon follow. Several hours had passed before Finnigan turned and stopped.

Felix lowered the cart. "Is it time?" He asked, staring ahead through the trees.

Finnigan nodded in the dark, "Short pass through up ahead, and the gates shouldn't be far off."

Felix turned to his men who were eagerly waiting for his command. "We are out in the open, keep your eyes sharp." He hissed, hefting the cart back up.

"Lead us in Finnigan."

Finnigan turned back to the trees and started forward, leading them through the brush and onto the proper path. Felix could hear his heart racing, it was the most exposed they had been in a long while, no trees to hide them from the watchful eye of their enemy and his Dragons.

It was all up to luck now.

The short pass through the trees and across the pathway seemed to take forever, they pulled the cart slowly, afraid to make too much noise as they approached the Village gates.

Letting the cart fall gently to the ground, Felix stepped forward, his fist hovering before the giant wooden doors before he knocked.

One deep breath in, and he rapped his knuckles against the wood. Waiting for a response.

It felt like a lifetime before the click of a latch was heard. Slowly a peep hole was opened.

"Answer." A deep voice called into the night.

"Felix, the King of the Fallen." He responded, the title seemed fitting to him, despite the protests of Finnigan and the others.

"You shall enter, my King." The eyes dipped down as the man behind the door bowed, a courtesy that Felix didn't feel worthy of. It appeared the Low Village would accept them, and that was all that mattered.

"Thank you." Felix whispered as the gates slowly opened, allowing their cart and men to pass through.

Beyond the gates, the Village was bustling with life, more than there had ever been on any evening when Felix had ventured over in his youth. Fires were lit, bread was baking, tables lined the street filled with foods.

A feast had been prepared for them, a welcome sight after the weeks in the woods, for his men much longer. There had been a time when he would have expected this kind of welcome, but with all of the trials that he had faced the mere sight of it all brought a tear to his eye.

"Come, King Felix, have a seat, feast." The Village Chief, Evan, bowed, approaching Felix with a smile.

Felix was breathless, he had done so many things to this very village in his time, and they had welcomed him with open arms, a fallen King.

He nodded to Evan, smiling as best as he could muster while trying to keep his tears at bay. "I will wait for the rest of my Knights. Thank you for such a warm welcome, I am sure these men could use the rest." He turned to the gates, nodding to his men that they may eat and rest while he waited for the rest of their party.

There were very few things that he had learned from his father, but in that moment he knew that he could not sit and eat without the Knights from the woods at his side, he owed them that much at the very least.

RISING

Felix stood silently by the gates of the Low Village, drowning out the sounds of the merry feast behind him as he waited for the last of the carts to arrive. It was difficult, his stomach rolled as each fresh scent filled the air, but he dared not turn and look, for fear that he wouldn't be able to stop himself. He still had to figure out what was going to happen next.

They had moved their camp, it was a choice that would keep them alive. But there was still more to plan, more to discuss, and Felix tried to busy himself with thoughts of plots while he waited.

The Knights from the woods were cheerful, more than Felix had ever seen them. At the sight of fresh warm food it was as though they had forgotten all of their troubles, if only for a brief while. It had been a good move to bring them to the Village, if only to boost their morale. They had been hiding in the woods for far too long.

But soon Felix would have to press forward with the rest of his half formed plan. Soon they would have to make plans to reach out to the High Village, the King of the Fairies, and the leader of the Clurichaun.

There would be no time for rest, as soon as the last cart entered the Village, he had to be ready to go. Though he had made a choice to move to the Village and recruit other creatures in Avidaura to fight for their cause, there was still the matter of how they could possibly take back the throne.

The Wizard was more powerful that he had imagined, his brief encounter in the throne room had shown just how useless he would be against a foe who could wield magic. Even with Ash and Piper, mostly trained Wizard's, at his side, there was no way they could ever fully defeat him.

He had tried to take Avidaura before, Felix had heard the stories around the campfire. Not even Fallon and his Father had been able to stop the Dark Wizard from rising, they had trapped him in a spell, a spell that had broken when the magic in Avidaura had nearly been drained by a mirror.

Felix couldn't make the same mistake, whatever happened to the Wizard it would have to be permanent. He wouldn't risk Avidaura being brought to its knees again, not in his lifetime, not in the next.

It was nearly an hour before the next cart arrived, announcing itself with a soft knock on the gates. The chatter at the feast had died down as the Knights had left to find a place to rest. Felix stepped forward, watching as the gate guards opened the hatch. They looked back to him as two soft eyes smiled in from outside.

"This one of yours?" The guard asked.

Felix nodded, "Let them in."

Piper was the first to enter the Village, racing straight to Felix as the caravan followed behind her and Ash took up the rear.

"We made it." She breathed, a smile plastered on her face as she looked about the busy Low Village. Already a second feast was being delivered to the tables to welcome more of the Rogue Knights.

"You didn't have any trouble, did you?" Felix asked, looking over Piper's shoulder at Ash, who seemed stiff as she made her way past the cart towards him.

"We found a Gwin on the trail." Piper whispered, "He seems to be injured." She pointed back at the cart, Felix could see the twisted shape of the Gwin, its wing clearly damaged as they rolled it past him.

"Are they taking it to the medic?"

"Yes." Piper nodded.

"It carried no message." Ash added, joining them.

"No message at all?" Felix wondered why it had found them.

"It has said nothing." Ash shook her head, "I even tried to get it to talk." She added, flustered.

"I see." Felix stared after it, he had been worried that the Gwin had carried bad news. Not that there was really any bad news left to be had.

"Was he alone?" Felix asked after a moment.

"He was alone." Ash confirmed, "I don't know where the rest of the Gwin have gone, but he will be safer here." She added.

Felix nodded, he was curious where the Gwin had all disappeared to, it was clear that it was unsafe for them to fly and take messages across the land, but he had never really considered where they came from before. Perhaps it was time that he found out.

He watched as the cart passed him, the Gwin resting atop the supplies from the woods. He looked wounded, singed by a fire, Felix could smell it on him. But the Gwin had closed its eyes, if Felix was going to talk to it, it would have to wait until later.

"You two should eat." Felix changed the subject, directing the sisters to the table where the Knights they had traveled with were beginning their feast, "You've had a long day."

"They finally made you that feast..." Piper laughed, remembering the Prince when she had first met him.

Felix chuckled, "I was hoping you didn't remember that."

"How could I forget." Piper raised a brow, "Are you coming?" She asked, turning to follow Ash to the table.

"I should wait for the other caravans."

"Okay." Piper smiled and sauntered off after her sister.

Felix stayed at his post by the gate, waiting for the next caravan. He couldn't help but feel relieved that Piper and Ash had made it through without any trouble, but Zarah wouldn't be arriving until the last caravan came tumbling through the gates. If the Wizard caught wind of their move, he was the one facing the most danger.

Felix had his sword at his side, he thumbed the hilt, hoping that he wouldn't need to use it. As the King, it was his job to ensure the safety of all of his Knights, and there were still many wandering through the woods towards the safety of the Village.

Soon the caravans began to arrive at regular intervals, each more tired than the last. Felix had begun to lose count as each had crossed into the village, but he knew that he hadn't seen Zarah arrive yet, so there would still be more to come.

Each meal that Felix stood through was harder than the last, his stomach ached with the pains of hunger, but he kept his mind on the task at hand. He still had to have a plan when Zarah arrived, and he couldn't let the delicious scent of food distract him from the real reason they had moved to the Village.

Avidaura was still in trouble.

***

It was well into the early morning hours when the last of the carts ventured through the gates to the Low Village.

Each cart had seemed more tired than the last as Felix had watched them, greeting each with open arms. The Village had quickly become full, Felix had never seen so many people in one place. He worried that they wouldn't have enough room, until the villagers began ushering Knights into other areas, preparing small tents in the streets to accommodate their army. It seemed that for once the Knights would have somewhere warm to sleep.

Felix was still standing at the entrance, his stomach rumbling, fighting off his tiredness when he saw Zarah enter. The last of the Fallen Knights. Felix felt the relief wash through him, his tired stiff muscles finally relaxing as he saw the face he had been waiting for.

Leaving Zarah behind had been one of the hardest parts; but to ensure that all of the Knights made it safely through the move they had decided that Felix would lead, and Zarah would take up the last, making sure that everything ran smoothly, and no one was left behind.

The Villagers had kept the feast going, the tables had been replenished with each wave of Knights, those that had been fed were given a place to sleep. Shops had been transformed into sleeping quarter for the Fallen, the Village had become a refuge for all those who had and would fight for Avidaura.

Zarah approached, looking just as weary as Felix felt.

"Your travels went well?" Felix asked, welcoming him with a bear hug.

Zarah seemed taken back by Felix gesture. It hadn't been that long ago for Felix that Zarah had seemed a pain in his side, but the Royal Advisor had grown on him, become family.

"Yes. The camp is gone." Zarah confirmed, they had left no man behind.

"Then let us feast." Felix smiled, finally allowing himself to feel the hunger pains that had been rolling through his stomach all night.

As Felix and Zarah sat at the table with the last of the Fallen Knights, a silent hush fell over the town. Felix looked to Zarah, all of the Knights had turned to him.

"They expect you to speak, King." Zarah whispered under his breath.

Felix nodded, taking the time to stand and appear bold while he thought about his words.

"To the ones that fight for Avidaura." Felix's voice boomed across the table, he raised his glass to them, "We shall have our land back, our new journey begins today!" He raised his glass higher and dipped his head, hoping that that was enough of a speech to appease the Knights.

"Here, here." They cheered, raising their cups as Felix returned to his seat.

"Was that okay?" Felix leaned towards Zarah, lowering his voice as he reached for a piece of bread.

"It was exactly what they needed to hear." Zarah nodded, a small knowing smile upon his lips.

Felix filled his plate, it seemed like he had been waiting for this very feast since the day he had left the castle on his first quest. He finally felt like he had earned a hot meal, and each bite seemed to warm him to the bones.

Living in the woods had taken its toll, he watched the Knights at the table with him, ripping through their food like they might never see another morsel again. He felt the same, and tried to restrain himself. He was the King, he was expected to appear well mannered and presentable. Though he wished for nothing more than to fill his stomach and have a long rest.

When the last feast had finally ended, dawn was already breaking over the Village walls. Though Felix was exhausted, those that had rested were expecting him to have a plan.

"Zarah, I have to call a meeting. Could you gather the others?" Felix leaned over to his companion, he could see the rest of the Knights watching expectantly.

He rose from the table, "Rest, we have much to do." He called across the table to the last of the Fallen. Nodding to them as they rose from the table.

He would find the Village Chief, Evan, while Zarah gathered the others.

Evan was waiting by the Gate at the guard post, well rested and smiling when he found him.

"Did they all make it?" He asked, glancing at the guarded gates.

"Yes. Thank you for welcoming us."

"It was the least we could do," Evan paused, "what happens now?" His voice had lost its cheerful edge, the reminder of the state of Avidaura hanging in the air.

"Is there a place we could meet with my council?" Felix inquired.

Evan nodded, "This way." He turned into the Village and led Felix through the crowd.

As they walked through the Village, Felix could see remnants of his past, buildings that he had visited often, ones that had burned from the fires. Finally Evan led him around a bend and held out his arm.

"The tavern should suffice." He smiled knowingly.

"You've rebuilt it!" Felix exclaimed, "It looks wonderful."

"I am sure the barkeep would be willing to accommodate us." Evan smiled, ushering Felix though the door.

The bar was exactly as Felix remembered, the musky scent of ale, the worn bar stools, the dim windows. It was hard to believe that the last time he had seen it it had been a pile of ash scattered across the ground.

It had been his own doing that had ruined the tavern, and much of the Low Village. He had been a brazen Prince, who had only wanted to see how fireworks looked, he hadn't known that the consequences of lighting them off inside of a tavern would be so devastating.

That event had shaped his life, it had been the final straw for his father, the reason that Felix had been sent across Avidaura on his quest. That moment had changed him forever.

Felix stopped inside of the doorway, looking across the dim lit bar as the memories came back to him. If that one moment hadn't happened, he wouldn't be where he was, Piper might not have made it alone in Avidaura, Ash might not have closed the mirror.

There was one thing that wouldn't have changed through, the Wizard would have still been freed; and Avidaura would still been conquered.

"Well," The barkeep leaned across the bar, "is that who I think it is?" He smiled with his crooked grin, staring at Felix across the room.

Felix snapped out of his daze and smiled back, taking another step into the tavern, "Fredrick." He beamed, "How are you?"

"I am well, you haven't brought any more fireworks? Have you?" He laughed.

"No." Felix tried to hide a blush that was creeping onto his cheeks, "Not this time." He shook his head.

"Fredrick, we will need the bar." Evan announced, approaching the bartender behind his counter.

Fredrick looked across the bar at Evan, his chipper expression turning grim.

"As you wish." He nodded, quickly ushering the patrons out of the building.

Zarah returned as the building was clearing, "They should arrive shortly." He nodded to Felix, looking for a table that would accommodate their council.

Felix followed him and sat. There was much to think about while he waited.

Finnigan arrived first, quietly taking his place at the table. He seemed off, like returning to his Village had not been as grand as he had expected it to be. Piper and Ash entered shortly after, whispering as they closed the doors.

Felix stood, waiting for them to take their places. When everyone had settled, he began.

"I call to order the first meeting of the Rising." Felix nodded at Finnigan, who smirked.

"We have made the move to the Low Village, a more appropriate place to base our operations, thank you to Chief Evan for allowing us to operate here."

Evan nodded.

"We have determined that there are others who may wish to join us in our quest for Avidaura. Piper, do you still have the list?"

Piper pulled the piece of bark from her robes, sliding it across the table to Felix.

Felix looked across the table, "It appears that we only have enough for two teams. Evan we will ask you to stay with your Village, Piper and Finnigan will be with me. Ash and Zarah, you travel together. Find one of the Knights to bring your party up to three." Felix looked at the list again.

"I am familiar with the High Village," Ash interjected, "And Zarah has ties there, would it be best if we made that journey?" She added as an afterthought.

"Felix has a way to travel to the Dark Fairies, and the Clurichaun are near there, we could cover them both with Finnigan." Piper added, nodding to Ash before Felix could change his mind.

Zarah looked across the table, "Are you sure about traveling into the Forest of Night?" He asked Felix, his voice filled with concern.

Piper spoke up, "The Fairies have been affected just as much as the rest of Avidaura." She sounded like she knew what she was talking about, "I don't know if they will join us, but they will at least know of a way to help."

"They seemed to know a lot about Dragons." Felix added thoughtfully. "And we will need a way to keep the Dragons at bay. I am sure they would be willing to share some of that information with us."

"The Fairies do not deal with Humans." Evan shook his head, "They only take what they need." He added, his face sour.

Felix smiled, "I would like to try."

"Are you sure?" Zarah asked again, he seemed to be worried about Felix departing without him.

"I will have Piper and Finnigan with me, there is nothing to worry about." He decided.

"And what of the Village?" Evan asked, "Is there anything we can do here while you are away?"

Felix nodded, "You have Smiths, we will need them to repair some weapons, anything you have really."

"I can have that done." Evan agreed, clearly expecting more.

"Lodgings," Felix added, "and anything that the Knights need to prepare for the final battle. We need netting, something heavy that can contain a Dragon, we need to stop the Dragons from traveling."

"I have heard that there are ways, I will put my best men on it." Evan nodded sternly.

"The rest of my Knights are at your disposal." Felix added to Evan, "Have them fortify your Village, make them useful."

"That I will." The Chief nodded again.

"How soon should we be prepared to depart?" Ash asked, looking across the table. Felix and Zarah had yet to sleep, though morning had reached the Village.

"Then I suppose there is nothing left to discuss, prepare to depart at dawn." Felix tilted his head to the gathering at the table, "we have a long journey ahead, all of us."

The meeting ended soon after the sun had risen over the wall. Ash and Piper had departed to prepare for their trips, and Zarah to rest. There was still one last thing that Felix wanted to deal with before he even considered resting or preparing to travel through the forest of night.

The Gwin.

Felix crossed the Village, slipping though the morning rush and into the medical building before anyone noticed that he was there. The building was full, Knights from the woods having their wounds treated properly after their time in the wilderness, wounds that hadn't quite healed since the siege on the castle.

When he entered, the front room seemed to grow silent.

A medic approached, hands covered in brine from a dressing that he had been applying.

"I am here to speak to the Gwin." Felix said softly.

"He's at the end." The medic nodded, returning to his patient.

Felix crossed though the room, not daring to glance at the patients being treated, they were in enough of a fragile state, he didn't need to gawk. When he reached the last bed the curtains were drawn nearly the whole way around.

Felix stepped past the curtain, the Gwin was perched on the end of the bed, his wing's wrapped, a pained look in his eyes.

"Hello." Felix stepped closer, the Gwin raised its head and looked at him, startled to see someone standing before it.

"King Felix" He gasped, bowing his head, though it looked as though it caused him pain.

Felix pulled up a chair and sat before the Gwin, meeting him at eye level.

"What happened to you?" He asked, curious of the strange wounds on the Gwin, that had been covered. He appeared to be missing quite a few feathers.

"The Dragons, they ran me right out of the sky."

"Were they chasing you?"

"No." The Gwin's eyes fell.

"Are the rest of your kind safe?" Felix asked after a moment.

The Gwin looked up, the expression on his face unreadable, "For now." His eyes looked haunted.

"Is there anything I can do to keep you safe?" Felix asked.

Gwin in Avidaura were like nothing Felix had ever known. They were messengers and until he had seen one injured he had never really considered that they too were a race that fell under the protection of the throne. He wouldn't allow himself to be the kind of King that left the Gwin when the world was falling apart.

The Gwin's beak twisted into what Felix could only assume was a wild smirk, there was a fire in his eyes.

"We can fight." He answered.

QUEST

Ash was prepared to leave the Village before the first signs of dawn had appeared across the darkened sky. Zarah had found a Knight to accompany them in their quest, a young lad by the name of Tor who had been raised in the High Village. He was eager, and waited at Ash's side for Zarah to gather his thoughts that morning.

They wouldn't have time to say goodbye to Felix and Piper, the two were on the other side of the Village preparing to depart into the woods. They had said their farewells the night before at their final meeting of the Rising.

"Zarah, are we ready?" Ash asked as he approached, adjusting the satchel at her side, it seemed heavy since her last travels.

"As ready as we'll ever be." He smiled, leading the way to the wall that towered over the Village.

There was a secondary exit to the Low Village, that was not often used. It opened up into the forest, only a half an hour walk from the main path that led to the High Village.

Evan was there to guide them through the exit, and make sure that it was secure once they had left the Village. They would have to take the long way on their return, but if the quest went well, there would be many of them returning, they wouldn't be so exposed and alone.

"Safe travels." Evan smiled, opening a small door in the wall.

Ash wouldn't have ever noticed that there was a door there if it hadn't opened before them, it was so small and blended perfectly with the rest of the wall, it was easy to see how it had been kept a secret.

"Thank you, we shall return as soon as possible." Ash smiled back, ducking under the door and into the woods beyond.

When the door closed behind them Ash turned back. The door had vanished, and they were alone in the woods. There would be no turning back for them, not until they had managed to make it to the High Village and seek help.

They had not been able to send a scout to the High Village to announce them, they were showing up unexpected. The Gwin had all gone into hiding, somewhere in Avidaura that not even Ash knew about. They hadn't seen one overhead in weeks. Even the last Gwin to reach them in the woods had traveled on foot, fearful of the Dragons that had taken over the skies. It was clear that Avidaura had become a dangerous place in the years that Ash had been away, it still seemed so surreal to have returned to such a different world.

"Should be a short trek up this way to the path." Zarah called out, still keeping his voice from carrying too far.

The forest was thick and overgrown, the path had not been used in a long while, if it had ever been used at all. Zarah tried to lead the way, soon allowing Tor to take his place so he could strike his sword through any overgrowth that stood in their way.

What was supposed to have been a half hour through to woods soon turned into a full hour, and they had yet to see any sign of the path ahead of them.

Finally Ash could see a break in the trees ahead, she was sweaty and covered in twigs and leaves, it was about time they found a clear path.

Ash was about to walk through the trees when Zarah stopped suddenly, holding his arm out to keep Ash from walking forward.

"Wait." He whispered, holding his other hand up to stop Tor from passing him.

"We should scout the path out first, maybe stay to the trees." He added, listening through the silent woods.

Ash perked up, there was a muffled sound coming from the break in the trees, it could just be an animal, but Zarah was right. There were too many of the Wizard's followers wandering the paths to be sure what was up ahead.

"You're right." Ash agreed, nearly forgetting the Dark Knights that traveled the pathway, still searching for the camp of the Rising. It would do them no good to come across the minions of the Wizard, there were only three of them, and they were not prepared to fight; not yet at least.

Tor stayed with Zarah while Ash went ahead to scout out the pathway. She had the advantage of being a Wizard, and could make herself unseen if there were Knights walking the pathway. She could also make them forget.

Her spells had come a long way since she and Piper had returned though the mirror, spells that her father had taught her in her youth and she had long forgotten had come back to her while she had been teaching Piper to control her powers. Spells that she never thought she would have a use for, like the shield they had used in the castle siege.

Creeping through the brush she found herself holding her breath. There were noises on the pathway, someone was talking. They had nearly walked into a group of the Dark Wizard's men.

There were five of them. Four stood over the last one who was huddled on the ground in a heap. Ash couldn't quite hear what they were saying, so she moved a little closer, careful not to make a sound.

"...you picked your side." One of them yelled, kicking the Knight on the ground.

"The winning side." Another added, crossing his arms.

"They ain't gonna take you back Phil, nobody's gonna take you back." The first one turned away. "I hope you rot out here." He turned away, towards the castle path. "Come on, let's leave him." He called to the others.

Soon the Knights were walking away, leaving the heap of their comrade laying in the middle of the path. Ash stared at him, the one they had called "Phil" he was squirming, his voice muffled.

They had tied him, and left him to die.

Clearly he had defied them, by the sounds of it he had changed his mind about following the Dark Wizard. And now he was paying the price.

Ash returned to the woods quietly, to bring news to Zarah and Tor.

"We'll have to wait." She whispered as she neared them in the brush.

"Wizard's Knights?" Tor asked, peering past her, hand on his hilt.

"Yeah, looks like they had a deserter. Left one tied up on the path." She looked at Zarah, he always knew what to do.

"We can't risk him seeing us, even if he was left there. He could tell them that he saw us, and then the whole mission would be ruined." Zarah seemed pensive.

"Well we can't free him, he's clearly not to be trusted, flipping from one side to the other..." Ash defended.

"If he sees us at all, then our cover is blown. The whole Village could come under attack." Tor stepped in.

"What are you saying, *kill* him?" Ash questioned.

"No, we can't just kill him." Zarah shook his head, a look flashed across his face that Ash could read instantly.

"You want us to take him *with* us?" Ash stared at Zarah who was nodding, like he had grown a second head, "That's a terrible idea." She shook her head.

"I don't know…" Tor cut in, "It could prove useful, like a spy on our side…"

"My thoughts exactly." Zarah had already made up his mind.

"And you think he won't lie to us…" Ash huffed, following Zarah and Tor as they started walking, "…great." She crossed her arms, already unimpressed with their decision, it appeared that they weren't even going to hear her out.

Zarah led the way to the path crouching at the edge, still inside the brush. Tor and Ash stooped down beside him, watching the Dark Knight floundering on the path. Ash wasn't set on the idea, but Tor was already scouting out the path for the other Wizard's Knights.

He returned shortly with news, "The path is clear, he is alone." Tor turned to look at the abandoned Knight. "Should we reel him in?" He asked, wondering how they were going to approach the Knight without risking being seen if his men returned.

"That's probably a good idea." Zarah considered, "Can you manage on your own?" He added.

Tor looked out at the Knight, he wasn't that big, maybe nineteen and as scrawny as they came. "I've got this." He smirked, towering over Ash and Zarah.

Ash watched, slightly amused as Tor broke through the brush onto the path. The Dark Knights eyes grew wide, the gag in his mouth shifting as he tried to protest a hulking beast like Tor manhandling him. Tor didn't say a word, he simply stooped down, threw the kid over his shoulder and returned to the trees.

Tor set him down on a log next to Ash and untied the gag.

"Please don't kill me." Phil pleaded, his arms and legs still bound.

"What did you do to end up on the path like that?" Ash asked, watching his face carefully. It was quite possible that he was a troubled youth caught on the wrong side, but it was just as possible that he was a trader.

"I...I..."He looked away, obviously not wanting to tell them.

"We're going to take you with us." Zarah explained, reaching forward to untie his hands.

Ash shot him a loathing look.

"You only get one chance with us," Zarah added, rolling his eyes at Ash, "we could just as easily leave you back on the path." He stared at Phil, waiting for him to agree.

Phil nodded, "Thank you." He muttered under his breath, rubbing his sore wrists before he leaned down to untie his legs. "I thought I was going to die out there."

"You very well could have." Ash cut in.

"I know..." Phil added slowly.

"We still have quite a way to go, we should get going before we waste any more time." Ash waited for Zarah to agree.

Zarah nodded, "We're going." He mumbled. "Stick to the side of the path, it seems clear for a ways, but we need to be able to take cover, just in case."

"Agreed." Ash, turned to lead the way out of the woods, carrying on up the path that led to the High Village without looking back.

Footsteps followed quietly behind her, she kept herself alert, waiting for something to go wrong. It had to be a trap, the boy on the path, no one could be so cruel to leave a boy like that out in the hot sun to die. Not even the Dark Wizard, Darius, her uncle.

She hadn't told Zarah of her encounter at the camp, it hadn't seemed like the place or time. They were already moving out, so the risk of him finding them had been null. Zarah had to have known who he was, he had been fighting for Avidaura far longer than she had, thanks to her trip into Piper's world. Zarah had to have known that it was her uncle who had taken the throne, he would have been around when the Wizard had been imprisoned, if that is what had really happened.

Yet, Zarah hadn't told her, he hadn't warned her that her uncle, seemingly dead to her, had returned, or that he was a villain. She had always thought he was a good person, sure he disagreed with her father about everything, the two could never be in a room together without an argument arising, but she would never have imagined that he had tried to take over Avidaura, that he had been sent away to rot in a prison that he would one day escape from; that he would *kill* her father in cold blood.

She hadn't said a word to anyone about the conversation that they had had, it just spun around in her head like a loop, taunting her with every repeat.

She was still going through the conversation when Tor tapped her on the shoulder, "Ash?" He tried, obviously not for the first time.

Ash stopped, snapping back to reality, "What?" She snipped, caught off guard.

"We're taking a break, are you going to join us?" He asked, carefully.

Ash looked up to the sky, high noon had come and gone while she had been lost in her thoughts, her mouth was dry. She looked back at the path, Zarah and Phil were sitting off to the side drinking from a canteen and talking.

"Are you coming?" Tor asked again, he glanced back at Zarah hopefully. Clearly he had been told to follow Ash if she had continued on without them.

"Yeah, let's take a break." She smiled, walking back to join Zarah and the new kid.

"Well, Ash." Zarah stood to greet her, "I thought you were never going to stop walking." He laughed, passing her the canteen. "It's nearly time to find a camp for the night, we've made good time." He nodded.

Tor sat, pulling a map from his satchel and handing it up to Zarah.

"We'll have to stay off the path." Ash leaned in, looking over his shoulder at the map to see where they were.

"There is a dense forest near the Lagoon," Zarah suggested, pointing to an area ahead of them on the path, it would take them a couple of hours to reach it. But it seemed to be as safe a place as any, and they had enough daylight left to get there and settled before night fell.

"Sounds like a plan." She agreed, passing the canteen over to Tor.

***

After they had rested and taken a break to relieve themselves they continued on down the path with a destination in mind. Ash had never been to the Lagoon, she had heard wild stories from her father about Mermaids and their powers when she was younger. There were even rumors that they had a pearl that could amplify a Wizard's powers tenfold.

Secretly she wondered if they would be willing to let her borrow one. It would give her an edge against her uncle, a way to stop him from overthrowing Avidaura, maybe a way to save the land.

If they were making camp there for the night, she might have a chance to ask one of them.

As the sky began to turn the orange hue of pre-dusk Zarah turned from the path and began to lead them through the woods towards the area they would make camp.

"Here." He said, finally stopping in a small clearing. There was only a thin line of trees between them and the Lagoon, Ash stared out at it, it was truly breathtaking.

Tor looked at the clearing and nodded, "I'll find firewood." He decided. "You." He pointed at Phil, "You're with me."

The kid nodded, following Tor back into the trees to scavenge for wood.

"You still think it was a good idea bringing that kid with us?" Ash asked, when the coast was clear.

"I didn't realize he was that young." Zarah looked surprised, "I couldn't imagine what his parents must be thinking."

Ash paused. It hadn't occurred to her that Phil, as young as he was, was also someone's child. His parents could be fighting on their side, or his parents could have fallen at the hands of Darius.

"I guess." She mumbled, letting the conversation fall flat. She stepped towards the Lagoon, taking in a deep breath of the fresh air.

The Lagoon was larger than she would have imagined, with pristine blue waters, so calm that she could see the clouds reflecting from overhead. It was nothing like the dark murky waters that surrounded her home, choppy and icy cold. She could already tell that the Lagoon was warm, inviting, calm.

White sand met her at the tree line as she continued forward. She kicked her boots from her tired feet and let her toes run through the soft sand. It was certainly an acceptable choice to make camp for the night at the shore of the Lagoon, they would be protected by the waters and would only have to guard the woods.

Ash walked to the water, sitting herself in the sand as she allowed the water to trickle over her feet, just as warm as she had expected. For a moment it felt like she was the only one left in Avidaura.

When she could hear the fire crackling behind her, and the waft of dinner being cooked, she rose, returning to camp as the sky began to turn purple overhead.

Zarah was taking a rest, so he could keep watch for some of the night. Ash joined Phil and Tor at the fire, warming her feet as they dried before she returned them to her soiled boots.

"So where are you from?" Tor was asking Phil.

Ash leaned in, waiting for his answer.

"High Village." He garbled, through a bite of food. "You?"

"Born in the High Village, served the true King until recently." Tor nodded to Ash. She had been the one who had freed him from the dungeons at the castle.

"Really?" Phil seemed surprised, "I don't remember you." He added.

"I was probably gone before you were even walking." Tor laughed, turning a spit over the fire.

"Are your parents still there?" Ash asked, wondering how Phil had ended up the way he had.

"Yea, my mum and dad are still there." He hung his head, "I ran away during the uprising." He admitted, under his breath.

"How old were you?" Tor asked, surprised.

"Fourteen."

"And they let you *fight?*" Tor shook his head, "Pathetic."

"I was ready." Phil was getting defensive, but Tor looked right at him.

"You were *fourteen.*" Tor replied.

Phil looked at his feet, the conversation was replaced with the crackle of the fire and the wafting scent of diner.

After they had eaten and night had fallen absolute, Ash offered to take first watch. She didn't trust Phil to watch the camp, he had been with the Wizard's Knights for too long to be trusted with their safety. Tor had agreed with her. Ash would watch first and then Zarah would take over, after he had rested for a while.

Ash settled in with her back to a tree listening to the forest around her while she watched the Lagoon. The water hadn't darkened with the coming of night, instead it had stayed a pristine blue that glowed lightly in the dimness around it.

She could see into the depths of the water, deeper than anything she had ever seen before, it seemed bottomless. She had yet to see any of the Mer-folk beneath the surface.

Shortly after the moon reached its peak Ash heard a rustling in the forest behind her. Standing slowly, she gazed through the trees, watching, waiting. Hands at the ready.

"Ash." Zarah whispered, walking towards her. He had woken from his rest and was walking towards her in the darkness. Ash let her shoulders relax.

"I'm here." She answered, stepping from her cover behind the tree so he could see her.

"Oh, good." Zarah approached. "I've been wanting to talk to you… alone." He added, his small frown showing in the moonlight.

"About what?" She inquired, settling down beside him.

"There are some things I need to tell you," Zarah paused, "In case I don't make it through." He added quietly.

"What?" Ash felt her face grow warm, the thought of losing Zarah had never crossed her mind before.

"I'm not planning on going anywhere." Zarah assured her, "But if I can't be there for Felix, there are some things he needs to know about being the King. You're the only one I can trust with this." He added, looking at her pointedly.

Ash may have been named the High Wizard of Avidaura, but she was knowledgeable enough to know that she didn't know half of what it took to rule a Kingdom. Felix knew quite a bit less than she did. If they were to restore the Kingdom after the Dark Wizard was gone, they would need all of the insight that Zarah could provide them.

Zarah and Ash talked until her eyes grew droopy from tiredness, she fell asleep with her back to a tree, still listening to all that Zarah had to offer. He talked of the old days, how the Wizard had come to be known as a Dark one, stories that Ash had never heard before. Stories that she wished she never had to hear again.

She understood as she drifted to sleep, why Zarah hadn't told her about her uncle, why no one had really.

He hadn't been a good man, he hadn't been the man she had remembered.

FAIRY

Piper watched Ash and Zarah leave across the Village. A lump had risen in her throat, she knew that she didn't have it in her to say goodbye to them one more time. She hoped that they didn't run into any trouble along the way.

As they disappeared into the crowd and away, she turned back to Finnigan and Felix, her company for the journey into the Forest of Night. Felix was scouring over a map with Finnigan, trying to remember just which way they would have to go to get to the Kingdom. The forest was not a safe place for humans, and their last journey though had been guided by the Fairy Knight Eniki, even then they had run into dangers.

This time they would be alone.

She adjusted the satchel at her side, a reminder of the quest ahead of her. It had been only a short while ago since she had ventured into the Forest of Night, the memory was confusing to her. She hadn't been in Avidaura long enough to understand what was really going on, Felix and Zarah had still been strangers to her. This time it would be different, she knew what to expect as they tried to find the Kingdom of the Dark Fairies.

Felix was still looking over the map when Evan returned and Finnigan turned away to talk to him.

Piper made her way over to Felix, looking at the map he still held in his hands.

"Did you find it?" She asked, quietly so the others didn't overhear.

"It's a human made map…" He shook his head, "None of the paths through the dark woods are on here." He looked over at Finnigan carefully. "If we can find the path from the side wall we should be able to make it to the Kingdom."

Piper nodded, "It's too bad they fixed the wall, we'll have to go around the long way."

"Exactly." Felix shook his head, tucking the map away carefully.

"You have the coin?"

Felix patted his cloak, "Always." He smiled.

Felix had picked himself to lead the journey into the Forest of Night for that very reason. Though the forest itself was warded against human trespassers, he had been given a coin by the Fairy Eniki that would grant them safe passage. He still wasn't sure if it would work for the three of them, they had only tried it briefly; he Ash and Piper, while they had been hiding from Dragons on their way through the Badlands. This journey would certainly put the coin to the test.

Finnigan and Evan walked towards Felix, ready to open the gates for the quest.

"Did Ash and Zarah get out okay?" Felix asked, knowing that Piper was nervous about them traveling alone.

"They seemed to be fine." Evan smiled.

Dawn was still breaking over the tired village, though the Knights were already bustling about to prepare for the final battle. Evan seemed hesitant to let them go through the gate, watching Felix with a concerned look twinkling behind his tired eyes.

"Are you sure you can get through the Forest of Night?" He asked finally, his uncertainty showing.

"He's done it before." Finnigan assured Evan, though it seemed like Evan had already heard Finnigan's story.

Evan laughed, "I know, I've heard the tale." He shook his head lightly, "But will they allow you to pass through their woods unannounced? It is warded against humans…" Evan seemed to have his own worries about allowing the King to travel into the unknown and the dangers that they might face.

Felix pulled the coin from his pocket, turning it over in his hand with a smile. "I am sure that we will have no troubles in the Forest of Night." He assured Evan, "They will receive us at the Kingdom." He added, looking down at the coin in his hand.

Evan sighed, staring at Felix again as he contemplated, "I am still not sure about this." He admitted, finally turning towards the gates, "but I must trust the King." He waved at the gate guard, letting him know that they would be leaving, "Safe travels to you all." Evan bowed his head, "I hope we see you soon."

"Thank you Chief Evan," Felix tipped his head in return, walking towards the gates as they finally opened, "we shall see you soon." He assured the Village Chief one last time as he passed through to the path on the other side.

Piper followed behind him with Finnigan on her trail, she was eager to get their quest underway. They would have a few days of traveling ahead of them if they planned to visit the Fairies and the Clurichaun before returning to the Village.

The gates stayed open, just long enough for the three to pass through before they began to close again, quickly clicking into place as they were locked. Piper looked back, listening as the locks were put into place, it seemed so final. The Village had expelled them for their quest, they wouldn't be returning until they were finished.

And if it all went well, they wouldn't be returning alone.

"Piper, come on." Felix called to her, snapping her out of her daze, he and Finnigan were already a few paces up the path.

Piper jogged up the path, stopping next to Felix and Finnigan who were bracing themselves for the border crossing into the Forest of Night.

"Are we ready?" Felix asked, looking at his companions standing at the edge of the forest. There was a short walk before the Forest of Night began, though the coin in his hand was already starting to take on the blue tinge, so he knew that it was working.

"I've always wanted to see the Forest of Night." Finnigan started walking forward eagerly, leaving Felix and Piper in his wake. There was a bounce in his step as he marched through the woods towards the boundary.

"Wait up." Felix called after him, rushing ahead of Piper to catch Finnigan before he walked through the barrier and into trouble. He reached his arm out and stopped Finnigan from breaking though the barrier.

"Just right through here, right?" Finnigan smiled, his eager excitement to venture into the Forest of Night showed Felix just how naive he really was about the dangers that waited on the other side of the barrier.

"Yeah, right through there." Felix confirmed, keeping his hand on Finnigan's arm before his companion started walking again, "You have to stay near me once we enter the Forest of Night, this," Felix showed Finnigan the coin, "will keep us safe from the wardings in the forest." He explained, watching as it dawned on Finnigan what he was about to venture into.

"So *that's* how you did it." Finnigan seemed impressed, staring at the coin as it slowly pulsed blue, not quite at full power yet. "They always told us it was dangerous out there…" He mused, staring out at the border where the forest turned to night.

"It is very dangerous…" Felix trailed off, reminded of his encounter with the wild vines and the creatures that called the Forest of Night home. "Everything they told you was true."

Felix added, seeing the look on Finnigan's face as he remembered the horrible stories from his youth.

"Everything?" Finnigan seemed unsure, and Felix couldn't really know what stories he had heard. Living so close to the barrier in the Low Village he was sure they heard more scary stories about the Forest of Night than he had at the castle.

"Most of it." Felix confirmed.

Piper had caught up to them while they had been talking, there the three stood, the wall of darkness sprawled out before them like an omen. Piper looked at Felix and nodded, she was ready to enter.

"Do you know which way it is to the Kingdom path?" Piper asked Felix under her breath.

"I think I remember." He seemed unsure.

"We'll find a way." She reassured him, reaching for his hand.

Piper held her other hand out to Finnigan, still not sure how far the coin's powers would reach, it was better to be safe.

Together they stepped through the barrier, darkness washing over them as they passed into the Forest of Night.

Finnigan gasped, "Wow." He breathed, holding Piper's hand tighter, "It's *really* dark in here."

"You'll get used to it." She promised, blinking to let her eyes adjust to the perpetual darkness.

Beside her Felix's coin was growing bright, the glow washing over them, shedding light onto the forest around them.

It was exactly as Piper had remembered it. The trees with their purple leaves, the canopy covering any trace of light from the sun, blue and pink orbs flickering in the darkness like fireflies that had forgotten their colors.

"We walk until we find a path." Felix decided, starting forward and tugging Piper and Finnigan along behind him.

It was as good a plan as any. This was not the same place that they had entered the forest on their first mission through it, there had been a path that the Fairies had taken to lead them to their Kingdom. If they followed the Village wall, they would surely find the place where the path began.

It wasn't as easy as Felix had hoped, the Forest of Night was thick with brush and foliage, there was no clear way to follow the village wall and the boundary of light. It was a tedious task to maneuver through the woods with Piper and Finnigan in tow, especially with them still holding hands.

Until they reached the proper path he wasn't willing to put the coin to the test and see if they would be safe, there were too many ways to get maimed in the Forest of Night.

The underbrush was hard to pass through, the prickly bushes caught on their robes and held them fast, making it slow going as they trailed along the border of the Low Village making their way to the place where the path had begun.

Though Felix hadn't said anything to Piper and Finnigan, he was starting to wonder if the path was still there. It had been years since their first trip through, and the Village had clearly repaired the broken wall shortly after they had passed through the mirror. It was a possibility that it had grown over and hadn't been used since that day.

Evan had given them no indication that the Fairies had been back since that day. Felix watched the forest carefully, searching for an overgrown pathway, just in case. Without the paths on his map is was nearly impossible to guarantee that they would make it to the Kingdom at all, but Felix was still willing to give it a try.

"Hold up." Piper winced, tugging at Finnigan who was tangled up in a bush. Felix took a step back to give them room to untangle him before they continued forward.

Finnigan grunted, pulling at his robe until it finally tore free with a dramatic ripping sound. "Is it like this the whole way?" He grumbled, reaching for Piper's hand again before the forest realized that he wasn't attached to the small train.

"Once we get to the path it will clear up." Piper promised, giving his hand a tug to help him over a fallen log. "It should be easy from there."

"How much longer until the path?"

"Soon." Felix answered, turning back to search through the trees ahead for a clearing amongst the forest. He still couldn't see anything in the darkness ahead of them.

As they continued forward the underbrush seemed to come alive with the blue and pink bugs that reminded Piper of fireflies, they swarmed from the bushes as Felix tried to lead them through, circling the trio and nipping at their faces.

They must have wandered into a nest of the tiny bugs, because out of nowhere it seemed that they were covered in the tiny flickering things.

The bites stung like an electric shock. Piper yelped as one nipped her on the neck. Her hands were still clutching Finnigan and Felix, she couldn't even swat it away.

"I don't remember these being so evil." She hissed, twitching her head to keep them away.

"What *are* these things?" Finnigan, swatted one off of Piper's back saving her from the sting.

"I think we're almost at the path." Felix panted from the front, pulling Piper through another bush.

Finally they landed on a clearing, collapsing into a heap as Felix finally let go of Pipers hand.

"I think you found it." Finnigan huffed, rolling over to look at the path leading into the woods.

"It's about time." Piper picked herself up off of Felix, rubbing her neck where the light bug had bit her, it still stung.

"All right, all right." Felix stood up, wiping the dirt from his pants. "It should be easier from here," He looked at Finnigan, "Stay close though, and stay *on* the path." He warned.

"First, water." Piper panted, pulling the canteen from her satchel. She was covered in sweat and dirt, twigs tangled in her hair and twisted in her cloaks. It took her a minute to set herself straight after she had taken a deep drink of the fresh water in her canteen.

One look at her and Felix and Finnigan realized what she had meant. Though their hair was short and hadn't caught as many stray branches, they both looked like they had just dragged themselves through the woods, not exactly an image that provoked a feeling of alliance. They needed to appear properly when they presented themselves to the King of the Fairies, or he wouldn't be willing to join them.

They spent a good ten minutes in the dim blue light of Felix's coin picking branches off of one another before they finally looked presentable enough to carry on down the path.

Thankfully Finnigan took the warning seriously, staying to the center of the path as he began to walk slowly into the Forest of Night more cautious than he had ever been before.

Piper and Felix fell into step behind him. Piper was watching the forest, wondering what other troubles they would encounter before they reached the Fairy Kingdom, and how long it would take for them to reach their destination. In the everlasting darkness time didn't seem to matter, she couldn't be sure how long they had already been there, or when they would come back out.

"Do you remember the last time?" She turned to Felix.

"It wasn't that long ago."

"Do you think they remember us?" She asked, thinking of the Fairy Eniki who had taken them to the Shore of Sorrow on their quest to save Avidaura.

"I sure hope they do." Felix chuckled, turning the coin over in his hand again. Eniki had given it to him so he could return one day, he hoped that it meant something, and they hadn't forgotten about him.

"You're right." Piper poked at a fallen branch with her toe before stepping over it. "How far is the Kingdom?"

Felix didn't answer, he had been trying to figure out how long the journey was going to be for a while, "I have to admit," Felix leaned in towards Piper, lowering his voice so Finnigan didn't overhear "I don't really remember how long this journey was."

She turned towards him, his face portrayed the worry that they all felt. Would they have enough time to gather allies before the Dark Wizard made his next move?

"I don't either, Avidaura was so new to me..."

"I can't believe it was only a couple of weeks ago." Felix shook his head, time had been different for them. Though the Fairies hadn't seen them in years, it had only been a few short weeks since Felix and Piper had made this same journey from the Low Village.

"Do you think the elders will remember us?" Piper asked.

"It hasn't been *that* long..." Felix laughed, wondering the same thing. They had only spoken briefly with the village elders on their first trip to the Fairy Kingdom. And they had spent a short while with Eniki in the woods. Would the Fairies remember him? Or were they walking into danger? Only time would tell.

The path through the woods was much easier to travel on, soon they had fallen into a rhythm and were making good time. The noises in the dark forest were strange, Piper didn't remember them from their last adventure, but then they had been surrounded by Fairies, whispers and feet patter had probably drowned them out.

Finnigan was still in the lead, slowly getting farther and farther away as his strides took him quicker than Felix and Piper. She was watching him, worried that he didn't understand how important it was to be near Felix and the coin.

She was about to call ahead when suddenly he was no longer in view, it was as though he had disappeared.

"Felix," She turned, "Finnigan's gone."

Felix had been staring into the trees, his head snapped forward, searching for Finnigan on the path as his steps became a run.

"Where was he?" Felix was turning on the path, looking for the place where Finnigan had been only moments earlier.

Piper was a few steps ahead of him, the last place she had seen him. "He was right here, I just saw him, and then he was gone."

Felix looked up and Piper followed his lead, overhead there were vines, thousands of vines, wrapping themselves over tree trunks and down into the abyss.

"The vines…" Felix whispered, a ghostly look on his face. Piper knew instantly what he was afraid of.

They stayed together, protected by the coin as they stared into the forest watching the vines and searching for Finnigan amongst the chaos.

"He should have stayed with us." Piper shook her head, turning to search for him amongst the next pile of vines.

She held her hands out, casting a glow from her hands that made the forest pause as the light touched it. She hadn't wanted to use her magics in the Forest of Night, Ash had warned that the forest would know and turn its own magics on her. But she couldn't leave Finnigan, and the blue light from the coin wasn't quite enough to search with.

With the glow from Piper's hands they could see a little farther into the woods.

"I can't believe he wandered off." Piper hissed, "We *did* warn him"

"He knew what he was getting into." Felix stared into the trees, "There, look." He pointed, slowly moving towards a lump in the vines, just off the forest path.

"Is it him?" Piper was right behind Felix, as close as she could muster without stepping on his heels.

"Finnigan?" Felix called out, peering into the heap.

A muffled cry answered him.

"It's him." He turned to Piper, pulling his sword out as he handed her the coin.

Soon Felix was hacking at the vines, trying to release their fallen comrade, the vines recoiled with each strike, slowly revealing Finnigan. His face was pale, eyes wide with shock, trembling as Felix reached down to take his hand.

"I know you're numb, but we need to get you back on the path." Felix smiled, helping Finnigan as he fumbled to get to his feet.

Felix remembered the feeling all too well, the vines had once taken him, and he would never forget the feeling of being swallowed alive, unable to fight back, and the numbness that had followed when he had been found.

Slowly Finnigan managed to walk back onto the path. With Felix and Piper at his sides they managed to get him a little ways up the path and away from the vines before they set him back down to let him recover.

"What was that?" Finnigan gasped, his body was still shaking.

Piper pulled the canteen from her satchel and uncorked it, handing it to Finnigan carefully, "Drink up." She suggested.

He brought the canteen to his lips, shaking like a leaf, soon the tremors had subsided and he seemed to have calmed down.

"What was that?" He asked again, looking to Felix for answers.

"Vines, just one of the dangers in this forest." Felix was staring off into the trees, watching something intently. "We're going to have to take cover." He announced suddenly.

As quiet washed over them, Piper began to hear the flapping. "Dragon." She whispered, searching the side of the path frantically for a safe place to take cover.

Piper tucked the coin into her pocket to hide the glow, and slowly they moved from the path into the brush, just as the trees overhead began to rumble with the downdraft from an incoming Dragon.

LAGOON

Morning came to the camp by the Lagoon quite suddenly. Ash awoke sweating, her cloak wrapped around her and her skin blazing hot. It took her a moment to remember where she was. Sitting up and tossing her robes from her arms, she stared across the clearing. She was too close to the fire, the heat radiating from the embers warmed the ground beneath her.

She moved away, taking her cloak with her before it caught fire from the hot red embers drifting out of the fire in the morning breeze. She was surprised no one had woken her and asked her to move.

Ash hung her cloak on a tree nearby, staring into the woods. She could smell food, breakfast was being prepared and the sun was already high, it was well past mid-morning. And yet she felt like she hadn't slept at all.

Nightmares had kept her from getting a good night's rest. Memories of her Uncle Darius from her youth somehow twisted to reflect the Dark Wizard that had taken Avidaura in his grasps.

When she closed her eyes she could see the Dragons, attacking her home, fire bursting from their lips, smoke curling from the towers. She could see her father's final moments, racing through the castle, trying to escape, and the final blast of fire at the front door consuming him. And then she had watched Avidaura crumble, standing on the edge of End Key, a small helpless girl, as the world had burned and turned to ash.

Waking from the nightmare had left her feeling bitter and on edge. She must have fallen asleep sometime after Zarah had taken over watch, though she couldn't remember leaving the Lagoon and walking back to the camp and lying next to the fire. She only remembered the nightmares that had followed.

Now awake, she couldn't shake the feeling that something bad was about to happen. She felt like her dreams had been an omen, she could still see Avidaura crumbling before her. No amount of fresh morning air could wash away the feeling that her dreams had left with her, Avidaura was in trouble.

They had left the Low Village to go on their quest, leaving the Knights of the woods exposed in the Village. Though the Village was welcoming and had supplies, they were not as protected as they had been at their camp in the woods. The Knights could be found by the false King, if they hadn't been already. Ash had a sinking feeling that they had messed up somewhere in their hurry to save Avidaura, that they had slipped up and something was about to go wrong.

If it wasn't the Knights at the Village then it was her friends. Piper and Felix had left the safety of the army to travel through the Forest of Night, that in itself was enough to worry about. Would Felix's coin get them to the Fairies safely? Or would there be other dangers lurking in that unknown forest?

It had been a long while since the three of them had been apart, she worried that they weren't safe without her. What if they needed her? What if Piper's powers couldn't be contained? Would Felix know how to calm her, or would something catastrophic happen because Ash wasn't there to help.

Ash herself had only been in the Forest of Night during their travels through the Badlands. She didn't know enough about it to feel confident that her companions were safe.

Though Felix and Piper had traveled through the lands before, then it had been with a guide, they had been protected. Ash remembered the feeling the forest had carried, even at the border, she knew that it was powerfully warded against humans. Even Piper's power wouldn't be able to protect them while they were in the Forest of Night, they would have to hope that Felix's coin was enough to get them through.

Though Piper had promised that they would be safe, Ash still worried that her sister's magic wouldn't be enough, that they would face danger without her there to protect them.

That they might not come back.

There was a heavy feeling in the pit of her stomach as she thought of them alone in the dark woods. She tried to push it to the back of her mind, but that uneasy feeling that something was about to go wrong just wouldn't go away.

Ash returned to the camp after taking a quick lap around the outskirts to clear her mind.

It was as though Tor and Phil knew she hadn't slept well, as she stepped back into the clearing they both grew silent, looking up at her as though they were afraid she had snapped.

"Good morning." Tor offered his greeting carefully, not making eye contact with Ash as she walked towards him.

Ash nodded in greeting, staring at the fire. It had been reduced to nothing while Ash had been clearing her head, the embers barely glowed.

Phil was standing over the fire pit, poking the embers with a stick as he tried to bring them back to a roaring blaze with no wood to burn in sight.

Ash stared at him for a moment, he didn't seem to know what he was doing, without any fresh wood on the fire he wasn't going to be able to get the fire started again. But the determination on his face was something to be admired, it was as though he believed he could will the fire back to life again.

Tor had turned back to his food preparations, ignoring Phil in his valiant attempt to get the flames back, though Ash could only watch him struggle for a moment longer before she stepped in.

"You're going to need more wood for the fire." She observed.

Phil jumped, he hadn't realized he was being watched, "I've got this." He nodded, poking the ashes again with more vigor.

Ash shook her head, "It won't' start if there is no wood to burn." She explained, searching the clearing for the supply they had gathered the night before, "Are we out of wood?"

"Yeah, I think we used it all up." Phil looked around the clearing, "We'll need more." He agreed with Ash.

"Where is Zarah? Did he go to collect wood?" Ash had yet to see him that morning, though she had only just realized he wasn't there.

Tor answered before Phil could make a sound. "He's over there, looking at the maps." Tor pointed across the clearing, "I wouldn't disturb him." He added with a knowing look in his eyes, clearly Zarah had too much on his mind to be bothered at that moment.

Ash glanced over at Zarah, practically hidden behind the brush, he was pouring over a map, his shoulders stiff and his brow furrowed. It was clear that he did not want to be bothered.

"You mind getting some more wood, this fire ain't going to cook anything." He added, passing Phil a disappointed glance.

"Sure." Ash agreed, there was still one thing she wanted to do before they left the Lagoon and continued on to the Village, and she was running short on time.

She dashed into the woods, quickly making a pile of wood that she could carry back with her when she was done with her mission, and then she made her way down to the lake, eager to have one last moment there before she had to face reality.

The water was just as clear and blue as it had been the day before, not a single ripple crossed the surface. She walked along the shore, watching the water, staring into the depths below.

Really she was looking for any sign that the mermaids still lived in Lagoon Lake. It seemed so still and glass-like that she couldn't be sure that *anything* was living beneath the surface. She had heard stories when she was a child, though she had always believed them to be fairy tales, until she had found the entry in her father's journal, the one she kept tucked safely at her side in her satchel.

He had listed the many powers of the mermaids and their origins to Avidaura. In the book, Lagoon Lake was listed as their Kingdom. And according to her father's notes, there was something that they could offer her, that would make it impossible for the Wizard to keep the throne.

If she could only find a mermaid to ask.

The lake was so silent that she could hear her feet in the sand, the depths beside her so blue that she couldn't even see the bottom of the lake.

When she had walked far enough up the shore to muffle the sounds of Tor and Phil arguing, Ash stopped. She pulled off her boots, rolling her pant legs up to her knees and stepped out into the water.

The sand carried a few feet out before it dropped off into the abyss. She walked along the edge of sand, splashing her feet in the water as she stared into the depths of the lake wondering what the merfolk looked like.

She wasn't sure how exactly she was supposed to call a mermaid to her, or if they would even bother to notice that she was there. There was no note in her father's journal to tell her how she could make contact with them and she couldn't hold her breath long enough to dive down into their Kingdom. So there she stood, splashing her feet and hoping that they would notice she was there.

She splashed her feet around for another ten minutes staring into the deep before she finally decided that she should return to camp. Tor was probably waiting for the fire wood, and she was sure that Phil hadn't bothered to help, leaving Zarah alone to be in charge. She knew that Zarah would get the fire started without her, he would probably be coming to get her soon. She sighed, looking up the shore to where she had abandoned her boots.

She splashed her way back towards her boots, the warm water running over her feet and splashing up the back of her calves. She was nearly back to her boots when something in the deep caught her attention out of the corner of her eye.

A strange white glow, orb-like and moving fast, began drifting out from the deep blue depths of the lake. Ash stepped back towards the shore, carefully watching as it drifted upwards and towards her at the shore.

The shape began to become more clear, taking form as it reached the surface. Teal hair that gleamed in the sun as though it was polished, skin so translucent that she swore it glowed from within; a mermaid.

It was gliding along the surface of the lake through the still water to meet her, leaving a slow ripple in her wake. Ash felt her breath catch in her throat.

They were real.

The mermaid stared at her for a good long while, not saying a thing, and Ash was too surprised to find the words to greet her.

Finally the mermaid spoke, her voice soft like the tide rolling in on a summers eve, "Who are you that dares trespass in our lake?" The mermaid inquired, her statement intended to be fierce, though her voice was far too melodic to sound harsh in any way.

Ash gasped, stepping out of the water onto the shore, she didn't want to offend the mermaid, she hadn't realized stepping into the lake had been trespassing, though she should have known.

"I am Aishwarya," She introduced herself with a small bow, "we are traveling to the High Village." She explained.

"Who travels with you?" The mermaid pulled a triton from beneath the water, holding it at her side defensively.

"I travel with Zarah, Advisor to the King, Tor, Knight of the Rising and Phil.." She trailed off not wanting to explain how they had come across one of the Dark Wizard's deserters.

"What is your intention here?"

"We are just passing through." Ash paused, afraid that her question would be too direct.

"You appeared to be summoning us, I could feel your magics pulling with wonder." The mermaid stared at Ash, seeing through her.

"I was hoping that I would have a chance to talk to one of you." Ash sat on the sand. "I *do* have some questions." She admitted sheepishly.

The mermaid smiled, "And what questions would you have?" She asked politely, resting her elbows in the sand as she propped herself against the shelf where the abyss began.

"Well, you see," Ash wasn't sure where to begin, "we are traveling to the High Village because of the Dark Wizard."

"The Dark Wizard?" The mermaid, looked about the lake, gripping her triton tightly in her thin hand, "Did he send you here?" She seemed shaken, backing away from the ledge in the water out into the deep.

"No, he didn't send us." Ash leaned forward so the mermaid could hear her better, "We are looking for allies, we are King Felix's friends." She explained, hoping that the mermaid knew who Felix was, or at least that he was not the Dark Wizard.

"You fight for the *True* King?" She asked to be certain.

"And I was hoping that you might be able to help." Ash offered.

"Help?" The mermaid looked confused, "How could we possibly help?" She asked, leading Ash into the question that she had been waiting to ask.

"I read about the mermaid pearls in my father's book."
Ash explained, "A pearl would help us to defeat the Wizard."
She added, watching as the mermaid's face grew dark, "My
sister and I, we are Wizards, it would make us more powerful
than him." She finished, surprised at the scowl that the mermaid
displayed on her once beautiful face.

"The dark one asked the same thing." She frowned,
staring at Ash as though she didn't trust her, "How do I know
that you are not here for him?"

"I would never follow him." Ash was quick to reply, "He
killed my father..." She added, her heart breaking at the
memory, "I would never..." She whispered, looking across the
lake.

"Wait." Ash turned back to the mermaid, "He was
here?"

If Darius had already been to see the mermaids and
gotten a pearl, then he would truly be unstoppable, Ash needed
to know if they had helped him.

"We were visited by his force earlier this week. His
Dragons have returned daily since we denied him a pearl." She
frowned, looking out to the forest beyond the Lagoon.

Ash followed her gaze, noticing the charred trees on the
other side of the lake, a sign that there had been Dragons there,
quite recently even. Perhaps it hadn't been the safest place for
them to make camp after all.

"You said no?" Ash needed to hear it again, she had to
be sure that her uncle hadn't gained the ability to amplify his
powers.

"And we would say it again, even if this lake dried up
under his Dragon's fire." She said boldly.

"Would you consider allowing *us* to use one?" Ash
inquired hopefully.

The mermaid sighed, "A pearl is not something that is
often given," She explained cryptically, "and yet it cannot be
taken either."

"We only want to save Avidaura, before it is too late." Ash pointed out.

"I can see that you have a good soul." The mermaid nodded, "But the Kingdom will not allow it." She added, again, leaving Ash confused as to how a pearl was obtained.

"Would you ask?" Ash asked carefully.

The mermaid looked away, Ash turned, catching the silhouette of a Dragon twisting over the trees in the distance. "You need to leave." She turned back to Ash urgently, "Quickly." She breathed.

"Will you ask?" Ash called out to her.

"I will ask, but don't hold your breath." The mermaid nodded, "Hurry now, before they arrive." She hissed, backing into the deep. "Save travels, Ash. I wish you the best of luck." She called, diving beneath the waves.

Ash watched as she plunged into the deep, staying only for one brief moment longer than she knew she should have. There was a Dragon coming, and where there was one, there were more behind it.

She reached for her boots, not stopping to put them on her feet. She needed to warn Zarah, they had to move before the Dragons spotted them, they had to get to the Village.

Ash ran back into the woods, her bare feet breaking across the forest floor without a sound. She raced into the camp, boots in hand and every head turned towards her.

"Dragons incoming." She whispered, reaching for her cloaks that she had left on the tree.

Breakfast was still cooking on the fire, without a second thought Tor and Zarah began tossing dirt on top of it to douse it, the spiral of smoke escaping from the canopy overhead was a dead giveaway that they were there. They would have to leave quickly.

Zarah raced about the camp, gathering the few things that had escaped from his satchel while he had been cooking. The flapping overhead grew louder, it was close enough to hear them.

Ash turned, watching Tor and Phil, she lifted her hand, warning them to stay silent as the canopy overhead began to shake from the breeze. Carefully the four crept from the camp, each step they took with care. Dragons had incredible hearing, and the fire had already given them away.

Overhead there came a deafening screech as the Dragon swooped over the top of the camp, still above the trees. A moment later two distant screeches replied.

There were more Dragons coming.

Move, Ash mouthed to Tor behind her, carefully picking up speed as she moved away from the camp.

They couldn't return to the path, it was too open, the Dragons would spot them in a second. Instead they stayed in the woods, wandering amongst the trees and hoping that they weren't spotted.

Zarah had taken the lead, Ash followed behind him, making sure that he didn't stray too far from the pathway. Eventually they would have to move to the pathway to get to the village gates, but they would have to be sure that they were safe first.

Zarah stopped after half an hour, crouching in the trees he waited for Ash to join him before he dared even whisper to her.

"We're going to have to wait them out." He whispered, only loud enough for Ash and Tor to hear in the still forest.

Phil had gone silent, staring into the trees. Ash watched him, knowing that he believed at least one of those Dragons had been sent to finish him. He had been left, abandoned, and the Wizard had wanted him dead. The look on his face was haunting.

"You think he'll be okay?" Ash leaned forward, her voice reaching only Tor.

He looked over his shoulder, moving slowly as he watched their other companion, before he turned back to Ash, shrugging his shoulder. He had no idea.

Around them other forest creatures were fleeing from the sound of the impending Dragons. Ash could hear them screeching by the lake and felt bad for leaving the mermaid alone with the beasts.

Dragons didn't swim, they wouldn't dare enter the Lagoon itself, their fires would be doused if they even tried. But they could heat the water enough to boil the lake, and the mermaids within it.

Ash hoped that they had a way to defend themselves.

ELDERS

From beneath the bushes Felix could see the Dragon swooping into the forest, grazing the tops of the trees as it penetrated through the dark shield overhead.

The forest had grown dark with the absence of their blue coin, even the light bugs had scattered at the sound of the Dragon in the trees.

Something was in the forest, on the other side of the pathway, the bushes shook quietly as it tried to sneak beneath the beast.

The Dragon circled again, the down draft from its wings rattling the forest as it turned, diving into the canopy. Tree branches snapped as it came in for a rough landing only a few steps up the path from where they had been standing.

The ground shook as its massive body landed on the path, sending a ripple through the woods.

Even with the canopy above destroyed, not a single drop of daylight escaped into the Forest of Night. The Dragon appeared as though it were a shadow, moving in the darkness.

Piper gripped Felix's hand, he held his breath, hopeful that the beast wasn't looking for them.

It turned on the path, staring through the trees as the forest came back to life.

Light bugs swarmed it, though with its thick scales it didn't seem bothered in the slightest. The trees had taken on the mystical glow that had once entranced Felix long enough for the vines to take hold of him. He could hear them slithering across the forest towards the Dragon, reaching for the intruder in the woods.

The Dragon turned again, it was looking for something, smoke rising from its nostrils as it poked its snout into the trees. Felix could already smell the fire, building up in the beasts belly. They would be lucky if it didn't char them to the bone.

Without warning a burst of flame shot from its mouth, illuminating the forest as the trees caught fire. Felix could finally see what it was after.

A Dark Fairy stood, petrified, surrounded by fire as it faced the Dragon alone. A hollow scream broke through the trees as the small Fairy realized that it had been spotted, just barely missed by the blast of fire that had brightened the woods.

She looked small and frightened, with no weapons in her outstretched hands. There was no way that she would be able to defend herself against a Dragon.

"We have to do something." Felix whispered. He couldn't just stand by and watch one of the Fairies fall at the flame of a beast, though he knew that they didn't stand any better of a chance. At least they still had the element of surprise.

"I don't know how to stop a Dragon." Finnigan whispered, obviously scared.

"It takes them a while to regenerate their fires, we have to strike now." Felix didn't wait for confirmation that his companions were going to join him, he leapt to his feet, hand at his hilt.

His sword was drawn before he had crossed the path to the Dragon, he moved so swiftly that the beast had yet to notice him when he thrust his sword into its thick side.

He remembered Eniki's fear of the beasts, and his plea for human weapons. He knew that his sword would work before he had even tried.

The Dragon hissed, its head turning away from the Fairy towards him. Piper and Finnigan were already at his side, their swords drawn, ready to strike. Without a word the three began to fight.

Felix pulled his sword back, covered in blood from being embedded in the Dragon's side. He moved over a step, aiming for its neck as he thrust again. A wing snapped out, swiping at him as the beast pawed at the ground, three times his size.

Piper and Finnigan were somewhere on the other side of the Dragon's head, he could hear them panting, their blades, striking the beast. And still he didn't stop. He wasn't sure that they could kill the creature, or even harm it, but they would at the very least make it reconsider its attack on the lone Fairy.

Felix thrust again, he was panting, trying to strike a creature of such magnitude took more energy than he had anticipated. It was hard to aim his sword to strike between the scales, he had been lucky with his first blow, but the scales were thicker than he had the strength for.

The Dragon turned back to him, hissing again, its tail came swooping in as the creature turned again, tromping down the path away from them.

Felix ducked as the tail passed overhead, a spike scarcely missing his neck.

With a few thunderous strides that shook the forest, the Dragon unfurled its wings and leapt into the air, breaking through the canopy and leaving a scattering of falling branches and a raging fire behind.

Felix was on his knees, watching the Dragon depart and hoping that it didn't return with reinforcements.

They would have to move before it had the chance to return.

The forest was still ablaze, everything was in sharp relief. It didn't seem so dark anymore, the Fairy had made it to the path, away from the fire, before it had collapsed.

Felix approached her and knelt back to the ground.

"She's breathing." He called back.

No one answered him.

Felix turned to find Piper and Finnigan were trying to put out the blaze, tossing dirt onto the fire to keep it contained.

He turned back to the Fairy, her breaths were shallow, her eyes only slightly opened. He could smell blood, but he wasn't quite sure where it was coming from.

"You're okay." He whispered, "The Dragon's gone." He leaned in, placing his hand lightly on her shoulder.

Her eyes flickered, confusion crossed her face and he could see panic as her eyes darted about trying to place herself.

"We're in the Forest of Night." He assured her. "I have come to speak to the Village Elders, we are visitors." He added, watching as her face relaxed.

"The Dragon is gone?" She sounded surprised, trying to sit up. Felix placed his hand on her back and helped her into a sitting position.

The fire was nearly out, the forest growing darker by the second, reminding Felix of the other dangers.

"Piper, the coin." He called to her before it was too late and the dark world came back to life.

As the flame flickered out, the orange glow in the forest slowly turned to blue as the coin took over.

"You." The Fairy was looking at Felix with an intensity that made him nervous.

"Prince...King Felix." He corrected himself, bowing his head.

"You're the one they've been waiting for." She breathed.

Felix looked up, "Waiting for?" He tried to hide his surprise.

"Is she okay?" Piper came closer, cutting their conversation short.

"Yes, yes." The fairy tried to stand, but her leg appeared to be injured.

"I can carry her." Finnigan suggested, looking at the small Fairy.

"We aren't far off from the Kingdom." The Fairy informed them.

Finnigan stooped down and scooped her up in his arms. "Lighter than I'd thought." He laughed, "We'll get you back in one piece."

"I thought I would never get back," the Fairy admitted, "that Dragon had been following me for two days." She shook her head.

"Two days!" Piper stared, "What did it want from you?"

"We refused to join the Wizard, they've been plucking us off one by one." She frowned, a pained look crossing her face. "The Kingdom is protected, but the woods…" She trailed off.

They had already started walking up the path, the dim blue light barely covering the four of them as they crept at the center of the path towards the Fairy Kingdom.

The Fairy was still talking to Finnigan and Piper, but Felix had gotten lost in his own thoughts. How could the Fairies have known that he would return, in Avidaura he had been gone years. He wondered if they were looking for him as an ally in the fight against the Dark Wizard, or if they had finally decided that the humans were just too much trouble to deal with.

He felt the same nerves that had coursed through him the first time he had traveled to the Fairy Kingdom, he was never sure what to expect. But this time he was King, and he had made them promises, he would have to follow through.

They had been walking for nearly half an hour when the Fairy, who had introduced herself as Zia asked them to stop.

"Up ahead there is a fork in the trail, it will be hard to see, but we need to take the smaller path, it leads straight in to the Kingdom." She explained, "Be careful though, this is where the Dragons like to wait."

Felix nodded, it had been a stroke of luck that they had found Zia, not only had they managed to save her, but she had told them that there were Dragons in the dark woods. It was something that they wouldn't have been expecting to find with all the other dangers that were present.

Carefully they crept forward, Finnigan in the back with Zia in his arms. Piper and Felix took the lead with their swords at the ready, they could fight their way through if they had to, but there was no guarantee that any waiting Dragon was without its fire.

The path quickly turned from lush wild forest to charred trunks and coal. It looked like the Badlands at night, and Felix could see that the Dragons had clearly visited recently.

Piper slowed at his side, scanning the darkness for any signs that there were Dragons present. They had kept the blue coin out, for their own safety from the woods. Zia had suggested that the dark forest wasn't too pleased with the Dragon's presence. If there *were* Dragons nearby, the light of the coin wouldn't be the only thing that gave them away. Zia was still bleeding from her leg, and it was nearly impossible to cover the scent along with the sound of them moving through the charred forest.

If there were Dragons they would know soon enough.

They had reached the opening, Zia pointed to a small break in the trees, "There." She hissed from Finnigan's arms.

Hurriedly they rushed forward, breaking through the tree line into a blue lit oasis.

A line of Fairies was standing before them, weapons in hand, their faces angry and unpleasant. The line drew forward, one Fairy stepping into the lead before Felix.

"Who dares enter the fairy Kingdom unannounced." His tiny voice demanded.

"King Felix, I have come to speak to the Village Elders." He bowed his head, their rage washed away quickly.

"We found this one in the woods." Finnigan stepped forward with Zia in his arms. "She is injured."

"Bring her this way." Another Fairy stepped forward leading Finnigan away.

He looked back at Piper and Felix, worried.

"You're fine, go with them." Piper smiled.

Finnigan soon disappeared into the Village with Zia, leaving Piper and Felix with the Knights of the dark Kingdom.

"King Felix?" The Knight asked again.

"Yes." Felix nodded.

"Then your father had perished." He bowed his head, the other Fairies followed, "We are truly sorry." He righted himself, turning to part a path amongst the Knights.

"You'll want to follow me." He added, waiting for Piper and Felix to follow.

Felix recognized the path from the forest to the tree of the Elders, this time when they passed through the small wooden doorway he was less surprised with the massive living space contained within.

The Knight led them to a chamber, not the same as the throne room where they had first met the Elders, but a large room with a table that was sizable enough for Humans to sit without crouching.

"I will announce your arrival to the Elders, and there is another who wishes to see you." He bowed his head and left, leaving Piper and Felix alone.

"This is much bigger than last time." Piper pulled out a chair and sat, sighing as she relieved her tired feet. Felix took a chair at her side and lowered himself in slowly. His whole body ached from their encounter with the Dragon.

"We made it." He smiled.

Piper reached for his hand, squeezing it lightly in hers, "I hope Ash and Zarah are doing well."

"They should be at the Village by early morning." Felix looked up, realizing that he had lost track of time since they had entered the Forest of Night, he had no idea what time of day, or even what day it was.

"Do you think the Fairies will join us?" Piper whispered, not wanting to be overheard.

"I don't see why they wouldn't, unless..." Felix's eyes grew wide, he had forgotten that the Dark Fairies couldn't travel in daylight. "I am sure they can assist in some way." He decided finally.

"When all of this is done, we're going to need a vacation." Piper laughed, the usual lightness in her voice undertoned with the worry that they all carried in these trying times.

"A vacation?" Felix was confused.

"On my world a vacation is when you get away and relax for a little while." She explained.

Felix smiled, "I like the sound of that…"

The door swung opened and Finnigan entered with another Fairy behind him.

"So this is where you've been." He smiled, crossing the room to take a seat at the table.

Felix let go of Pipers hand and stood, recognizing the Fairy that had followed Finnigan through the door.

"Eniki!" Felix smiled, walking around the table to greet him.

Eniki let his scowl fall for a moment, shaking hands with Felix, "It has been too many years." He bowed, "I hear you are the King?" He inquired, watching Felix's face carefully.

"I am afraid it is so." Felix answered, trying to stop the pain in his chest from taking him over. Carrying the loss of his father across Avidaura was a burden he had not anticipated, it was still so fresh that there were many that didn't know.

"I am truly sorry to hear." Eniki bowed again, "You will make a great King." He added, a small smile playing at the corner of his mouth as he moved to sit at the table.

Soon the doors had been opened again, Eniki rose from his seat and the three followed his lead, bowing their heads in respect as the Village Elders entered the room, taking their places at the head of the table.

When they had been seated, Eniki and the others returned to their chairs.

"Prince Felix," One of the Elders addressed the room in his reedy dignified voice, "You have become the King, and yet the throne has been occupied by another."

Felix remained silent, trying to read the Elders and see where they were leading the conversation.

"A Dark Wizard has taken the land, and will stop at nothing to see it in ruins." He continued, "We the Dark Fairies of the Forest of Night, cannot stand against this foe alone."

"We would like to stand together." Felix suggested, knowing that the Fairies were a proud people he didn't dare suggest that they stand by his side.

"Together indeed." The Elders nodded in unison. "What are the plans?" He asked finally, leaving Felix on the spot.

"We have built our base at the Low Village, from there we will storm the castle, with greater numbers we are sure to take the throne back, and restore Avidaura." Felix added, sure that they didn't care about the Human throne.

"He has Dragons on his side." The elders raised their brows, waiting to hear of Felix's response.

"And we have swords, your Knights would be outfitted suitably." Felix decided.

They would have enough metal to forge some short blades for the Fairy army, their magics didn't work against Dragons, so they would need another way to fight the beasts.

Eniki smiled from across the table, he had planted that very seed with Felix the last time they had spoken on the way to the Shore of Sorrow.

"Very well." The Elders nodded. "And what of us?" They asked, finally.

"Magic." Felix said plainly, waiting for the word to sink in, "We have two Wizards on our side, and with your magics we should be able to remove the Dark Wizard from Avidaura forever."

"Your Queen, she is a Wizard?" The Elders looked to Piper, who was blushing.

"I am not the Queen," She corrected them softly, "But I am a Wizard, as is my sister, Aishwarya, daughters of Fallon." She added, showing their lineage.

"I see," The Elder looked from Piper to Felix like he was seeing something that they did not, "entrapping the Dark Wizard did not work the last time, it would have to be something....more *drastic*." He whispered, suddenly looking fearful.

"Is there a way to strip him of his magic?" Piper suggested.

"There is one artifact, from the beginning of Avidaura's creation that can strip a Wizard of powers, but it has been lost to us for a millennium." He concluded sadly, "There may be a way to contain his powers, but it could fail...like it did the last time."

"What will you need from us?" Felix asked, they could deal with the defeat of the Wizard later, when they had amassed all of the troops, it would be more practical to meet in the Low Village with the Knights to discuss the final details.

The Elders looked to Eniki, their top Knight, leaving him the task of determining what his army would need.

Eniki cleared his throat, watching Felix for a moment.

"Weapons, made of iron, its the only thing that will damage a Dragon." He began, "A map of the lands, where the siege is to take place." He added, considering, "And a place to take refuge from the light." He said finally.

Felix nodded, "Iron weapons, they will do harm to Dragons?"

"It is one of the few things that can ." Eniki said.

"We can do iron weapons, a map will be made when we return to our base." Felix paused, considering how they could offer to protect the Fairies from the daylight, "Your forest, it reaches the walls of the Low Village?" He asked.

"Yes, but the threat of Dragons is still to be considered." Eniki answered.

"But this Kingdom is protected?" Felix continued.

"Yes."

"Could you protect a base camp in the same manner?" Felix inquired.

Eniki looked to the Elders.

"It would be allowed." They responded to Eniki before he could ask the question.

"Then we shall have your base camp in the Forest of Night, where it is safest for you to reside, next to the Village." Felix concluded. "Is this agreeable?" He asked, looking from Eniki to the Elders, waiting for their answer.

Eniki nodded.

"We shall join you." He announced.

With the basics aside, Felix and the others began to discuss tactics. The Fairies had a wide base of knowledge that Felix was only beginning to comprehend, and the Elders, like Zarah, had been around for the first rising of the Dark Wizard. They were able to shed light on some of his previous moves, helping to anticipate what he truly had planned for Avidaura, and how they might be able to go about stopping him.

The conversation continued on through three meals and two short breaks for fresh air, there was clearly a lot to discuss when going to war. Felix was quickly learning that there was more to leadership than being brave, the Elders seemed to think of every aspect, down to the most minute detail.

Felix was exhausted by the time they were done talking, unsure what time of the day it was, he was relieved when Eniki suggested that they take rest while he rounded up his troops. They would leave in a few hours to make a base camp for the Fairies outside of the Low Village wall, where they would be protected from the Dragons and close enough to assist with the war.

It had been the first true deal that Felix had ever made on his own, and with the Fairies at his side, he was sure that they would have the edge that they needed to unite the rest of Avidaura in their quest to bring order back.

He fell asleep soundly in moments, ready to take on the world.

RONAN

Ash was stiff from crouching on the forest floor, waiting for the Dragons to leave. The trees were shaking from each pass they made over the tree tops, she could hear the fire scorching the lake.

There were more than a dozen of them, she could tell by the steady sounds of fire hissing on the top of the lake. It took Dragons a while to build their fire back up before they could use it again.

It was a good hour before she realized that they were too preoccupied with the lake to bother noticing that there were Humans in the woods. Zarah seemed to notice too, he nodded to them and began to creep forward though the trees.

Slowly and carefully the four crept through the forest towards the path that would take them to the High Village gates. Once they were inside the Village walls they would be safe, but they dared not speak a word until they had reached their destination.

One small sound and the Dragons could easily change course. They were still an easy target, and once they had reached the path, they would be visible until the gates had been opened.

Phil leaned over towards Zarah, his failed whisper echoing through the trees. "Is it safe yet?" He realized a moment too late that his voice had carried.

Ash froze.

Zarah held his finger to his lips, hoping that Phil would stop talking. The forest fell silent as his words drifted away on a breeze. If they were lucky the beasts were too busy to notice. If they were unlucky, their last sight would be the Dragons' teeth.

Overhead the flapping shifted, the treetops ruffled as a snout slid by, poking through the trees as a Dragon passed overhead. A raging screech broke through the silence.

Ash closed her eyes, hoping that the Dragon wouldn't bother checking the woods. There was nowhere they could hide, nowhere they could run, if the Dragons found them they were done for.

An answering screech sounded somewhere over the lake.

A blast of fire shot down through the trees, right where their camp had been. Within minutes the forest was on fire. But they dared not move for fear of the Dragon noticing that it had missed them.

Instead they stayed still and silent as the woods filled with smoke, the fire raging through the wild, still far enough away that they were safe from the heat.

The fire crackled through the woods, too loud for Ash to hear if the Dragon was still watching them, though soon they would have to move, Dragons or not. Their cover had been blown.

Carefully she began to creep through the woods, the rest of her comrades close behind her. At least with the fire blazing the soft sounds of their footsteps wouldn't be heard.

With the Dragons so wild across Avidaura, they hadn't been able to send a Gwin to the High Village to let them know they were coming. Sending a scout ahead had been too dangerous to even consider, so when they did arrive at the Village, no one would be expecting them.

As they finally broke from the trees and approached the gates Zarah slowed down. Ash stared into the sky behind them, watching for Dragons, they would have to be ready to take cover if the gates weren't opened quickly.

Ash, Tor and Phil waited at the edge of the path, close to the woods while Zarah carefully walked to the gate.

He looked nervous, glancing back over his shoulder as he raised his hand to knock. The sound of his fist striking the wood echoed across the empty path, making Zarah jump at the sound.

He stepped back to wait, muffled voices on the other side told him that there were guards there, but the gate didn't move, and no one peered out to see who was there.

Zarah looked over his shoulder at his companions, they all seemed as baffled as he was. Tor walked past him and hammered on the gates again.

Still nothing.

Tor pounded his fists on the wood, "Hello!" He shouted, expecting that someone might hear him on the other side and let them in.

He was about to knock again when the small hatch finally opened and they were greeted with the eyes of a hesitant guard.

"Oh!" His eyes grew wide with surprise as they passed from Zarah to Tor. The hatch closed and they could hear the gates being unlatched.

Finally the gates opened, just enough to allow the four to pass through in single file.

"Quickly." The waiting guard hissed, looking out over their heads into the woods.

Zarah rushed through the gates, into a waiting crowd of guards, weapons at the ready. He looked back at the gate, unsure why there were so many guarding it so prepared for a battle.

The gates closed behind them quickly, latches were back in place moments after it was sealed. They clearly weren't taking any risks.

The guard from the gates approached once he was sure that everything was secure. "A bit dangerous out there to be traveling don't you think?" He raised his brow at Zarah like he was scolding him.

"We are here to see Ronan." Zarah replied dryly.

"Ronan?" The guard looked surprised, "You'll have to wait here..." He trailed off.

"Then we will wait." Zarah nodded impatiently, encouraging the guard to hurry.

The guard walked off into the Village, clearly not in any sort of hurry, leaving Zarah standing by the front gates, waiting.

"Where is he going?" Ash asked, leaning in towards Zarah.

"To get Ronan." Zarah replied.

"That seems...odd." Ash stepped closer, the crowd of guards at the gate were back in their positions, watching the four visitors with wary eyes.

"Something is not right." Zarah whispered, confirming Ash's suspicions.

Something was off at the High Village, and they were right in the middle of it all. Ash looked around, they were surrounded by guards, they were watching their every move with an intensity that was usually reserved for prisoners.

Tor and Phil had crowded in with Ash and Zarah, uncomfortably the four stood in the center of the circle of guards, waiting for Ronan; if he was even coming.

The guards had begun whispering, making the situation even more uncomfortable when there finally fell a hush over the crowd. Ash looked up through the guards and into the Village, her hands ready to cast if she sensed danger, beside her Tor and Zarah had slipped their hands beneath their cloaks onto the hilts of their swords.

The guards parted and Ronan walked through. His face was more serious than Zarah had ever seen it, his eyes steely as they stared at the four travelers, finally resting on Zarah.

His face grew softer, eyes twinkling with a smile, "Zarah?" He sounded surprised.

"Hello Ronan." Zarah bowed his head, "It has been a while."

"Stand down." Ronan shouted, snapping his fingers.

Instantly the guards turned back to the gates, leaving the travelers to Ronan.

"We have had quite a few unwelcome visitors recently." Ronan explained, gesturing for Zarah and his company to follow him, "You can never be too cautious." He added, falling in stride beside Zarah.

Zarah nodded thoughtfully and followed Ronan through the Village. It was quite unlike the last visit to the Village, smoke curled from the black smith shop that seemed to have grown in size. At least twenty men were working on swords as they passed it by. The Village looked darker, every person that they passed seemed busy, their usual cheerful manners had been replaced with blunt pointedness.

Zarah watched carefully as Ronan led them farther into the Village, towards the back walls, it was clear that the Dark Wizard had taken his toll on their lives.

A large building had been constructed along the back walls, it was clearly something that had been added to the Village recently, drapes hung across the front in place of a proper door.

Ronan paused, turning to his guests, "We have much to discuss, you have arrived at the perfect time." He looked at Zarah pointedly, "The Centaurs are forming a rebellion."

"The Centaurs?" Zarah couldn't contain his shocked expression.

"We have all had enough of the false King, join us and we will take Avidaura back." Ronan challenged.

Zarah smiled, placing a hand on Ronan's shoulder, "And we have come to seek allies for our own rebellion, it seems that we are on the same side."

Ronan laughed, "Then we should talk." He nodded, finally turning to the building, he pulled the coverings aside and waved Zarah and the others inside.

The building facade covered a hole in the outer wall of the Village that led into the forest beyond. Zarah heard Ash gasp, though he was not surprised after the revelation that the Centaurs had become involved.

Centaurs were not suited to be confined in a small Village, their sheer size called for more open space and they were quite content with their open range on the upper coast of Avidaura. Very rarely did they venture into the main land.

It was a shock indeed that they would choose to rise against the Dark Wizard, as the Human side of Avidaura meant very little to them with the exception of the trade agreements.

Clearly the Wizard had threatened their way of life.

Zarah passed through the fake building and into the woods, waiting for Ronan to follow behind him.

"Follow me." Ronan appeared at his side and led the way through the woods to a wooden table that had been built to accommodate their meetings.

Zarah took a seat, Ash and Tor on either side. Phil looked uncomfortable, sitting next to Ronan, a man that he had turned against when he had joined the Dark Wizard.

Two Centaurs were approaching from within the trees at a slow trot. They seemed surprised to see extra visitors at the table, but still they approached with kindness.

"Gatlin," Ronan stood, nodding to the taller of the Centaurs, "this is Zarah, former Advisor to the fallen King, leader of the Rogue Knights." Ronan introduced him.

"And his companions?" Gatlin asked, looking each over in turn.

Zarah stood to address the question himself, "Ash, daughter of Fallon, Tor of the true King's Guard, and Phil, a deserter of the Dark Knights." Zarah nodded to each in turn allowing Gatlin to process the introduction.

"Fallon's daughter?" Gatlin seemed impressed. "And she fights against her Uncle?"

"I fight for Avidaura, and the true King." Ash nodded.

Tor was staring at her as though she had grown a second head. Though some of the older inhabitants of Avidaura, those that had been there for the first rising, knew that she was related to the Dark Wizard, it hadn't been made common knowledge amongst the Knights that had rebelled with them.

Zarah had kept it under wraps, even Piper didn't know that they were related to the man who had taken the throne; he was an outcast, he was not family.

Gatlin however, seemed to be uncertain of Ash's loyalty, and rightfully so. The Centaurs, who had very little interest in Human affairs, could not be certain that the Dark Wizard's niece, her bloodline, would choose a side other than his. She could see the concern in the Centaurs eyes as he watched her, considering her a traitor already.

"And who is the true King?" Gatlin asked, watching Ash intently.

"King Felix of the Fallen." She responded with a smile.

Gatlin stared at her, searching her features for a glimmer of doubt. Centaurs were notoriously well known for being able to detect a lie, most of their wealth in Avidaura came from trade agreements, being able to detect false words gave them an edge in their business.

The moment lasted a long while before Gatlin finally nodded, satisfied that Ash was indeed on their side.

"I see." Gatlin smiled, finally at ease with the Wizard before him. "She can be trusted." He confirmed, turning to Ronan with a nod of approval.

Ronan smiled, "I suspected as much." He agreed, "She is an ally of the King, I could see no reason that she would abandon her friends." He added with a knowing look.

"Where are King Felix and Piper?" He asked after a moment.

"They ventured into the Dark Woods to talk to the Fairies." Ash replied, receiving a strange look from Gatlin.

"The Dark Fairies?" He didn't seem sure.

"Yes." Zarah answered proudly, "He has spoken with them before."

"Interesting." Gatlin seemed thoughtful for a moment.

Ronan stepped forward, a grin plastered across his face as his new ally heard about the Human King and his accomplishments.

"They have allies in the east." Ronan stated, "It appears that there are more on our side than we had thought."

"Where are you based?" Gatlin asked.

"We have made our base camp at the Low Village, closer to the Wizard's place at the castle." Zarah confirmed.

"Is it fortified?"

"The Knights are working on it as we speak." Zarah nodded.

"And your numbers?" Gatlin was straight into business.

Soon he and Zarah were conversing like old acquaintances. Though it had been many years since Zarah had had contact with the Centaurs, they easily fell into conversation discussing the one thing that Centaurs knew best; weapons and war.

The Centaurs, though usually a kind and gentle race, lived on the western shores of Avidaura, where sailors and shipwrecks were a daily occurrence. They had protected Avidaura from invasion for centuries, and amassed quite an arsenal of weaponry in the years that they had been there.

Normally they were known to trade with the Humans, mainland resources like food and fresh water for scavenged weapons from their battles. To see the two races united for battle was something that had never been done before.

Zarah had many questions for Gatlin, about how the Centaurs preferred to run a siege. Their style was quite different than those that they normally used, though the fresh perspective could clearly give the army of the Rising an edge that the Wizard wouldn't expect.

Centaurs had not been involved in the last rising, they had been mostly unaware of it until the Dark Wizard had returned and threatened their way of life. Ronan had filled them in on the Human history that had led to the Wizard returning to take Avidaura to its knees.

The history was fresh to them, making Gatlin more inclined to see it all as one large event, rather than two occurrences over a span of time, this gave him more rage behind his words. And Zarah soon came to realize that the Centaurs had indeed been threatened by the Wizard. He had visited them, like so many other creatures in Avidaura, asking them to step aside while he took their land; and Gatlin, would not go easy.

Zarah couldn't recall a time in the history of Avidaura when the Centaurs had gone to war, with anyone. Though they were brutes who had a hold on the weapons trading in the land, they very rarely had a need to use that strength. Most of Avidaura understood not to bother them.

Zarah was both impressed and nervous that the Centaurs had decided to join them in the war to take Avidaura back. Though he knew that they could fight like nothing else, he couldn't be sure that they would care about the Humans enough to keep his army safe from cross fire casualties.

Talks with the Centaurs went better than expected, Ronan had been talking with them for some time before Zarah and his crew had arrived, so the way was already paved for them to join the alliance.

In a matter of hours they had determined, not only how many of the Centaurs would be joining their ranks, but the weapons that they would bring to equip the Human army in turn.

Gatlin seemed to know a thing of two about Dragons, and claimed that the iron ore would be better to damage them, should they have to take on a Dragon. The Village had already been filling the armory with iron laced weapons for a week, their inventory was massive.

When they had finished speaking with the Centaurs, Ronan led them back to the Village to look at some of the swords that had been forged in the previous days.

"They seem eager to join." Zarah commented when they were through the curtain and back in the Village.

"They took his threat very seriously." Ronan nodded, "A bit intense for me, but they should be of great assistance." He added.

Ash had been silent since she had spoken to the Centaurs, Tor and Phil were looking at her as though *she* were a deserter. And Zarah could tell that the common knowledge of the Dark Wizard being her Uncle amongst the older generation of Avidaurans was something that bothered her.

She was a good Wizard, and had been raised away from the darkness. But discovering that a part of her past had been a lie to protect her seemed to be bothering her more than Zarah would have expected.

"I just need to have a word with Ash, we'll join you shortly." Zarah patted Ronan on the shoulder, allowing him to continue on with Tor and Phil as he fell into step beside Ash who had been walking in the back looking desolate and abandoned.

"We'll see you at the blacksmiths then." Ronan nodded, walking away in a hurry, far too excited to show off his weapons.

"Ash, are you okay?" Zarah waited until Ronan and the others had distanced themselves, stopping on the road at Ash's side.

"Yeah," Ash lied, "it's just strange that some people know me as *his* niece." She admitted a moment later.

"More of them know you as Fallon's daughter, and the High Wizard of Avidaura." Zarah assured her.

"I just.." Ash looked around, wondering who was staring, "I didn't know he was alive…" Ash admitted.

Zarah was really the only person that she could talk to about her confusion. Piper, though they were sisters, didn't know their uncle. She didn't know any of her family from Avidaura because she had been raised in another world by their mother. The burden of being the Dark Wizard's family fell on Ash, and she hadn't been prepared to handle it. She had thought he was dead.

"I know that must have come as a shock to you." Zarah agreed, Ash hadn't told him of her encounter with the Wizard and how she had really found out. He must have assumed that one of his Knights had slipped, she could see that he felt guilty for her knowing.

"I'll be fine, it's just….it's strange." She shook her head, plastering a neutral look on her face. "We should go and see the weapons, Ronan seemed pretty excited about them"

"Okay." Zarah patted Ash on the shoulder, "I just wanted to make sure you were alright."

"Thanks Zarah." Ash smiled, thinking of her own father for a moment and how much Zarah reminded her of him.

Zarah and Ash walked to the blacksmiths in silence, the streets growing hushed as they passed. Surely the villagers had heard of their arrival and the true purpose of their visit by now, word traveled fast within the walls of a Village.

"The weaponry." Ronan announced, greeting them outside of the blacksmiths up the street, it appeared that he had already given Phil and Tor the tour and had waited for them before he continued.

Beside the Blacksmiths, several carts had been placed, each heaping with mounds of iron lace weapons. Ronan pulled back the cover on one of the carts, showing Zarah what they had been at work making.

Zarah reached forward, pulling out a sword. The balance was impeccable, the weight was easy to strike with and he was impressed with the quality of the blending of two metals; a thick strip of iron ran through the center of the sword, from the tip to the hilt. Perfect for piercing a Dragon's hide.

"Impressive…" Zarah breathed, mesmerized by the blade.

Ronan took it gently from his hand and placed it back onto the cart, covering it back over.

"We are prepared." He admitted, patting the cloth proudly.

"When would you be ready to depart?" Zarah asked turning the conversation back around.

"We've been ready for weeks." Ronan smiled, "I give the signal and they are ready to march at dawn."

"It's time for the signal." Zarah declared.

"Then we shall march at dawn." Ronan nodded.

KINGS

Felix was still half asleep when he heard the knock on the door. He had only closed his eyes for what felt like a moment, though he really couldn't be sure how much time had actually passed.

The rapping on the door continued, sounding urgent.

"Just one moment." Felix called, announcing that he had heard the caller and wasn't in fact still asleep.

"It's time to go." Eniki's voice called urgently from the other side of the door.

Felix reached for his cloak, tossing it over his shoulders as he pulled his satchel up from the ground and took the two steps to the door. The room was small, no bigger than a broom closet at his home. And yet it had served its purpose, allowing Felix to rest his eyes for a few moments while Eniki had prepared his army to depart.

"The King would like to see you before we depart." Eniki announced as Felix opened the door.

He looked nervous, his eyes wide, face scrunched up trying to look as though it were just a normal day, but Felix could see through it. Eniki was stressed.

Felix nodded, he had expected that he would have to meet with the King, ruler of the Fairy Kingdom, before he departed with a small army of his men. Although his meeting with the Village Elders had been insightful, the King had the final say on what happened to his people, and Felix would have to appear before him if he wished to have the Fairies by his side for the final battle.

He would have to appeal to the King, and promise him the safety of his warriors. While Felix followed Eniki through the winding passages inside the Kingdom tree, he remembered his first visit to the Forest of Night.

He had met with the King of the Fairies once before, during his quest to stop the mirror from draining the magic from the land. The King had treated him with respect, it had been the first time in Felix's short life that he had even pretended to be of the royal bloodline, a Prince who had finally accepted his role in his Kingdom.

And now he returned, only a few short weeks in his time, as a King, and still as naive as he was the last time he had visited; the only difference was that he had grown enough to recognize how little he actually knew. He remembered the first time they had met in the great throne room, the King had seemed so much wiser than Felix. He was sure that he would look like a fool, even now with an army behind him, he didn't have the wisdom of a true King.

Felix still followed Eniki through the small passage, not saying a word. He seemed to be in a hurry to deliver Felix to the throne room, his eyes darting back to Felix frequently as though he expected that he was walking too fast for the Human to keep up to him with his short little legs.

"Is everything okay?" Felix wondered aloud, not really expecting the Eniki would answer.

Eniki huffed, moving faster as he turned down another hall without a word in response. He twisted and turned through the halls without another sound until they had finally turned into the familiar hallway that led to the throne room doors.

They reached the doors quickly, Eniki rapping his knuckles against the door without hesitation. Instantly the door began to open and Eniki finally turned to Felix, his eyes bearing down on him with an intensity that told Felix how serious his meeting with the King was to his Fairy friend.

Eniki stepped aside, his voice stiff, "You have been announced." He declared, leaving Felix to enter alone.

Felix passed Eniki, taking a deep breath and straightening his shoulders as he entered the Fairy throne room. It was exactly as he remembered it, mossy green spanning out before him as a carpet that covered the ground that he walked on, a single throne rising in the center of the room made of vines that twisted from the ground beneath them.

The King was already waiting for him.

There he stood at the center of the room, dwarfed by his throne as he waited for Felix to cross the room and stand before him.

Felix walked before the throne, bowing his head as the King nodded to him in return.

"Welcome back to Avidaura, *King* Felix." He addressed Felix formally. "It has been a long while since we last met." His eyes passed over Felix growing wide for a brief moment, "But perhaps it hasn't been so long for you?"

Felix faltered, "I don't understand?"

"It seems that you have not aged, not as much as this world has." The King leaned towards Felix taking a closer look.

"It is true." Felix admitted, "Time is different on the other side of the mirrors."

"Through the mirrors?" The King smiled, "You crossed to another side?"

"Yes, only for a day." Felix nodded, "But here, it seems that time moved faster."

"Avidaura has indeed changed in your absence."

"I have seen." Felix stared at the mossy ground, he hadn't expected the King of the Fairies to have known that he hadn't aged in the years that had passed. He wasn't sure that the King would allow him use of his army, not knowing that he was still the same foolish Prince that had only just left on a quest that he had failed to complete alone.

"It appears that Avidaura is about to go to war." The King waited for Felix to look up and meet his eyes again, "Are you prepared to lead this army?" His brow raised, watching Felix intently waiting for a response.

"Yes." Felix answered, he had never felt more sure of anything in his life. He could feel it in his bones that he was ready for the war and the command of the army that followed him. He could tell that the King was pleased with his answer, his face grew soft, a small smile fluttering under his beard.

The King lowered his voice, leaning forward, "I do believe that with your *limited* experience." He tipped his head, his voice growing softer, "Eniki may be of great assistance to you." He nodded knowingly towards Felix, offering him a Knight who could help with his tactics.

"It would be of great use to have Eniki on the council." Felix agreed, assuring the King, that though he himself was new to his role, he had already entrusted others who carried the knowledge to lead an army successfully.

"Eniki shall lead my army." The King announced, leaning back, his voice returning to a normal volume. Felix nodded, suddenly realizing why Eniki had seemed so distressed. He had been put in charge of the Fairy army, and any loss would reflect back on him. His loyalty to his King would be put to the test, Felix could understand the tension that his comrade must have been feeling.

"It would be an honor to work with Eniki." Felix smiled, at least he would know the Fairy in charge. He was sure the King had chosen Eniki for that very reason.

"It seems we have reached an agreement." The King nodded, "I shall send you with an army, and an arsenal."

"Thank you, you will not be disappointed." Felix bowed, relieved that the King, even knowing that Felix had not aged, had backed his cause with an army of Fairies.

The King nodded, his face growing soft.

"When the land is restored, I would like you to visit again. It has been a long time since the Fairies and the Humans were united." He smiled, "You have brought us together, and as the King of the Humans I feel that we can work together in the future…when times are not so trying. Perhaps Avidaura could be what it once was."

Felix wasn't sure what to say, he was honored that the King of the Fairies remembered him, and uniting with the Fairies would bring great benefits to the lands. Not even his own father, a great King in his time, had managed an alliance of this sort.

Felix bowed, "We would be honored to work with you." He breathed, holding back his shock.

"It seems that you have a great mission ahead of you, King Felix. May the land be at your side." The King stood from his throne, bowing to Felix, "I hope I shall see you soon."

"Thank you." Felix bowed again, excusing himself from the throne room into the hall.

The King of the Fairies had given him his blessing to take an army to the Low Village, and offered to remain united after the war. Eniki stood on the other side of the door, looking nervous as he waited for Felix.

"Well?" He hissed, searching Felix's face for an answer to a question he hadn't asked.

Felix smiled, "We march when you are ready." He answered.

Eniki sighed, "I had hoped so. Though we have been preparing to leave some Knights behind to protect the Kingdom."

"Absolutely." Felix nodded, "When can we depart?"

"Within the hour." Eniki lead the way towards the exit into the court, "Your party is waiting for you outside." He added, opening the door to the outside.

Darkness waited on the other side of the door. The dim lit clearing was alive with life, Fairies bustling about in a hurried fashion that Felix had never seen before.

Fairies dressed in armor, carts of weapons and bottles of healing elixirs passed by the door before Felix stepped through and spotted Piper. She towered over the small Fairies, helping with one of the carts that they couldn't pull, it seemed too easy for her in comparison.

When Piper spotted Felix across the court she waved, the cart behind her not teetering an inch, though the Fairies seemed to panic thinking that she was about to spill their precious parcels all over.

Piper pulled the cart across the court, setting it gently down before she took the final steps to reach Felix and Eniki.

"Is everything okay?" She asked Felix, looking at Eniki's face with concern.

"Yes," Felix smiled, "Eniki says we should be good to leave within the hour.

"Why does he look so worried?" She wondered aloud.

"I'm not worried." Eniki snipped, staring across the clearing with a scowl, "There is just much to prepare."

"Where is Finnigan?" Felix asked, changing the subject before Eniki changed his mind about joining them.

"Finnigan is helping with their supplies." Piper pointed across the clearing, where Finnigan, towering over the Fairies, was helping fill a cart.

"Should we patrol the perimeter, check for Dragons?" Felix suggested to Eniki, who's face was still quite serious.

"Yes, that would be of great assistance." He answered, "We should have the carts ready soon. I will come and find you." He added, seemingly glad that they had been willing to scout for Dragons rather than sending his Fairies to do the task.

Felix walked towards the edge of the Fairy Kingdom, trailing along the line where their land changed from the protected Kingdom to the rest of the dark woods. He stayed just inside the line, knowing that he was safe from the forest and the vines while he remained inside of the Fairy safe haven.

Outside of the Kingdom, the forest seemed still and quiet. Piper walked alongside him, staring into the trees, watching the light bugs flickering in the dark.

He knew that they reminded her of her home world, the light bugs that blinked in the darkness, she had called them fireflies once. He watched her face, glowing softly in the flickering glow from the forest as they reached the path that carried out into the woods and the main path.

Felix turned, taking the path away from the Kingdom, into the dark woods.

Piper fell into step beside Felix, waking to the edge of the Kingdom, "Here's your coin back." She held out Felix's coin, it was already starting to glow blue as they neared the edge of the dark woods.

Felix took the coin from Piper, looking it over, "This thing is pretty handy." He commented, smiling.

"I know," Piper laughed, "Eniki gave me one of my own." She pulled a second coin from inside of her cloaks showing it to Felix.

"Really?" He looked at Piper's hand, the soft blue of a coin resting on her palm.

"Yeah." She blushed, "He seems to think that I am the Queen…." Piper trailed off looking away.

Felix smiled, "I can see why."

"What?" Piper was still blushing when she turned back to Felix.

"You're always there, right in the thick of it. I wouldn't be the King without you…" He trailed off, trying to keep the flush from creeping onto his own cheeks.

"You would still be King."

"I wouldn't have been ready to be a King if I hadn't met you." Felix admitted.

They has stopped walking, standing in the middle of the charred wasteland outside of the Fairy Kingdom. Light bugs twinkled outside of the blue glow that surrounded them.

Felix leaned in, "Would it be so bad?" He asked, "To be the Queen?"

Piper smiled, leaning towards Felix as their lips met.

Somewhere in the silence a flute had started playing, a thin cold tune that filled the clearing. Felix looked up, Eniki was standing at the path to the Kingdom.

"Well don't stop on my account..." He said dryly, a pan flute at his chin.

Piper turned away, her face red with embarrassment, Felix stepped towards Eniki.

"Are they ready?" He asked, clearing his throat.

"Are *you* ready?" Eniki smirked.

Felix rolled his eyes.

"We're ready." Piper decided, walking back to the path where Eniki stood.

"The coast is clear." She added, though she and Felix had been too distracted to really check.

Eniki raised the pan flute to his lips, letting out a shrill note that seemed everlasting. The light bugs fluttered off, and behind him, the sound of feet and carts began to grow closer.

"Then we march." He smiled, returning the flute to his belt.

Soon Finnigan appeared, leading the army of Fairies, with the largest of the carts trailing behind him.

"Lead the way." He called ahead as the Fairies began to pile up in the clearing.

Eniki took the lead, with Felix at his side, the rest of the army soon fell into step behind them.

Finnigan waited, taking the last place in the line with Piper, their final line of defense should they run into trouble along the way.

Eniki seemed to have a bounce in his step as he led the way through the Forest of Night. The blue glow from Felix's coin disappeared amongst the blues and purples of the Fairy staffs, they were safe from the woods.

"I thought you said she wasn't the Queen..." Eniki leaned over after they had been walking for a short while.

Felix frowned, "She isn't....that doesn't mean..." He trailed off before he could get himself into any more trouble.

It was true what he had said to Piper, he wouldn't have been the King if it wasn't for her, and he certainly wouldn't have been ready to take on Avidaura if he didn't have her at his side. There was just too much to worry about to even consider rushing into things like that just yet.

"Perhaps one day." Eniki said, the knowing look on his face causing Felix to blush again.

"Perhaps." Felix smiled.

***

The journey back to the Low Village was near half a day, though the darkness in the forest made it seem like it was much quicker. As they reached the break in the trees, Felix could finally see the light of day on the other side.

"Should we stop here?" Eniki inquired, reminding Felix that they dare not pass into the sunlight.

"Yes." Felix waited for Piper and Finnigan to make it through the crowd of Fairies before he passed through into the light.

"Finnigan." He called, waiting for the Knight to join them.

"That was fun." Finnigan smiled, blinking as his eyes adjusted to the sun after the trek through the dark.

"Would you stay with the Fairies, as their liaison?" He asked, turning to knock on the gates to announce their return.

"I would be honored." Finnigan nodded, "They're nicer than I thought they'd be." He added as an afterthought.

The hatch opened, and a pair of eyes peered out at them for a brief second before it closed back over and the latches began to come undone.

When the doors opened, Ronan was already waiting for them on the other side.

"Did it go well with the Fairies?" He asked, looking skeptical.

"They will make their base camp on the outskirts, where their forest meets your wall." Felix announced with a nod.

Ronan's eyes grew wide with surprise.

"They were willing to join us?"

"They sent what they could." Felix nodded.

"Do they need anything." Ronan scrambled, he clearly hadn't been expecting the Fairies to be willing to join the Humans. Immediately he seemed to be panicked, rushing to find something to offer them, a sign of his role as a Village Chief wearing through his tough demeanor.

"Finnigan knows what they will be needing, refer to him and they should be settled in soon enough." Felix turned to Finnigan.

"Anything they need." He reminded his companion, Finnigan nodded and turned back to the woods.

"And what of you and Piper?" Ronan asked.

"We will continue on to the Clurichaun." He turned to Piper, making sure that she agreed.

Piper nodded, "I'm ready."

"We will see you when we return." Felix looked back at the gates, they had already begun to unlatch them again for his departure.

"I shall go with Finnigan to greet our new companions then." Ronan stepped towards the gates, talking to the guard who nodded to him with understanding.

The four passed back through the great gates of the Low Village and onto the well-worn path.

"Best wishes on your journey." Ronan bowed as the gates closed before he and Finnigan disappeared back into the dark forest.

Felix watched after them for a moment, listening for Ronan's gasp as he crossed through the barrier.

Felix chuckled, "I don't think he was expecting that."

Piper laughed lightly, "No, I don't think he was."

Before they started down the path Felix paused. "It would probably be faster to cut through the forest." He observed, reaching for his copy of the map from his satchel.

"It would save us the trouble of running into the Wizard's Knights." Piper agreed, waiting for Felix to unfold the parchment so she could look it over.

"Back to the old camp, and out the other side." Felix pointed, "It would cut off a half day." He added.

"Agreed." Piper nodded, searching for the place where they had come out at the Village when they had moved the camp, "It's a little ways up." She pointed to an opening in the trees a few steps up the path.

Felix tucked the map away and they started to walk.

LUCINDA

Dawn hadn't arrived at the High Village, though the Knights were already crowding at the gates, ready to depart. Ash had lost sight of Zarah while she had been preparing herself for the journey back to the Low Village and she was having trouble finding him in the chaos that had taken over the paths at the gate.

She searched for him in the crowd, though he was indistinguishable from the Knights, all dressed in the same garb in preparation for their final battle. The crowd jostled Ash as she tried to weave her way through, searching for him.

Ash wanted to talk to Zarah before they departed, she still hadn't been sleeping well, and there was a sickly feeling in the pit of her stomach that something was going to go wrong. She wanted to be sure that they had covered everything, that they had a backup plan in place if something went wrong on their journey. She needed to know that they could still save Avidaura if Piper and Felix didn't return, she still couldn't shake the feeling that they were in danger.

Pushing her way through the crowd, Ash finally spotted Zarah talking with Ronan and Gatlin at the back wall of the Village. She squeezed through the crowd, trying not to lose sight of him as she tried to get free of the Knights pressing their way towards the gates. It was like swimming upstream, everyone was heading in the other direction. Finally she broke free, racing to the back wall before Zarah could disappear again.

"Ash!" Zarah spotted her and waved her over, calling over the crowd.

"I've been looking for you everywhere." Ash breathed, finally catching up to him, "Is everything ready?" She asked, nodding to Ronan and Gatlin in greeting.

Gatlin stepped forward proudly to answer, "Everything is ready, we are prepared to move on your command." He bowed his head to Ash.

"And your men?" Ash asked Ronan, glancing back at the crowd of Knights saying their final goodbyes to loved ones they would be leaving behind.

"We are ready as well." He confirmed, "The men should be prepared to depart shortly." He added, seeing that they were beginning to line themselves up at the gate.

"Then we shouldn't waste any more time." Ash decided, watching Zarah shake his head in agreement. "Prepare to leave immediately." She decided, giving the final word that they had been waiting for.

"As you wish." Gatlin turned to Ronan, waiting.

"Send the signal." Ronan nodded, stepping back as Gatlin pulled forth an arrow and his bow.

Gatlin leaned forward, striking the tip of the arrow against the ground, somehow igniting it. Ash stepped back, watching as he turned it in his bow, drawing it back as he arched it towards the sky and released it. The arrow burst forth in a high arc over the Village before exploding with a loud pop, sending a shower of deep red sparks into the sky before it disappeared into nothing.

The crowd went silent, staring at the sky in awe as the Knights turned to Gatlin and Ronan as though they had been called.

Ronan stood tall, raising his voice as he spoke, "It is time." He announced, watching as the crowd nodded, turning to the gates wordlessly to sort themselves as they had been asked.

The crowd began to move, the silence that had washed over the them disappeared as the Knights finished their final goodbyes and moved to wait at the gates for the doors to be opened.

"Safe travels." Zarah patted Ronan on the shoulder, ready to depart, "We will see you at the Low Village." He nodded solemnly.

Ronan nodded, watching as Ash and Zarah departed, leaving him at the end of the line to protect their ranks with Gatlin at his side.

Zarah and Ash walked through the crowd, the Knights parting for them as they made their way towards the gates. As they approached the doors, the guards began to open them and silence washed over the crowd again.

Ash had never seen both of the doors to the Village opened at the same time. As she walked towards the front of the crowd, the opening continued to grow wider as the wooden doors were pulled out of the way, revealing the wide open path ahead. She and Zarah didn't slow when they reached the gates, they continued out onto the path outside of the Village, listening to the shuffle as the Knights at the front began to follow behind them. Ash held her head up high, trying her hardest to keep her eyes on the path ahead and not look back, all the while knowing that she may never see the High Village again.

It was a strange feeling walking at the front of the line, knowing that an army walked behind her. She had only been a Wizard in training until her return through the Mirror and her father's untimely demise, the way that she was treated now, with such authority, was taking some getting used to.

Mavera, Gatlin's second in command, trotted alongside Ash and Zarah at the front of the line. He kept pace with them easily, watching the horizon as they led the Knights down the path.

"I have never been into these parts of Avidaura." He admitted, not looking down, his eyes still trained on the distance, searching for threats, "Is it much different?" Mavera asked, his voice peaking with curiosity.

"Not really," Ash answered, glad for the distraction, "the Low Village is quite a lot like the High Village." She added, not quite sure what Mavera was accustomed to in the Centaur's Village, she had never seen their land to know how different it may be.

"And in between?" Mavera asked, still watching the path.

"There isn't much." Ash answered, "Just this path."

Mavera seemed surprised, he glanced down at Ash, "There is *nothing?*"

"Well there is the Lagoon, a little ways ahead." Ash explained, "But it is not a Human inhabited place." She added.

"Oh." Mavera sighed, "I see." He nodded and returned to his watch as they walked.

Behind them the army of Knights from the High Village walked, their whispered conversations buzzing through the crowd. Many of the men had never left the High Village, let alone traveled across Avidaura. Ash could hear them wondering about their sister Village and what they would find there.

Beside her, Zarah had stayed silent, his face set in a look of determination, but Ash could see through it. He was worried. Taking the castle path was a bold move against an opponent who had trained Dragons, though they had been walking for nearly an hour, the risk of being discovered by the Dark Wizard was as high as it was the moment they had left the Village.

"Are you okay Zarah?" Ash whispered, trying to shake him out of his thoughts.

Zarah sighed, a smile growing on his lips, though it was just for show.

"I'm surprised we haven't seen anything yet." Zarah admitted, keeping his voice low, he turned, looking back over the trail of Knights as though he expected that they were under a quiet attack that he had missed.

"They are fine." Ash waited for Zarah, he had slowed his pace to look back.

"I see." He joined her again, quickening his pace to reach Mavera who had not slowed to wait. "I am just surprised that ..." Zarah trailed off.

"That he hasn't noticed us yet." Ash finished his sentence quietly, "You think he will?" She asked.

"We would be lucky if he didn't." Zarah's voice was flat and tired, Ash could tell he was bracing himself for the worst.

"And if he does?" Ash considered, "Are we ready if he does?" She asked.

"We have a plan for it." Zarah answered quickly.

"And why was I not aware of this plan?" Ash stepped closer to Zarah, lowering her voice to keep their conversation as quiet as possible, she found it hard to believe that Zarah could go making plans without her, especially important plans like he was talking about.

Zarah passed her a look, she could see him hesitate.

"Well?" She asked again, "Shouldn't I know what the plan is?" She was starting to get frustrated. She was supposed to be the High Wizard of Avidaura, and Zarah was keeping battle tactics from her, they were supposed to be on the same side, she couldn't imagine why he wouldn't just tell her.

Zarah cleared his throat, still stalling though Ash could tell that he was about to let her in on the plan.

"If we are found, Mavera is to take you and run." Zarah spoke slowly and clearly, watching Ash as her face went blank.

"What?" She asked, though she had heard him quite plainly.

"You are the High Wizard of Avidaura, *you* are our number one priority." Zarah added for clarity, "We need you, and you will be protected."

"That's the plan?" Ash was appalled.

"That is as much of the plan as you need to know." Zarah confirmed that there was more, perhaps he wasn't telling her because he didn't want her to protest her departure.

Ash bit her tongue, she had things she wanted to say, but she knew that her words wouldn't change the situation. Zarah didn't want her facing the Dark Wizard, not yet. So if they were confronted on their journey, she would have to leave, she just didn't know if she could if it came down to it.

Zarah expected her to put her own safety above those of the Knights that had given up their lives for Avidaura, those who had volunteered to fight with them. She didn't know how she felt about it, though for a moment she considered what her father would have done.

Fallon would have known that saving the High Wizard would give them another chance in the fight, he would have left and retaliated in his own time. If her father had still been there she would have expected him to go with Mavera.

"Okay." Ash breathed, surprising Zarah with her answer.

"It is good to hear that you have some sense." Mavera commented, clearly he had been listening, though he had appeared to be concentrating on the forest ahead of them.

Ash went silent, she still wasn't sure what she would do if the situation arose, but there wasn't much point in talking about it any longer, they still had a long walk ahead of them, and they needed to stay alert.

They fell silent, walking down the long path towards the Low Village at the other end. Ash stared ahead, avoiding eye contact with Zarah and Mavera, she could tell that they both had more to say, and she didn't want to hear it.

It had been nearly an hour of silence, the sun rising high in the sky and with it the heat on the open path was becoming nearly unbearable when Mavera paused suddenly.

Ash stopped beside him, turning to see what had caused him to halt so abruptly.

"Do you hear that?" He whispered, staring into the trees beside the path, searching for the source of the sound he had heard.

Ash and Zarah both turned towards the trees, trying to hear what he was referring to, but his Centaur ears had clearly picked up something beyond their range of hearing.

"Do you?" Mavera asked again, turning to regard his companions.

"I don't hear it." Ash whispered, still straining to pick up the sound.

"There is something in the woods." Mavera announced, slowly trotting over to the side of the path, his head tilted to pick up the sound.

Though Ash still couldn't hear the sound that had caused Mavera to stop so suddenly, she knew that he wouldn't waste their time if it was just an animal scampering in the trees. She turned to Zarah, seeing the same concern on his tired face.

"We should check this out." She decided, stepping towards Mavera at the edge of the path.

Zarah turned to the closest Knight, "Wait here." He ordered, following Ash towards the woods.

They were near the place they had stopped to make camp before arriving at the High Village, Ash could see the burn marks from their fire as they entered the woods to discover what had caught Mavera's ear.

Finally Ash heard it, through the trees off in the distance ahead of them, the flapping of wings. "Dragon?" She hissed, instantly lowering her voice as they crept forward to see.

There was another sound coming through the trees that Ash couldn't quite place, it sounded like hissing, though she was sure that Dragons didn't make a sound like that.

Carefully they crept towards the opening on the other side of the trees, where the Lagoon waited, staying under the cover of the branches so they wouldn't be seen. Though realistically, if they could see the Dragons, then the Dragons from their height could see the army of Knights waiting on the path beyond the trees.

Things were about to go very wrong.

Ash could feel the tension in the air, as Zarah began to pass looks to Mavera, prepared to make the call to have Ash whisked away.

They reached the edge of the trees and Mavera held his arm out, warning them not to step farther into the opening. Ash stared past him, the Lagoon before them was smoking, steam rising from the waters creating an eerie scene in the bright mid-day sun.

"That's the Lagoon." Ash hissed staring at the chaos in horror. She tried to look though the canopy overhead to see how many Dragons there were she could hear their wings, and knew that there was more than one on the attack.

"Oh my." Zarah was still staring at the Lagoon, the steam and smoke covering it so entirely that it looked like dusk beyond the clearing.

"What are we supposed to do?" Ash turned to him, "We can't just leave them like this, they'll all die if the water gets too hot." Ash watched as another Dragon swooped, blasting a stream of fire atop the water, it hissed and bubbled, steam rising as the temperature rose. "They'll all die." Ash breathed, realizing that there was nowhere for the Merfolk to go, the Lagoon was all they had, there was no escape hatch, they couldn't just run, they needed the water to survive.

"They won't survive this." Mavera agreed quietly watching the skies. It looked like he was trying to see how many Dragons there were, and from his vantage he could see more clearly then Ash who was only up to his waist.

"How many?" Ash asked, when he looked like he had made a full assessment.

"Two." He confirmed, reaching for his bow and pulling an arrow from the holster on his back.

He crept forward, not quite breaking through the line of trees that wrapped around the open Lagoon, watching for the Dragons. Mavera paused, waiting for each Dragon to take a blow before he rushed through the line of fire at the edge of the trees with his bow at the ready.

One quick draw and he had struck the first of the Dragons. With a screech they both turned towards the Centaur at the edge of the woods. Mavera drew again, striking the second Dragon in the wing as it swooped, sending it off course.

Ash pulled her sword from her hip and charged to Mavera's side, ready to strike.

The first Dragon screeched again, both turned and drifted off over the forest away from the Lagoon, the one with the injured wing listing to the side.

"We should send word through the ranks, have the archers ready." Mavera turned to Zarah. "They may turn back."

"Yes, we will do just that." Zarah breathed, staring at the lake with a pained expression on his face.

Ash stepped forward, the familiar glow from the depths drawing her in. She was nearly in the water when she realized that she was booted and cloaked.

"Ash, we should return." Zarah called, turning with Mavera back to the forest.

"One moment," Ash looked back. "I need to talk to her."

Mavera stepped forward, to Ash's side, "The Merfolk talk to no one." He shook his head at Ash like she was dreaming.

A moment later two heads broke free from the water.

"You have returned." The same Mermaid that Ash had spoken to before was bobbing in the water with a companion at her side. Both were carrying spears.

"Yes." Ash breathed, still taken by their beauty.

The Mermaids looked around for a moment, "The Dragons, they have gone?"

"They may return." Mavera spoke, "But for now they will not bother you."

"Is this the resistance?" She turned to ask Ash.

"Yes, we are great in numbers." Ash smiled. "Are you sure that you could not offer your assistance?"

"I spoke with the council." She shook her head pausing to look at the Centaur, it was clear that she had never seen one before.

"Would they allow us a pearl?" Ash asked, hopeful.

"They would not." The Mermaid frowned. "Do you know what a pearl is?" She asked.

Ash considered the question, it seemed to out of place. "It amplifies magic." She answered, sure that she was correct.

"This is true, but do you know what a pearl *is*?" The Mermaid asked again, watching Ash's face.

"Well it is just a pearl....isn't it?" Ash was confused.

The Mermaid moved closer, pulling her tail on the ledge where the water was shallow.

"A pearl," She looked back at her companion, "is the soul of a Mermaid." She watched Ash again, "To take a Mermaid's pearl, is to condemn them to the land."

Ash gasped, "I had no idea..." She apologized, she hadn't realized that she had been asking a Mermaid to give up its life, all for a bit of magic.

"It is never done." She added, "But Avidaura is falling..."

Ash shook her head, "I shouldn't have asked..."

"We wouldn't survive if the Wizard won..." She looked sadly at her companion. "I would offer myself for your cause." She finally declared, her sad eyes boring into Ash's soul.

"But," Ash was shocked, "what would happen to you?"

"I would be land ridden," The Mermaid stared into the woods stoically, "until my pearl was returned." She added, looking pointedly at Ash.

Ash sighed with relief. "So I could *borrow* your pearl..." She trailed off.

"And return it when the Wizard has been defeated." She concluded.

"You would be willing?" Ash asked, Zarah was at her side, his face nervous with excitement. A pearl would give them an edge that they could use to defeat Darius. But the cost was quite steep.

"Would you protect me while I am land-ridden?"

"At all costs." Zarah agreed, looking at Ash.

"Yes." Ash agreed, glad that Zarah would allow her the men to protect the Mermaid.

"I shall see you soon." The Mermaid had turned to speak to her companion, confirming that she would allow Ash the use of her pearl.

"Lucinda, are you sure?"

"Yes. Tell the council that I will return." She reached for her companions hand, squeezing it tightly. "And Avidaura will be saved." She breathed quietly.

Her companion nodded. Still waiting at the surface as Lucinda pulled herself to the shore.

Ash stepped forward, drawing off her cloaks to cover the Mermaid from the chill of the land. A great white light overtook the waters as Lucinda pulled herself from the waters, her face growing pained for a moment as her fin was drawn from the lake.

Lucinda gasped, collapsing to the ground, her fins no longer present. Ash covered her with her cloak, drawing it tightly across her bare legs.

"This is yours...for now." Lucinda held out her hand, a large pearl rested in her hand. Ash reached forward gingerly taking it from the Mermaid.

"Thank you." She breathed, staring at the gleaming pearl before making sure that it was held safe in her satchel wrapped inside the leather pouch of her canteen.

"Zarah." She called back.

Mavera stepped forward. "She may ride with me." He announced, in awe of their transaction.

"Thank you." Ash stepped back as Mavera leaned forward, his brute strength, lifting Lucinda from the shore and onto his back.

ALONE

"Are you sure that it was a good idea to go alone?" Piper whispered, following Felix along the trail back to the old camp. It was safer to travel through the woods than on the main path, she was quickly learning more about Avidaura than she could have ever learned on her own.

Though Zarah's team had done a decent job at hiding their tracks from the move, the brush had been cut back, making a clear path for Piper and Felix to travel on. It was easier than finding their own way through the woods, and safer than the guarded castle road.

Felix paused, waiting for Piper to catch up to him before he answered her so his voice wouldn't carry.

"The Clurichauns trust us." He whispered back to her as she stopped beside him, "I don't know how they would react if we went in with an army." Felix imagined the raging Clurichaun attacking his Knights like they had the Giant.

They had to go in alone to talk to Murray, otherwise it could go very wrong, the Clurichaun could be savage.

And savage was exactly what Felix needed to give his army an edge.

Piper nodded in agreement, "As long as you thought it through..." She mumbled, falling into step beside Felix silently.

"I also brought ale." Felix muttered, reaching for an oversized canteen at his side. "I thought it might soften Murray up a bit." He smiled.

Piper laughed, "That should do the trick." She chuckled, remembering the Clurichaun leader and his thirst for ale with fondness.

They had turned out to be a kind people, Piper recalled the first time she had met them, Felix hadn't been with her then. They had given her cloaks and food, though she had barely made it out of the Village, they had been eager to have her stay. She had been new to Avidaura then, and unsure who she could trust. The second time she had met them it had been very different, they had been wild, untamed, the very thing that nightmares were made of. If Felix could manage to get them on his side in the war, she didn't doubt that they would do some damage.

She was sure that Murray would at least hear them out.

Piper resumed the walk through the woods in silence with Felix, the old camp wasn't too far off, but with only two of them walking through the trees, everything seemed so much louder. Piper found herself walking more careful to try not to make so much noise, but each step she took was followed with the sound of her cloaks dragging behind her, scraping against the layer of leaves beneath her feet.

There was still the chance that the Dark Knights had found the remnants of their camp, it was only a matter of time before they did, and Piper was nervous traveling through the forest that they would be discovered.

There was an edge in the air, that hung heavily on Felix's shoulders. They hadn't run into any trouble yet, though without Finnigan he knew that they had perhaps spread themselves too thin for their journey. Felix held his head high, keeping an extra careful watch on the forest around them, he could feel that something was coming, he just hoped that they reached the Clurichauns before they ran into trouble.

By the time they had finally reached the old camp in the woods, Felix was tired and parched. "You up for a quick break?" He whispered, settling onto a log before Piper could agree.

"You know it." She smiled, sitting down next to him and reaching for her canteen while she looked around the clearing.

It had been hard, walking in silence for so long, so much hanging in the air. There was a war coming, their mission to recruit the Clurichauns made it all the more real. Walking through the quiet forest seemed so out of place, so unnatural with the looming threat of a battle hanging in the air.

"It shouldn't take us long to reach the Village." Piper stared at the old camp around them, there were nearly no signs that anyone had ever lived in the clearing, save the track marks from the carts barely hidden beneath the leaves.

"We still have to cross the path." Felix reminded her, taking another gulp from his canteen. "We'll have to be careful." He added.

Piper nodded with understanding, the nervous expression on her face reflecting exactly what Felix was feeling about the next leg of their journey. They would have to cross the path near the bridge to the castle, where the Dark Wizard's Knights would be keeping guard. He was sure that their numbers would have grown since the siege on the castle, they would be hard to avoid.

But if they could make it past, they would be able to win over the Clurichauns, the small army of roughens who were capable of taking out a Giant for no other reason than a search for ale.

"Do you think Murray will join us?" Piper asked, tucking away her canteen as she prepared to move again.

"I think they would," Felix admitted, "they seemed to have some conflict with the Dark Wizard that took their ale." Felix reminded her.

Piper chuckled, "Do you think they'd be willing to give up their fountain to join us?" She asked seriously looking worried.

"I'm sure we can make it worth their while." Felix smiled.

He had already prepared for the Clurichauns at the Low Village, with the help of Ash they had recreated the Clurichaun fountain, a small offering for agreeing to help them recover Avidaura from the grip of the Dark Wizard. He hoped that it would be enough to appease them in their move to join forces.

"You sound like you have something up your sleeve." Piper stood, waiting for Felix to join her.

"Felix shook out his cloaks, staring at his wrists, "Nope." He answered.

"Oh, I mean, it sounds like you *planned* something." Piper chuckled, "For the Clurichaun." She added.

"Oh," Felix nodded, "just wait and see, I think they'll be happy to join us." He added with confidence.

"You've already got the Fairies." Piper nodded, "They seemed pretty eager to join you, Finnigan was surprised." Piper added.

Though she herself wasn't aware how the Kingdoms within Avidaura normally interacted, having grown up in the other place, Finnigan's reaction to Felix's success at securing the Fairies as allies had seemed to impress Piper.

"The King has asked me to return when Avidaura has been restored." Felix admitted, feeling proud of himself, though Piper wouldn't fully understand the implications of such a request.

"Wow." Piper seemed more impressed than Felix had expected her to be, "It sounds like you've made an alliance."

"I think so." Felix beamed, proud of himself for accomplishing something good amongst the horror that had overtaken Avidaura, "We just need to save Avidaura first." He added quietly, finally standing to join Piper.

"You ready to go?" She asked.

"Yeah. Let's take it easy though," Felix listened to the forest, again worried about the stunned silence.

The next part of their journey would have to be timed just right. They were about to pass over the castle road where the Dark Wizard's Knights patrolled. They had already lost their backup when Felix had asked Finnigan to stay with the Fairies and get them settled at the Village, it was just Felix and Piper, and neither were very good in a fight.

Piper walked quietly behind Felix as he led the way to the edge of the clearing towards the small break in the trees that would take them to the castle road. Each twig that snapped beneath their feet caused Felix to pause. He could feel that something wasn't quite right, the stillness of the forest around them set him on edge, he was waiting for something to go wrong.

Felix paused before they reached the road, turning to Piper to make a plan.

"Are we ready?" She asked, peeking over his shoulder with curiosity.

"We'll scout it out first." Felix decided, turning back towards the road.

When they had neared the castle road and were able to see it through the trees they settled in to watch. The Knights of the Dark Wizard tended to patrol in perfectly timed rounds. They would wait for the patrol to pass and then they would have a clear shot at the path to the Clurichaun Village.

Felix's legs were beginning to cramp when they finally spotted a set of Dark Knights departing from the castle bridge to take their patrol of the castle path. Felix and Piper ducked down, staying quiet as the two slowly made their way past, watching the woods carefully, looking for the Knights that opposed their King.

It was a long while of silence that followed, while they waited for the Knights to get far enough down the path not to see them when they left the woods.

"I think we're clear." Piper stood from her place in the brush, holding a hand out for Felix.

Felix reached for her hand, pulling her back. Something was off, he could tell that they were being watched.

"What?" Piper whispered as Felix pulled her back behind the cover of the trees.

"Look." Felix pointed to the sky, a Dragon was coming, and it was aimed right at them.

"It's coming right for us…" Piper tensed.

They didn't have time to run, the Dragon was already swooping in for a landing in the center of the wide open path, it circled low twice before landing with a thud that rattled the forest.

Dark eyes stared at them through the trees, though the Dragon stood eerily calm, Felix knew that it had seen them. Felix froze, it was too late for them to duck behind the cover of the trees. Piper was still gripping his hand, the pressure increasing as she stared into the eyes of the beast.

Felix slipped his hand from her grasp, slowly moving it towards the hilt of his sword as the Dragon finally moved, tucking its wing in towards its side, revealing the Dark Wizard.

Felix felt his heart in his throat, his hand moved past the hilt of his sword, reaching again for Piper's hand before he even knew what he was doing.

Her palm in his, he stared at the Wizard, knowing that this was his last moment, his last chance to fight for Avidaura. It was as though he was back in the throne room, bound and bleeding, though this time his inability to move was sparked by the fear that coursed through his veins and not the Wizard's magic.

Piper took a side step towards Felix, her eyes trained forward on the Wizard, her movement stiff with fear. Felix could tell that she was feeling the same fear.

The Wizard watched them, stepping from the cover of his Dragon's wing, but he did not cross the path to greet them.

"You are a hard lady to find." His eyes fell on Piper as he finally spoke, his voice filled with amusement at their predicament.

Piper whimpered, realizing that the Wizard was there for her. Felix squeezed her hand and took a step forward, blocking her body from their oncoming foe. Though he knew that his stance wouldn't do much to protect her against the Wizard, he hoped the gesture would help her stay calmer.

"Oh, and the fallen Prince…" The Wizard shook his head, mocking Felix, "Still trying to be brave for your people I see." A small smirk played on his lips.

Felix growled, "Avidaura will not be yours." He snarled, glaring at the Wizard while knowing full well that those may be his last words.

"Oh, who *cares* about Avidaura…" the Wizard brushed off Felix's words, stepping to the side so he could see Piper better, "I've come to talk to *you*." He smiled at Piper like she was a friend that had been long forgotten.

Piper tensed, gripping Felix's hand so tightly that he could feel pain shooting up his arm, if the Wizard noticed he didn't seem to care. He took another step, still staring at Piper, a whimsical look on his face.

"Still happy living under your sister's shadow?" He continued as though Piper had responded.

"What?" Piper whispered, she sounded confused.

Felix had no idea what the Wizard was getting at, it seemed so strange that he would want to speak to Piper, even stranger to imply that she had been living under Ash's shadow, when she had just arrived from another world a few short weeks earlier, at least in Felix's time line that is.

"I know it was you that freed me, I thought maybe you had grown tired of living under the shadow of Fallon's first born…" He trailed off, lazily stepping closer to Piper.

"I don't know what you're talking about." Piper hissed, the edge in her voice clear.

"We would make a great team, you and I. I could show you what *real* power feels like…" He smiled again, it didn't look natural on his pointed face, "No more hiding in the shadows, no more riding your sister's cloaks…true power." He offered, waiting for Piper to agree with him.

Piper looked surprised, "I would *never* join you." She breathed, daring to defy him, "I would *never* take a Kingdom so cruelly." She stared at the Wizard, her eyes gleaming with hatred.

"We will take Avidaura back." Felix declared, still standing between Piper and the Wizard, "I wouldn't get too comfortable in that throne, it won't be yours much longer." Felix dared.

"You can have your throne." The Wizard laughed, "It won't mean much when the land is gone." His snide voice cut Felix like glass as he turned back to Piper, "You are the one that freed me." His voice had grown soft, stepping towards Piper again, "It is because of *you* that I will be able to achieve greatness in this universe." He stepped closer again, only a breath away from Felix who still stood his ground.

"Are you sure that you don't want to join me, and see how we can rule over *everything*." He whispered, his eyes twinkling with mischief.

Piper had gone ridged, her hand still in Felix's, had grown cold.

"I would never join you." Her voice carried across the clearing, filled with rage.

"Just like your sister." The wizard smirked, "Then you shall fall together." He stared at Piper, allowing her the chance to change her mind.

Piper gripped Felix's hand firmly, staying silent. Her other hand raised into the air, facing the Wizard, and she released a gust of wind strong enough to make his Dragon take a step back.

But the Wizard didn't budge, his cloaks whipped around him, and still he stood, watching Piper with amusement. When the gust had died down he smiled.

"As you wish." He snarled, flicking his wrist.

Piper shot back into the trees, nearly taking Felix with her as he tried to hold on to her hand.

Felix fell to the ground, staring after Piper into the trees, a hand landed on his shoulder and he felt his body grow ridged.

"I'll need to borrow you for a little while." The Wizard whispered in his ear, leaving Felix on the path frozen in place as he mounted his Dragon.

A thick clawed hand reached out for Felix, the Dragon gripping him in its front claws.

Piper rose from the ground, her hands both shooting forwards, power flowing from her like the stars in the sky. Felix felt it as it radiated through him, knocking him unconscious. Her magic was unable to reach the Dragon through its protective scales.

With one lurching leap the Dragon was back in the air, Felix teetering high above the land.

Piper screamed, trying to chase after the Dragon, her energy expelled, there was nothing she could do to get Felix back. The Wizard had taken him, and without him there was no Avidaura worth saving.

She fell to her knees, the Dragon disappearing into the woods that surrounded the castle. She had to get him back, without their King, the army had no one to lead them into battle, no hope for a future. She had done her best, and it hadn't been enough; Avidaura was going to fall.

Piper stared at the trees, the turrets of the castle rising over them in mockery, she had lost sight of the Dragon, though she knew where it had taken Felix.

She didn't know what the Wizard wanted him for, though she imagined that it wouldn't be long before Avidaura was without a King again. She had promised Zarah that she would protect him, her eyes burned with tears as she replayed the exchange with the Wizard over again in her head. Maybe if she had agreed to join him, Felix would have been safe, maybe if she had trained harder her magic could have saved him.

They shouldn't have gone alone to the Clurichaun Village, to take such a risk had been foolish. And now Avidaura was without a true King, and she was alone on the path, the very same path where she had first met Felix, except this time he wasn't coming back.

Piper was still staring at the castle piers, lost in herself when she heard footsteps on the path behind her. She didn't bother to look. If it was the Wizard's Knights they could have her. She was done with the war. She was done with Avidaura.

Her eyes stayed on the castle, unmoving.

A hand rested on her shoulder, "What are we looking at?" A small voice asked.

"He took Felix." Piper turned, looking into the eyes of Murray.

He stared out at the castle, patting Piper on the shoulder roughly. "We'll get em back." He snarled, holding out a hand to help her to her feet, though she was twice his height.

"He took Felix." Piper repeated, finally snapping out of her daze. Dusk had fallen and she had been staring at the castle for hours. She was surprised none of the Wizard's Knights had found her, she was out on the open path before the bridge, just staring.

"Come with me." Murray tugged at her hand, "We've got your back, we've always got your back." He mumbled, tugging Piper from the main path towards the Clurichaun Village, "You look pale." He tisked, tugging her faster, "We'll have to feed you up."

Piper was still in shock, she couldn't find the words to thank Murray, she just followed him wordlessly towards the Village, and away from her worst mistake.

As they entered the Village Piper froze, the Clurichaun were dancing, music echoed across the clearing, it was as though nothing was wrong in the world. The whole Village laid out before her, a reminder of what she was fighting for, a glimpse of what Avidaura had once been to her.

Then one at a time the Clurichaun glanced towards Murray standing next to Piper and the Village fell silent.

WIZARD

Felix regained consciousness on a stone floor, his eyes were open and his body stiff. He could feel the stone beneath him, cold and unwelcoming. He rolled his eyes, trying to stop the dryness from spotting his vision so he could see the room around him.

He was still half frozen, his body unable to move or respond to any of the commands that his brain was screaming. When the panic finally subsided, he began to remember how he had gotten where he was, and then the worry started to set in.

It had all happened so fast that Felix wasn't sure of his memories. One moment he had been toppling onto the castle path, frozen, and then he was in the air, watching as Piper blasted her energy towards him. There was nothing after that, he tried to turn, wondering if Piper was there with him, or if she had managed to escape the Dark Wizard when he had been taken captive.

He cursed himself for not holding on, not staying conscious long enough to know what had become of Piper. Had the Wizard let her live? Had she reached the Clurichauns? Or was she a charred pile on the side of the path, the same as Fallon had been at his castle.

He should have seen it coming, he had known that something was off. The woods had been too quiet, the walk too easy. There had been no sign of the Dark Knights, and they had been circling for weeks. He should have known that they were being watched, that someone was following them. The Dark Wizard had known where they were, someone had told him where to find Piper and Felix.

It had been too easy, traveling through the woods, stopping at the camp. He had let his guard down, and it had cost him dearly.

Felix was still struggling to make his body work. He grunted, the only thing that his body could actually manage in its paralyzed state. Though he was still frustrated, it felt good to be able to do *something*.

As the dizziness subsided from Piper's spell, Felix began to feel the room around him. It was like a sixth sense, telling him that he was in an open room, somewhere spacious and cold. Though he still couldn't move his body to check, Felix knew that Piper wasn't there with him.

But he wasn't alone.

If Piper had survived their encounter with the Wizard then Felix knew that she could be fine. If they weren't back by nightfall, Finnigan would send someone. Piper hadn't known, but three of the Rogue Knights had been ordered to leave a few hours after them, in case they ran into danger.

It certainly hadn't helped them when they *had* run into danger, but at the very least Piper wouldn't be left alone.

As long as she was okay.

Felix knew that he was done for. The Dark Wizard had taken him, the Rogue Knights wouldn't find him, the fight would have to go on without him. He was sure that this time he wouldn't get away with his life.

The last time Felix had been bound by the Wizard his body had been coursing with rage, now all he could feel was defeat. If Avidaura was going to be saved, it would be without him. There was no one to rescue him this time, he was on his own.

Felix tried to move his body, wondering how long the effects of the Wizard's magic would last, and why he had been taken alive at all.

He couldn't feel his limbs at all, they no longer registered with his brain as part of his body, they had been frozen so long. As he stared across the room, trying to concentrate on wiggling his fingers, everything began to come into focus.

The large doors across the floor from him were familiar, though they seemed out of place. The room had changed, but it began to come back to him.

He was home.

The windows were still the same, the high arching stone ceilings and the polished floor with the interwoven map of Avidaura. He was in the throne room, the same place he had encountered the Wizard last.

The banners had been removed, paintings taken from the walls. The room was barren and looked as though it had been abandoned and collecting dust for years, though it had only been a week since he had been in that very room, in the very same predicament; frozen by the Wizard and ready for his final moments in the world.

Felix didn't know if the Wizard was there with him or not, there had been no sound in the room save his grunt and the distant sound of Dragons screaming.

He knew that this time he wouldn't be leaving the castle. Without Ash and Piper at his side to help him, he didn't stand a chance. The Wizard had finally taken him, and alone he would be defeated.

The memories slowly came back to him, how it had all begun. He had been on the path with Piper, she hadn't judged him the way that the others did. He had been foolish and naive and unruly, and that quest, that moment, had changed him.

She had been alone and scared, and when she had asked for help he had tried to deny it. But she had been persistent. And if Piper had taught him anything, it was persistence.

He struggled against the bonding spell, slowly feeling his fingers as they began to move. He had to get back to her before it was too late, he had to help, he wasn't ready to give up.

It took everything he had to make his arms move, sweat beaded on his forehead as he struggled, feeling his limbs slowly coming back to him. Finally he managed to turn his head, his gaze landing firmly on the throne as he shifted, blinking to save his dry eyes.

The Wizard was watching him, his legs tossed over the arm of the throne, laying back as though he hadn't a care in the world. His face was amused, watching Felix struggle to break free of the invisible shackles that held him. Felix could feel himself welling with anger.

"Well then, looks who is finally awake. I was worried for a moment that her spell had killed you..." He frowned as though it wouldn't have mattered to him either way, "At least now I get to say goodbye." He tilted his head down at Felix, a small smirk playing on his lips.

Felix grunted, the closest he could manage to a retort. He balled his fist, fighting to raise his arm from the ground in protest.

The Dark Wizard laughed, twisting himself from the throne as he raised his hand to Felix.

Felix felt the energy wrap around him, lifting him from the ground and placing him on his frozen feet. His legs stretched out stiffly to hold his weight. He was still immobilized, but now he was standing before the Wizard.

Felix grunted, his once free arms were now pinned to his side, but he wasn't ready to give up yet.

The Wizard stared at him, amused at his determination to break free, it only spurred Felix on. He wasn't letting the power consume him, not this time, his fingers twitched at his side, he was already breaking through the spell. It wouldn't hold him for long.

"This is a lovely castle you have here." The Wizard gestured at the throne room, looking around at the size with pleasure, "But the thing is…" he turned to Felix, his eyes going cold, "your family is quite good at hiding things. So many secret chambers and passages. Why, it could take *years* to find something if you didn't know where to look." He stepped towards Felix his eyes locked with determination.

"I don't have years…" He hissed.

Felix scowled, his face muscles finally free of the binding.

The Wizard turned, pacing away as he continued, "There is something hidden here, and yet, I haven't managed to find it. Even with magic…" He waved his hand, releasing Felix from the binding curse and turned to face him again, "That's where *you* come in…" He smiled.

"I would …never…help you." Felix struggled to get the words out, his body pulsed with pain, he struggled to keep his footing.

"I don't think you'll have much of a choice." The Wizard sneered.

Felix took a step forward, his legs felt heavy beneath him, "You won't win this war." Felix grunted, gritting his teeth to keep the words straight.

"War?" The Wizard chuckled, "I didn't ask for a war, that was *your* choice. I only want to restore the universe to what it was *supposed* to be, before Avidaura became corrupted." He stopped, turning back to Felix, his voice growing cold. "There is no one in this universe that can stop me now. It's too late." For a moment there was almost a glimmer of pity behind his eyes.

Felix grunted, taking another step towards him, his hand struggling to release the sword from his waist.

He felt his fingers on the hilt and tried to grasp it, but his fingers were still too numb to lift the sword. He stepped forward, agonizing pain shooting up his legs as he moved towards the Wizard, the sword slowly rising from the sheath at his hip.

"You know a sword won't stop me Felix." The Wizard shook his head in amusement, "But really, there are more pressing matters." He waved his hand towards Felix, releasing another wave of magic.

Felix blinked, he felt dizzy. His feet shuffled beneath him, trying to hold him in an upright position, though he felt like he was about to tumble forward. It was as though he had been sucked underwater and spun until he didn't know where he was anymore.

But the Wizard was gone.

He stepped forward, reaching for the throne, it swayed before him, still on the other side of the room. Felix stumbled, trying to keep his balance.

Something was wrong with him, he felt giddy, like there was nothing in the world in his way. He turned, the room around him looked different, yet strangely familiar. The pictures on the wall looked hazy, the banners out of focus; but it was home.

There was a strange sensation that something was different, something had changed, and yet Felix couldn't quite figure it out. Somehow it didn't seem to matter.

When he turned back to the throne there was a figure sitting there, as though he had always been there. As though he had never left.

"Welcome back Felix." His voice was light and airy, it sounded like he was far away.

"Father?" Felix squinted, trying to see him better, "What are you doing here?" There was a tickle in the back of his mind that told him his father shouldn't have been there, but he couldn't remember why.

His father smiled, "Oh Felix, you've had a great ordeal." He tilted his head, rising from the throne, "How was your quest?" He asked, a spark of pride in his eyes.

"Quest?" Felix stuttered, trying to remember.

"The Mirror Felix, you just returned from the quest."
The King explained, looking concerned, "Are you feeling alright
son?"

"Did I?" Felix looked around the room, he remembered
standing in the throne room when his father had sent him to
the Field of Mirrors, but there was something missing,
something he was forgetting. It felt as though he had never left.

"I heard you did quite well." His father continued,
stepping towards Felix slowly.

Felix stared at him, he seemed strange. His feet made no
noise on the stone floor. There was something different about
him that was bothering Felix.

"Did I?" Felix was confused, the quest at the Field of
Mirrors was coming back to him, it had been a long time ago,
though his mind was too fuzzy to recall the details.

"I know it has been a long journey for you." The King
stepped closer, his feet making no sound on the floor. "I have
another quest for you." He offered, his voice fading in and out.

Felix stared at him, he wasn't sure what had happened,
but he felt like something was wrong, "Another quest, so
soon?" He asked.

"Yes Felix, this one is important."

"Important?" Felix wondered what sort of quest his
father was offering.

"Very important." The King nodded his head, conveying
his seriousness.

For a moment Felix thought he flickered.

"Is everything okay?" Felix asked staring at his father,
wondering why he had a feeling that something was wrong.

"Yes Felix, but we must hurry." He took another step
towards Felix.

"Hurry?" Felix asked.

"I need your help Felix." His father sounded so far away,
though he stood only two steps before Felix.

"My help?" Felix was confused again.

"Well yes, we can't let that Wizard take over Avidaura." His father looked stoic, "I need you to find the carnelian crystal. It's the only thing that can stop him."

"The Wizard…" Felix knew that there was something in the recesses of his mind trying to get through, he couldn't place it, but there was something about the Wizard that he knew, something that he needed to remember.

"You remember the Wizard Felix." His father raised his hand, and Felix felt the memories return.

There was a Dark Wizard in Avidaura, and he wanted to take the castle. Felix wondered why he hadn't remembered about it until just now.

"How long do we have before the Wizard comes back?" Felix asked.

His Father stared at him, sadness in his eyes, but also a glint of something else that Felix didn't recognize. "Very soon Felix, he will be coming today."

"That soon?" Felix thought about it, "And Fallon cannot help?" He considered the options.

"We have been through this Felix." His father sounded angry for a moment, "The crystal is the only way."

"I don't think it is." Felix answered flatly. One Dark Wizard wasn't enough to call upon the most powerful thing in Avidaura. It couldn't be the answer. "There has to be another way."

"Felix, this is not a time to argue." His father sighed, "We don't have much time."

"We can't use the crystal." Felix remembered some of the lessons from his youth, "Where is Fallon? We need him."

"He will be here shortly." The King seemed rushed to get going. "Come Felix, we must get the crystal." His Father edged closer, still out of arms reach, and as Felix looked up at him he felt a wave of calm wash over him.

"The crystal." Felix repeated, the words feeling strange on his tongue, "Why?" He asked.

Somewhere in the recesses of his memory, he knew that he wasn't supposed to go near the carnelian crystal. It was kept in one of the most guarded areas of the castle underground. It didn't make sense to him that his father would be asking for it. But he couldn't find the words, or the energy, to defy him.

"Felix, it is the only thing that can restore Avidaura, we discussed this, remember?" The King had an urgency to his words that left Felix wondering why he couldn't remember, "We must hurry Felix, before the Wizard returns." He edged closer to the door, encouraging Felix to follow him.

"Oh, yes…" Felix could remember the Wizard, and how terrible things had been in Avidaura since his arrival. He turned towards the door to the main castle, nearly tripping over his own feet as he tried to walk forward. His legs were numb, he didn't know why. "Hurry." He whispered to himself, trying to contain a giggle.

Felix stumbled through the throne room doors, trying to tip toe through the castle so he would be quieter. He turned down the Hall of Kings to take a short cut and paused.

"Where are the Kings?" He turned back to his father, and then stared down the hall.

The paintings were all gone, the hall was dark and dusty. The candles seemed that they had all burned down a long time ago, wax drippings had hardened in the holders and no one had replaced them.

Felix looked back to his father, "Where are they?" He asked again. Something seemed suspicious about the whole thing, Felix listened to the castle, it was quieter than it had ever been. The usual scent of rising bread and mulled wine was absent too.

"They were taken down for protection." His father answered simply.

It seemed to make sense to Felix, but still the silence overwhelmed him, "Where is everyone?" He whispered, though his voice carried farther than it should have.

"In hiding Felix." He answered impatiently, "We really must be going." He added urgently.

"We can't stop in the kitchens?" Felix asked, he had been hoping to have some pastries before he went into the underground.

"No, we need to hurry." His father snapped. His face flickering again.

Felix had the strange sensation that he was in a dream, that he wasn't really standing in the castle at all. He reached his hand out and felt the stone wall. It *felt* real beneath his hand.

"What are you doing?" His father stepped closer, his anger growing.

"Something just feels wrong." Felix admitted, "Don't you feel it?" He asked.

"Of course something is wrong Felix, we need the crystal." The King was growing more impatient by the moment, Felix had never seen him like that before.

Felix nodded, taking his hand from the wall. Perhaps his father was right, maybe the Wizard had just set things in motion that Felix wasn't ready for. He had never seen the castle so empty and abandoned, but his father was right, they had to protect the people, and having them working in a castle during a siege wasn't the way to keep them safe.

Felix would just have to get used to the quiet halls and the empty walls, it would only be for a while, if the crystal worked, then the Wizard would be stopped and everything would go back to normal.

Though somewhere in the back of his mind, there was a voice telling him that it would never be the same again.

Felix turned down another quiet hall, leading his father through the castle towards the dungeon doors.

"It's down here." Felix whispered, surprising himself as his whisper echoed back up from the dungeon.

He descended the steps, the torches had burnt out and the dungeon was quiet. There was a feeling to it, a quiet desperation that tugged at Felix's chest. He glanced at the first cell and felt a surge of overwhelming loss, though he couldn't quite understand why.

It felt to him like something had happened there, something that had changed him, something that he should have remembered; something that he could never forget. Though the memory wouldn't come to him. He could smell metal, blood, stone, and the scents wanted him to remember. But it still wouldn't come. He didn't know how long he stood there staring into a dark empty cell, but his father hadn't said a word. He stood behind Felix, watching him, staring even, until his impatience grew again.

"Hurry Felix, we have to find it." His father was behind him, urging him to continue on.

Felix nodded, turning his eyes away from the cell, "This way."

RETURN

Ash stood outside of the back door to the Low Village, not quite sure where the opening really was. The Centaurs were already busy making their camp in the woods, preferring to be outside in the open woods than confined in the walled Village. It was probably for the best, Ash wasn't sure how much room was left in the Village anymore, and Centaurs were quite large.

When they had left the Low Village, it had already been full near the breaking point, and Ash had returned with the an entire army from the High Village, there wouldn't be room for Centaurs inside the Village walls, there might not be room for the Knights.

There was no visible line where the door was, it was rarely used, and quite well hidden. If Ash hadn't left through it, she might not have believed that there was a door in the back wall to the Village at all. She had been staring at the wall for nearly five minutes, trying to see any sign that would tell her where it was.

Behind her, Mavera pawed the ground impatiently with his hooves, eager to get on with his own preparations.

"Are you sure this is it?" He questioned.

"Yes." Ash sighed, "This is the Village." She stared at the wall a little while longer, trying to determine where the door was hidden.

"And they are expecting us?" Mavera sounded concerned, Lucinda rested on his back, she would need to be taken care of soon, she wasn't doing well out of the Lagoon.

"Just give me a minute." Ash sighed again, reaching towards the wall with her fist poised to knock. She hammered her fist against the wood, listening to it echo back across the clearing, she just hoped that they could hear it from the other side.

A moment passed, and Ash had yet to hear anything from inside of the Village, she moved up the wall and knocked again.

Soon she heard the scraping of the door being opened, still a few feet from where she stood. At least they had finally heard her.

Ash moved quickly towards the opening, waiting for the Village to come into view. Evan was standing on the other side when the door finally opened. He looked past Ash at the waiting crowd, his eyebrows rising with surprise.

"You did it." He whispered, turning back to the Village, "They are here." He called back to the crowd behind him.

A chorus of cheers followed.

"Ash, welcome back." Evan beamed, stepping out of the way to let through the travelers from the High Village.

It was clear to Ash that they were running out of room in the Village, as the Fallen Knights began to lead the newcomers to small tents that had been erected in the streets.

"Do you think we can fit them all?" Ash asked, scanning the clearing behind her. "We could probably fit more tents out here." She added, wondering if the Centaurs would mind if they had to move into the woods to fit everyone.

"We should be able to manage." Evan answered, staring back into the Village as it filled.

Their numbers had grown, and the Fallen Knights looked hopeful again. Ash smiled, watching them as she stood by the door while the High Villagers entered one at a time.

Most had never been to the Low Village, traveling in Avidaura was nearly unheard of amongst the Villages. Ash watched as they stared at the buildings, their faces wide with wonder.

Finally Zarah approached with Mavera at his side. The great Centaur twisting his body to fit through the small opening. "Where shall I take Lucinda?" He asked, his eyes landing on Evan.

Evan gasped, "A Centaur?" He whispered, turning to Ash as though he couldn't believe his eyes.

"This is Mavera," Ash introduced him, "The Centaurs will be making their base in the woods beyond this door." Ash confirmed, "But he carries a Mermaid, Lucinda, we must protect her at all costs. Is there somewhere suitable for her to rest?" Ash asked, watching Evan's face as he tried to process what she had just said.

Evan paused, for a moment it seemed as though he was frozen, he stared at Mavera and the traveler resting on his back and then slowly turned to Zarah, his eyes wide.

"A Mermaid?" He asked, his voice coming out in a hollow whisper.

"Yes." Ash rolled her eyes, "Lucinda needs to be kept somewhere safe, she is very important. Is there somewhere she could rest?" Ash asked again, losing her patience.

Evan righted his shoulders, nodding his head as he composed himself, "Well, yes..." He stumbled, turning into the Village, "I have a place for her." He nodded to Zarah, as though Zarah should know where he meant.

"Are you sure?" Zarah asked.

"Yes, take her there." Evan nodded, "I will stay with the Knights." He nodded, staying at the door as Zarah and Mavera carried on into the Village.

Many heads turned to watch as Zarah and Mavera disappeared into the crowd with Lucinda. Ash stared after them, amused at how the Villagers were reacting to a Centaur in their midst.

"Centaurs…" Evan breathed, returning to Ash's side, "I've never even *seen* one before…and here they are…" He still seemed surprised, more surprised than Ash would have guessed. "How did that even happen?" He asked, curiosity wearing through his shock.

"They were already at the High Village," Ash explained, "this threat affects everyone in Avidaura." She added, reminding Evan of the mission.

"You are right." Evan finally collected himself, staring out at the Centaurs making preparations in the woods. "It will be good to have them on our side." He noted.

"It will." Ash agreed. "Have Piper and Felix returned?" She asked, changing the subject.

There was much that had changed since she had left them for her quest. She wanted to tell Piper about the pearl and their stroke of luck in finding it. She would need to train Piper to understand how to use it. It would take them both to neutralize the Dark Wizard.

"They returned with the Dark Fairies." Evan nodded, "But I am afraid you have missed them, they departed for the Clurichauns some time ago. They should be returning soon." He added as an afterthought.

"The Dark Fairies have joined us?" Ash smiled, she had never spoken to a Dark Fairy before, though she had heard of Piper and Felix's adventures through the dark woods, and had been saved by the coin that Felix now carried.

"Yes, King Felix has managed the impossible." Evan looked proud, "He has come a long way from the boy he once was." Ash saw the twinkle in his eye, the memory of the Prince she had first met sparked in her mind.

Ash chuckled, "He certainly has." She agreed.

"I should attend to the newcomers." Evan nodded, about to depart.

"And there are things that I should see to before Felix and Piper return." Ash nodded in agreement, departing into the woods to talk to the Centaurs.

Though Piper and Felix had yet to return, Ash knew that the Centaurs and the Fairies should meet, along with the Chiefs of the Human Villages. If they hoped to work together to defeat the Dark Wizard they would all have to be in agreement. Ash knew that it would be best to secure their bond before they began talking tactics, and she knew that Felix would overlook their introductions.

Ash stepped through the clearing into the woods, searching through the trees for a Centaur to talk to. It seemed as though they had just disappeared, not a trace of them could be seen anywhere, though Ash knew that they hadn't left.

"Gatlin?" She finally called into the trees, wondering where he and the Centaurs had hidden.

A moment later she heard him galloping towards her. "Ash." He bowed his head, "How may I assist you?"

"Is there anything you will be needing?" She asked, realizing that she should first make the Centaurs feel at home before she began introductions.

Gatlin considered, "I believe we have everything that we could need, however if I think of anything…"

"Please let me know." Ash smiled. "If you have time, I would like to introduce you to some of our allies."

"The Humans?" Gatlin seemed surprised.

"There are others too." Ash nodded her head, walking back towards the opening to the Village.

Gatlin silently followed Ash back through the opening into the wall, walking into the Village as the Fallen Knights stared.

"There are quite a few here." Gatlin commented quietly. He sounded impressed.

"King Felix should be returning soon with others." Ash nodded, it sounded strange to call Felix the King, she was sure she would get used to it eventually.

Ash led Gatlin through the Village to the front gates on the other side, hoping that someone would be there to assist her. There she found Finnigan, his arms heaping with supplies, trying to convince the guards to open the gates for him.

"Finnigan?" Ash called, catching his attention. He turned, dropping a handful of the supplies teetering in his arms. Ash leaned over to help him retrieve them. "Are you back already?" She looked around, expecting to see Piper and Felix somewhere nearby.

"Yeah." Finnigan shot the guards at the gates another look, "I'm supposed to be delivering these supplies, but the guards won't let me through." He sighed, accepting Ash's help with the load. "Is that a Centaur?" He leaned in, whispering as he stared past Ash at Gatlin.

"Yes." Ash whispered, "Gatlin," She called behind her, "This is Finnigan, one of our higher ranking Knights." She introduced the two.

Finnigan blushed, "I'm not really a Knight…" He whispered, embarrassed.

"Of course you are, you've been with King Felix since his first quest." Ash smiled. "Speaking of, where are they?" Ash looked around again.

"They went to talk to the Clurichaun." Finnigan answered, the guards had heard Ash and were finally opening the door for Finnigan.

"And you weren't with them?" Ash asked.

"No, they asked me to stay and get the Dark Fairies settled." He hefted the load in his arms, taking the items from Ash's hands, "I've got to take these supplies out." He added.

"Oh, okay." Ash took a step back, giving him room. "We would like to arrange a meeting, if you wouldn't mind asking." She added.

"Sure," Finnigan nodded, stepping through the gate, "I'll talk to Eniki." And with that he disappeared.

"Eniki." Ash muttered, trying to remember the name, she had heard Felix talk about him before, he must have been the Fairy in charge.

"Would you go find Evan for me?" Ash turned to one of the guards at the gate, "Tell him we will be needing a meeting place." She added.

The guard nodded and disappeared into the crowd to do as Ash had asked.

"Clurichauns…" Gatlin stared at Ash pensively, "Do you really think that is a good idea?" He sounded concerned for Felix and Piper.

"The Clurichaun are a loyal people, you'll like them." Ash nodded, hiding her concern that Piper and Felix had gone alone on their mission.

Dusk was breaking across the Village, and soon it would be dark enough for the Fairies to leave their woods. Ash had little time to prepare for the meeting of the allies. She wondered when Piper and Felix were supposed to return.

Ash and Gatlin stood by the gates, waiting for Finnigan to return with Eniki. Many of the Knights and Villagers were staring, Centaurs were a rare creature that many of them had never seen before; Ash could tell that Gatlin was starting to feel uncomfortable when Evan approached them, appearing from the crowd.

"Ash," He smiled, "and this is?" He held his hand up to Gatlin, clearly over his surprise at seeing the Centaurs.

"Gatlin." Gatlin shook his head, nodding.

"Evan, great to meet you." Evan bowed his head.

"This is the Chief of the Low Village." Ash explained, finishing their introduction.

Gatlin bowed his head, "And you as well." He responded to Evan.

"Did the guard find you?" Ash asked, waiting for Evan to answer.

"Yes," He nodded, "I have prepared a meeting place that is suitable for us all. And now that night has fallen the Fairies should be able to join us." He added.

"Should we wait for them?" Ash asked.

"The guard will send Finnigan in the right direction." Evan answered, leading Ash and Gatlin back into the crowd.

***

Ash stood at the head of the table, staring out at the gathering of allies. As High Wizard she would take the place of the King until he returned from his travels.

Finnigan and the Fairy were the last to enter the building, taking their places at the table as a hushed silence fell over the room.

All eyes were on Ash. She took a deep breath and tried to steady her hands, she wasn't used to being in charge, she was more familiar with *taking* charge.

"I call to order the first meeting of the Rising." Ash declared, taking her seat as the meeting began.

"Where is King Felix?" The Fairy asked, looking around the table, he seemed concerned.

"He will return soon," Ash smiled, not knowing if she was being truthful, "though I thought it would be best to get the introductions out of the way, so he can focus on more pressing matters." Ash nodded to Zarah, who had agreed with her when she had told him of her planned gathering.

With so many leaders from across Avidaura gathering together, it was probably better to break the ice before Felix dove in and started talking tactics.

Ash remembered her father's teachings, it had been over a hundred years since the old Avidauran council had last met, there was a lot of ground to cover before they started forming their plan to take Avidaura back.

"I am Aishwarya, Daughter of Fallon and High Wizard of Avidaura." Ash began by introducing herself. Though she knew nearly everyone at the table, she had yet to meet a Fairy before.

Zarah went next, standing up to make his introduction, "I am Zarah, leader of the Fallen army… and Advisor to the True King." His voice broke at the memory of Felix's father.

"Gatlin, leader of the Centaurs at the Western shore."

"Evan, Chief of the Low Village."

"Ronan, Chief of the High Village."

"Lucinda, of the Mermaids."

"Finnigan, Knight of the True King."

"And I am Eniki, leader of the Dark Fairy army." Eniki bowed, introducing himself to the table. He looked up towards Ash, "You have certainly done well with the members present." He complemented, returning to his seat.

"Thank you Eniki, it is wonderful to finally meet you." Ash nodded, rising from her seat again to address the crowd. "Though we all come from different areas of Avidaura, and we all have different perspectives, I think we can agree that we are all here to save the same Avidaura from a terrible fate." Ash stared out at the table, all heads nodding in agreement. Is was a brief moment of unity, realizing that so many different groups from across the land were willing to fight for the same cause.

"Centaurs…" Finnigan stared across the table, "I hear you make the finest weapons, my father had a sword forged by your kind." He nodded to Gatlin, all heads had turned to follow his stare.

"It is true." Gatlin agreed proudly, "And we have already made arrangements to forge some weapons for this cause." He looked to Ash, revealing what the Centaurs had been preparing in the woods.

"Wonderful." Ash declared, her excitement showing, "Is there anything you will be needing from the Village to help?" She asked, looking to Evan who nodded in agreement of her offer.

"We have determined that iron will be needed, it is the only metal that will pierce a Dragons hide," Gatlin shared, "and we are aware that the Dark Wizard has gained their favor." He added.

Ash smiled, many had known about the Dragons, but not the iron. The table erupted with chatter, ideas, plans, information that would be useful when Felix returned and they began to make their formal plans. Ash took notes while the meeting continued, listening to all of the ideas and jotting them down so Felix could review them before their next meeting.

It was a brief discussion, the late hours and the tiredness from traveling soon had the table sitting silent in agreement. Ash rose from her seat again, addressing the gathering.

"I think we have made some good progress here, and there is much to think about. We will gather again when King Felix has returned to discuss the final plan." Ash nodded to the table, finishing the meeting.

Slowly the gathering dispersed, each left looking lighter, more refreshed. Soon only Zarah and Ash were left alone at the great table.

"Well done Ash," Zarah patted her on the shoulder proudly, "Felix is certainly lucky to have you on his side."

"Thank you Zarah." Ash smiled, tucking her notes away so she could give them to Felix. "When will they be returning?" She asked, wondering how their visit with the Clurichauns had gone. They should have been on their way back, she was starting to worry that they had encountered some trouble on the way.

"Soon." Zarah looked over his shoulder at the door as though he expected them to appear.

"There is one other thing I could use your help with..." Ash caught Zarah's attention again.

"Yes?" He asked, turning back to the table.

"The pearl." Ash placed her satchel on the table, retrieving a worn leather book, "I don't know how to use it." She admitted sheepishly.

"I wouldn't expect that you would." Zarah smirked, "A pearl hasn't been given since the beginning of Avidaura."

"That long..." Ash sounded nervous.

"Are those your father's notes?" Zarah stared at the book, curious if Fallon had known a way.

Ash nodded, turning the pages until she found what she was looking for; a passage, scrawled in Fallon's small neat writing.

"I haven't found anything yet, but here…" She pointed, "I think he is talking about a pearl." She added.

Zarah pulled up a chair, moving closer, "Let's see what we can find then." He was already poring over the passage, his face drawn in concentration.

Ash waited for him to finish reading.

"He talks a lot about the pearl, clearly he didn't know how to get one, or he would have mentioned the Mermaid's soul." Ash went on as Zarah reread the passage, "There are several spells listed, but none of them really make any sense, it seems more theoretical than anything."

"Perhaps Lucinda would know how to take this theory and apply it." Zarah suggested, finishing the passage. "I will talk to Evan, and make sure that these ingredients are available to you."

He pulled a parchment from his cloak, and began to write a list.

"I hope we can make it work." Ash was nervous, "Piper and I *need* it to work." She flipped through the pages in her father's book, looking for anything else that could help them.

"They'll be back soon." Zarah tucked the parchment away, "Why don't you rest for a while, then you can talk to Piper and Lucinda." Zarah paused, looking at Ash with pride, "We will find a way." He promised, rising from the table.

Ash stared at the book, alone in the great room with her father's thoughts, she wouldn't disappoint him.

CLURICHAUN

The Clurichaun hadn't needed an explanation from Murray. He had simply told them that Avidaura needed their help, and they had dropped everything and began to pack.

Piper hadn't moved, she stood at the path, watching as the Village became deserted, the Clurichauns lining up to leave for a cause that they had yet to know.

Their loyalty struck a chord with her, she was already trying to hold her composure after losing Felix to the Wizard; tears spilled silently over her cheeks as she realized how willing the Clurichaun were to help.

Soon the entire Village had been packed up.

Usually after a long day of traveling Piper would stop to rest before venturing back out onto the paths, but with Felix in peril she couldn't allow herself to waste any more precious time, she was thankful that Murray understood her haste.

Murray appeared at her side, a satchel nearly the same size as him was strapped to his back, brimming with supplies.

"Are we ready to leave?" Piper asked, her voice still hollow.

Murray nodded, his face still stuck with the sad expression he had greeted his Villagers with, "Let's go." He agreed.

Piper nodded and turned back towards the path, staring into the darkness. She could hear Murray behind her addressing the Village one last time before they departed.

"On yer toes, let's get moving." His voice echoed across the silent crowd, a moment later they were all marching forward, and Murray was leading Piper out of the Village.

As they reached the intersection at the castle path, Piper tensed. It hadn't been that long since Felix was taken, visiting the scene of the crime sent a twinge of guilt through her. Though she could still vividly recall the events that had transpired, the path looked unchanged, untainted, like nothing had happened there at all.

Piper glanced towards the castle, the towers rising from the trees on the island that held it. Their silhouettes against the deep purple sky reminded her that there was still a world worth saving, they still had to take the castle back; even if they had no King to rule.

If Felix was still alive, they didn't have much time to get to him. The army would have to march much sooner than they had anticipated. Piper only hoped that Ash and Zarah had returned with the re-enforcements from the High Village that they had left to gather. They would need all the help they could get to take Avidaura back from the Dark Wizard that had captured their King and their Kingdom.

The miniature army barely hesitated as Piper dove into the woods, leaving the castle behind as she took the more covered way towards the Village, leaving the castle road and the memories behind.

Murray didn't say a word as he followed her into the woods, which was good because Piper was still lost in her own head. She was going to have to explain to Ash and Zarah how she had lost the King; how she had failed, how she had ruined their plan. She was supposed to have been there to protect Felix, she had magic, and still she hadn't been able to do a thing as the Wizard had taken off with Felix in the claws of his beast.

Zarah was never going to speak to her again. Felix was like a son to him, he was the hope of the Kingdom. She should have done more, and she wouldn't blame Zarah if she was exiled, she didn't deserve to be a part of Avidaura, not after what she had done.

Piper was walking so fast that the forest was passing in a blur, Murray and his army were running to keep up as she led the way through the dark forest. She hadn't bothered to listen for danger, there was nothing that could happen that was worse than what had already transpired, she had already lost Felix, nothing else mattered as much. Soon she was coming out the other side of the woods before the Village gate.

Piper paused, staring at the gate, and dreading the moments that were about to follow. She took a deep breath and brought her fist to the wood, knocking on the gate while her mind reeled. Still, Murray was at her side, wordless, but there.

The peephole opened and a pair of familiar eyes peered out. "Oh Piper, you're back quick, I was about to send the Knights to gather you." Finnigan smiled, closing the latch so he could open the gate properly.

Piper could hear him on the other side, releasing the locks as he prepared to let them enter. Her heart was already racing, it wouldn't take them long to realize who wasn't with them.

"Murray?" Piper whispered as the doors began to open, "I need to find Zarah, Finnigan will settle you." She glanced at him expecting to see hurt in his eyes, instead she was met with fury.

"We'll get the King back Miss." He growled, nodding his head sternly at her, "You do what you have to do." He added, turning back to his people, he raised a hand, signaling something that Piper didn't understand.

"Thank you Murray." Piper took a short breath, trying to keep herself from crying again. She wasn't ready to face Zarah, but she knew that she had to, he needed to know what had happened, she had to be ready to face him.

The gates opened and Piper stepped inside, followed by Murray. The Village was bursting, there was not a clear space in sight.

"Welcome back." Finnigan smiled, looking at Murray standing at Piper's side, "Are these the Clurichaun?" He asked.

"Finnigan, this is Murray." Piper introduced them quickly, "Could you get them settled, I need to see Zarah." She added quickly before she lost her resolve.

"Yeah, Zarah's out by the back." He pointed through the crowd. "I've got this." He looked past the heads of the short Clurichaun. "Where's Felix?"

Piper didn't answer, she had already slipped into the crowd, making a beeline for Zarah. She had to talk to him before she lost her nerve. It was important that he knew what had happened to their King, regardless of the wrath she herself would face for losing him.

Piper pressed through the crowd, making her way towards the back of the Village, though part of her just wanted to disappear and never be found. She knew that she had to talk to Zarah, and it had to be soon. Finnigan had already realized that Felix wasn't with her, it would be long before word spread that the King was missing.

Zarah and Ash were at the back of the Village, standing by a small opening in the wall and conversing with someone on the other side. Ash turned, seeing Piper before Zarah did.

Piper froze, she had expected to talk to Zarah alone, it would have been easier. Admitting to Ash that she had failed, it was going to be harder on them both. Though she had only known her sister a shirt while, she knew that Ash would blame herself for not going with them, and Piper didn't want her to have to live with the guilt that she already felt. Felix's capture was her fault alone to bear.

"Piper!" Ash waved, her face was more cheerful that it should have been.

Piper stood there, at the edge of the crowd, watching as Ash sauntered over, her heart beating faster and faster.

"The High Village has joined us." Ash gushed with excitement, "And the *Centaurs.*" She added, gesturing towards the wall where Zarah was still conversing with an unseen ally.

"I'm so glad you're finally back." Ash wrapped her arms around Piper, embracing her with joy, "I need to tell you what happened on the way, we finally have the edge that we need to take the Wizard down." She whispered, turning back towards the wall to lead Piper to Zarah so they could talk.

Piper's face must have looked off, Ash stared at her for a moment, looking back into the crowd, "Where's Felix?" She asked, staring past Piper like she expected him to appear from the crowd.

Piper looked at her feet, taking one last deep breath to steady herself before she told Ash. "The Wizard took him." She breathed, slowly meeting Ash's eyes.

"What?" Ash's face fell so quickly that Piper was sure she was about to faint.

"He took him." She repeated, her voice wavering as she tried to hold back the tears. "On a Dragon." She added, remembering the claw ripping Felix from the path in front of her.

"Zarah!" Ash turned urgently, calling Zarah from his conversation at the door.

Zarah walked over, seeing the looks on the sisters faces he paused, "What happened?"

"The Wizard took Felix." Piper repeated for a third time, each hurting her more than the last. Finally the tears began to fall, she couldn't hold them back any longer.

"Piper." Zarah stepped forward placing his hands on her shoulders, his face inches from hers, "You need to tell me *everything.*" He turned her and began to walk away, taking Piper with him to a safe place where the overlooking Knights wouldn't hear them. Ash followed along behind, worried that despite her efforts they had just lost the war.

Piper followed Zarah silently through the crowd, her ears ringing as she thought about what she had just said. Zarah seemed to be taking it surprisingly well, she wasn't sure that he had understood that Felix was gone. She didn't know if she had it in her to explain.

He led her to a great room with a table centered in the empty space. Within a minute he had all the candles lit and the room glowed with anticipation.

Piper felt small at the table, her eyes welled over as Zarah sat beside her, holding her hand, "Tell me everything." He whispered, his eyes brimming with pain.

Piper closed her eyes, she couldn't stand to see Zarah looking so sad, it would have been easier if he was mad at her, the disappointment in his voice was too hard to hear.

Slowly she recounted the encounter with the Wizard and how Felix had been taken, opening her eyes as she finished. She knew that she should have done more, Ash was staring at her, the blank expression on her face unreadable, but Zarah didn't say a word.

"He just took him?" Ash asked, her face still blank.

Piper nodded, she didn't understand what they weren't understanding. Felix was gone, there was nothing they could do to get him back.

"He just took him..." Ash repeated, not asking, just observing.

"He's still alive." Zarah breathed. His eyes lighting up.

Piper looked at him, puzzled. "How do you know that?" She wondered.

"If he was going to kill Felix, you would have known." Zarah concluded, sure that he was correct. "He must need Felix for something. We'll have to move quickly, but there is still hope." He sounded hurried, rising from the table, his expression wild with urgency.

"Ash, go get the others, this cannot wait, we will need to gather the council." He rushed Ash to the door, sending her out into the night to gather their allies.

Piper waited for the room to go silent again before she spoke, "There was one more thing." She whispered, though her voice boomed across the room, causing Zarah to flinch.

"What is it?" Zarah slipped back into the chair facing Piper, his expression stoic.

"He said he doesn't want Avidaura..." She tried to remember how the Dark Wizard had said it, "He wants the ... universe." She added, watching Zarah to see if it made any sense to him.

"The universe..." Zarah muttered, looking off into the distance, his eyes glazed with thought, "If he took the universe... then Avidaura wouldn't..." His eyes snapped back to Piper before he could finish the thought.

"Is everything okay?" Piper asked, she wasn't sure what the Wizard had meant by his comment, but it was clear that Zarah had an inkling about what it meant, at least for Avidaura. Piper hadn't grown up in Avidaura, she hadn't even known that it existed until the day she had stumbled upon the mirror, the Wizard's words meant very little to her. She only knew that it didn't sound good, and someone like Zarah needed to know what he was up to, someone who understood the implications of his words. Zarah seemed to be taking the news quite seriously.

Zarah didn't look like he was going to answer Piper, but even if he was, the door swung open and Eniki walked in, quashing any chance for Piper to find out more about the meaning of the Universe, and what the Wizard planned to do with Avidaura.

"Is it true?" Eniki slid into a seat beside Piper, the concern in his face evident. He looked more alert than Piper had ever seen him

Behind him, Finnigan and Murray entered.

"He took the King?" Finnigan asked of no one in particular, sitting at the table beside Murray, who just looked angry.

Piper nodded, it was all she could do to keep herself together, she didn't know if she had it in her to recount the story again, not that it would matter. All they needed to know was that Felix was gone, and it was time for them to take back Avidaura, before it was too late.

The table slowly filled, silence took over the room as they waited with bated breath for the emergency meeting to begin.

Ash was the last to enter, following behind Gatlin, who looked as though he had been sleeping.

Ash took her place at the head of the table next to Zarah, she looked nervous about the conversation that was about to occur. All eyes were on her, half sat curious, the others who knew what had happened were waiting to hear what was going to happen next.

"I call to order this meeting," Ash began hurriedly, "I would like to introduce my sister Piper, daughter of Fallon, and Murray of the Clurichaun." She nodded to each respectively, not waiting a moment longer before she continued.

"Piper was traveling with King Felix earlier today when the Wizard took him captive." She declared, waiting for the backlash.

The room gasped, nearly in unison as the news hit their tired ears. Suddenly they perked up, understanding why the meeting had been called so quickly to assemble in the middle of the night.

"The time has come, and we must prepare to strike before the Wizard makes his next move." Ash spoke sternly with a tone in her voice that belayed her inner rage at their predicament.

"Where has he taken the King?" Evan asked, the worry on his face growing more absolute by the moment.

"To the castle we believe," Zarah replied, his voice flat and void of emotion.

"Then it is time to march." Gatlin stomped his hooves against the ground, the sound echoing through the room.

"We will have to scout out the path, prepare to march."
Ronan nodded.

It seemed that they were all in agreement, Ash was
relieved. She had half expected that Felix's disappearance would
put an end to the union of the council. Instead, it seemed that it
had only spurred them on.

The time had come to take Avidaura back from the
grasp of the Dark Wizard. Ash still wished that they had more
time, there was still so much to prepare, and she hadn't had a
chance to talk to Piper about the pearl, though Lucinda, at the
table with them for preparations, had assured Ash that she
knew how to use the pearl, and would take the time to show the
sisters before the march.

It wasn't long before the room erupted, the plans laid
out on the table, and the gathering alive with energy.

They would have to make sure that their plans were set
in stone, they needed to march before it was too late, their King
was in peril.

***

Ash had to excuse herself while the council continued to
make plans, she slipped from the building into the cool night
air, taking a deep breath as she steadied herself.

She had hoped that they would have more time before
they had to act, she had hoped that she and Piper would have
been able to practice more with the pearl before they were
expected to use it. But time had stood still since Piper had
entered the Village without Felix, and they had to move soon.

Zarah had given Ash a look at the table when it was
suggested that they send scouts out to watch the path, she had
taken his lead and as she walked towards the gate to talk to the
guards she realized how unexpected this all must seem to those
around them.

They had only just gathered, they had only just begun to
discuss what was happening to Avidaura. It seemed too soon to
be marching, but they were left with no other choice.

She approached the guards at the gate, their leader stepped down from his perch to greet her.

"What can we assist you with Ash?" He asked, though the look on his face made it clear that he had already heard of Felix's predicament, word traveled fast amongst the waiting.

"I will need a team of scouts sent out to watch the castle and report back to me if there is any activity." She kept her request vague and brief, not wanting to stir up too much excitement.

The guards eyes flashed for a second, he had read far enough into her words to know what was coming. He nodded sternly, "They shall be there within the hour." He nodded, "Is there anything else?" He asked hesitantly.

"That is all." Ash bowed, backing away to return to the meeting.

She knew the guard would do as she asked, soon there would be Knights on the path keeping an eye on the castle and they could prepare for the siege knowing that the Dark Wizard wasn't coming for them.

It was only a matter of time before the Wizard got what he needed from Felix, they had to act before he was ready.

Ash hurried back to the meeting, the sun would be rising soon, they would have to finish in time for Eniki to return to the woods. They had talked for nearly the entire night, preparing a plan to siege the castle and return their King to his throne, dispelling the Wizard in the process.

When Ash returned, Eniki was preparing to leave, the discussion had come to an end and they had come to a decision about how they were going to proceed.

"We will move to the outer woods, where the Forest of Night meets the castle path. There we will wait for your command." Eniki stood from the table, bowing slightly to Ash at her return, "We will be ready." He slipped out the door before the sun had risen disappearing in the pre-dawn darkness.

Zarah waited for Ash to be seated, "Is it done?" He asked quietly, though the whole table was watching.

Ash nodded, "The Knights will alert us if anything happens while we prepare." She answered.

"Very good." Zarah continued, he had taken over the meeting in Ash's absence, which was probably better, he had more experience with that sort of thing having led the Rogue Knights in the woods and advised the former King of Avidaura. If anyone knew what so do, it was Zarah, despite that fact that he lacked a title.

"There are Knights watching the path for any movement, and now the Fairies will be moving into position." Zarah addressed the table quietly. "There is one advantage that we may have against the Wizard." He continued his eyes landing on Ash and then moving slowly towards Piper.

"And what is that?" Gatlin asked, his interest piquing.

Ash looked to Lucinda, who was waiting at the table with bated breath.

"Ash had procured a pearl. A rare gem that will help her and Piper amplify their powers." Zarah announced, his eyes darted towards Lucinda, though he didn't mention where the pearl came from.

"Two Wizards against one." Evan sounded interested, "How do we use that to our advantage?" He wondered aloud.

"Ash has been working on a way to use it against the Wizard." Zarah admitted, allowing Ash to take over.

"We believe that we should be able to use it to null his powers." Ash admitted. "Perhaps Lucinda, Piper and I should go and discuss its use while you finish with this." Ash excused herself.

There was more that Ash needed to know about the pearl before she committed to using it, if she wasn't sure of herself then something could go horribly wrong, and she wasn't willing to risk that; not even for Avidaura. Plus there was the matter of Piper, who had only just come into her power, and didn't know about the pearl yet. Ash only hoped that Lucinda would be able to help them figure out how it worked, everything was counting on it.

"Very well." Zarah nodded, excusing the three from the table.

Ash and Piper rose, gathering Lucinda so they could help her while she got used to her land legs. Soon the three had disappeared out into another room in the back, Zarah was sure that they would come to find a way to use the pearl. At the very least they had given the army hope for Avidaura.

Zarah stared at the remaining allies, Gatlin, Murray, Ronan, Finnigan and Evan.

CRYSTAL

Felix had slipped into the underground tunnels with ease, it hadn't been long since he had traveled down there, though he couldn't recall the memory very well. There had been a very important something, he just couldn't place it.

The tunnels were wild and winding, he knew this, and still he found himself disoriented. His brain kept trying to direct him towards the exit, the one under the bridge, though he couldn't recall ever going there before.

He had to fight to concentrate on what he was *really* there for. The crystal, a relic that had been guarded beneath the castle as long as Avidaura had existed. It was older than Felix could know, more powerful than anything he could ever dream of. And for some reason, his father wanted him to find it.

It was hard to see, the farther they got from the dungeons, the more absolute the darkness seemed. His father had somehow procured a torch, through the glow was dim and didn't seem to help Felix much. His shadow seemed to lead the way, winding him through the tunnels as though it knew the way. But there was more to it than just picking a direction and walking into the dark. There were precautions to take, markers to read, and his father seemed to be in quite a hurry.

Felix didn't want to admit it, but he was having trouble navigating through the tunnels, the memories seemed too distant to remember, and in the back of his mind there was a warning of the dangers that lurked around him.

It had been a very long time since he had wandered in the depths of the castle, even longer since he had heard of the carnelian crystal. Trying to piece together a misadventure from his youth to find the destination his father was seeking was proving to be more of a task than he could manage. Trying to find the crystal without falling into peril was even more difficult.

Felix had already set off two of the underground traps by accident, it was pure luck that he was still standing and his father hadn't been maimed. The farther Felix got into the tunnels, the more dangerous it became. Even one slight misstep could end his father's quest quite abruptly.

Felix paused, listening to the tunnels. He could hear the scurrying movement of the Hobgoblins, and he knew they were monitoring him. He wasn't sure how far into the tunnels the vicious creatures dared wander, but he steeled himself for their appearance just in case.

Felix had barely managed to fend off the last Hobgoblin he had encountered, and it had only been with the help of Ash that he had managed that. He wasn't sure that he would be able to manage taking on one of the underground creatures on his own, perhaps his father had some experience with them.

Felix stopped walking, the thought lingering with him. When had he been in the tunnels with Ash, and who was she? The memory didn't seem to fit, it had no context to him, and yet he could remember drawing his sword on a creature in the tunnels, and Ash blinding it with light.

Felix looked over his shoulder at his father, the glow from the torch made him seem almost translucent, as though he were a ghost. His feet didn't seem to touch the ground as he walked.

Felix paused, staring.

"Is everything alright son?" His father asked, catching Felix's glance.

Felix shook his head to clear it. "Yes, I just need a moment to remember." He answered, scouring his brain for the way through the tunnels.

As hard as Felix tried, he couldn't piece it together, it was as though parts of his memories had disappeared. He could remember seeing the carnelian crystal as a child, but not his travels through the tunnel. He could remember the quest to the mirror, but not his return. It bothered him that he couldn't piece it all together, even more that he couldn't remember the way to the crystal. Normally he could navigate through the tunnels easily.

Felix walked until he reached a fork in the path, feeling for the marker, behind him his father sighed, clearly disappointed that he was taking so long. Felix closed his eyes, feeling the symbols as he tried to remember which one would direct him to the right path.

"Felix, we don't have time for this." His father hissed.

Opening his eyes, Felix made his choice, "This way." He directed, wondering in that moment why his father had needed him to guide the way.

It seemed strange, his father should have known his way through the tunnels, he had been the one that had taught Felix how to read the markers as a child.

Felix glanced over his shoulder again at the man behind him, he was sure that it was his father, but something was off about him.

"Why don't you take the lead," Felix suggested, "you could probably get us through faster." Felix suggested, stepping aside so his father could pass him in the narrow tunnel.

A flash of anger crossed his father's face, unlike anything Felix had ever seen. It was gone in a moment, replaced by the tired sad eyes that Felix knew all too well.

"Son, we don't have time for that, I haven't been down here in years." His father had stopped moving, waiting for Felix to guide the way, "Hurry Felix." His voice echoed through the tunnel.

Felix turned back towards the darkness and continued forward. Ahead of him something hissed.

Felix reached for the hilt of his sword, he had known the Hobgoblins were close by, he just hadn't been sure that they would travel so deep into the tunnels, so close to the dangers.

"Father?" Felix called back quietly. "We have company."

His father paused, not answering Felix. He stood still and silent, watching as his son prepared to protect him.

Felix drew his blade slowly, not making a sound. The flickering of the torch behind him was enough, soon he caught a glimpse of its reflection in a pair of large eyes, staring back at him from farther down the tunnel.

The Hobgoblin hissed, crawling forward into the flicker of the torch. It seemed protective, and it clearly wasn't going to let Felix pass, though its large eyes rested on his father.

Felix glanced back, his father was still standing there, still and silent, he stared past Felix at the Hobgoblin, looking indifferent.

"We're running out of time Felix." He reminded his son, waiting for Felix to clear the path so they could continue forward.

Felix turned back to the creature, taking a step forward to close the gap, his sword drawn and at the ready.

The Hobgoblin hissed, still staring past Felix at his father, the torch light cast lightly on the creature and Felix could see the wound, still healing on its side.

"It's you." Felix hissed, his memories of a journey through the underground coming forward as though they were new. "I've fought you before."

The Hobgoblin glanced at Felix, a glimmer of fear in its large eyes. But it didn't advance. It seemed that the creature was more interested in his father than Felix.

"Are you going to do something about this?" The King asked lazily, staring at the creature on the path ahead of them.

Felix edged forward, keeping his sword drawn, but resolved not to use it.

The Hobgoblin let him pass. He turned back waiting for his father to join him, but the instant Felix passed, the creature had taken a stance, blocking the King from passing.

"We don't have time for this." The King snapped his fingers and Felix felt a wave wash over him, instantly clouding his mind. The Hobgoblin disappeared, and Felix found himself unable to wonder why.

"Let's go son." The King marched towards him.

He turned, leading the way through the tunnel towards their destination.

Felix wound them through several more tunnels, trying to find his way towards the cavern that cased the crystal. He could feel the urgency to his task, not stopping for anything, not even traps. The faster he moved the more his mind focused.

"It's around here somewhere." Felix muttered, feeling at the walls as he moved down the darkest path.

A memory was coming back to him. As a child he had ventured into the depths of the tunnels, too far, he had been lost. His father had found him, the panic in his eyes had terrified Felix, he had thought that he was in deep trouble. Instead his father had helped him to his feet, and showed him the secret of the dark tunnel.

His father had led him deeper into the underground, showed him the door, and let him see the crystal on the other side. Felix remembered his father stepping into the room and closing the case, covering the crystal as he told Felix its history. The carnelian crystal had been used to create Avidaura, it had come from another world, a place called Eranox where the Wizards were. It was to be protected at all costs.

He had then warned Felix never to return to those depths.

The tunnel that surrounded Felix seemed familiar, it was the same tunnel that he had traveled in the memory. Though he was older, and the tunnel seemed somehow smaller in comparison, Felix remembered it well.

He brushed his fingers against the wall, finding the marker that he had been searching for.

"This way." He whispered, entranced as he stepped around the corner.

Cobwebs hung from the ceiling, the ground was woven with strange gold symbols that Felix recalled represented the Avidauran Universe and all of its realms.

"Be careful where you step." Felix called back, remembering the warning his father had given him in his youth. Though most of the underground tunnel system was guarded, the crystal was the most guarded of them all.

"Hurry Felix." His father hissed impatiently, reminding Felix that they needed to be quick before the Wizard returned.

Felix nodded, taking his time to cross the golden glyphs. As his father followed, the torch still sit in his hand, the end came into focus.

There Felix stood before the door.

The great ornate door seemed so out of place in the dank tunnels, the woven patterns that decorated it were covered in dust and looked aged. Felix stared at it for a moment, there was no knob, no handle, but Felix knew how to open it.

Felix brought his sword to his hand, grazing his palm, just enough to cause blood to rise to the surface.

He placed his hand against the door. It had been enchanted to open only for the royal bloodline. There came a boom that shook the castle, nearly knocking Felix from his feet. Dust fell around him, loose rocks tumbling from the ceiling. Felix stepped forward as the door began to open, entering the dusty room on the other side.

The room seemed to light itself, his father's torch was no longer necessary.

As Felix crossed the threshold into the room his mind began to clear itself. In that moment Felix knew that he was the only one in Avidaura that could open have opened that door.

He was the last.

He turned, realizing what he had done, a strange memory rising to the surface.

His father was dead.

Felix stared as his father entered the room behind him, wondering what he was really seeing. As he crossed the threshold the magic failed, and the Wizard appeared, standing in his father's place.

Felix held his gasp. The Wizard hadn't noticed that his magics had failed when he had entered the room.

"Son, you have done well, now where is it?" The Wizard asked.

Felix flinched, the memory of his true father's demise rising to the surface.

"It's not here." Felix lied, walking towards the chest in the center of the room, guarding the crystal inside. His hand rested on the hilt of his sword, he was ready to protect the artifact with his life.

The Wizard looked confused, he reached forward to touch the chest and Felix saw a glimmer in his eye. He had realized his magic had failed.

"Oh Felix." He tisked, "There is no sense in hiding the crystal from me now, it is too late." The Wizard opened the chest, revealing the crystal inside.

Felix stared as the room began to glow. There it was, the fire from the torch magnified in the deep amber stone. It was the size of a dagger, a grip carved into the stone at one polished end while the other remained ragged and untamed.

Felix breathed out, surprised at the beauty of it.

"This is it." The Wizard breathed. His hand trembling as he reached for it.

Felix drew his sword, whipping the blade through the air as he aimed for the Wizard's outstretched hand.

He was a moment too late. The Wizard's fingers clasped the handle of the crystal and Felix's blade was knocked away as a surge of power radiated through the room.

The Wizard met his eyes, "Clever boy." He smiled, his eyes reflecting the orange glow of the stone. "It's too late now."

Felix could feel the power growing in the room, the crystal amplifying the Wizard's power, the protection on the sacred room dissipating as the crystal awoke to its new master.

"You won't have Avidaura," Felix hissed, "they *will* stop you."

The Wizard laughed, his below echoing in the chamber, "I am unstoppable now, there is nothing they can do. It is time that Avidaura paid the price for neglecting the other realms." His eyes glimmered with victory, "You can have your throne, I won't be needing it anymore." The Wizard turned, "Enjoy it while it lasts." He chuckled.

Felix didn't know what came over him in that moment, his sword drawn he charged across the cavern, his blade striking the Wizard in the shoulder.

There was a blast, and Felix felt his feet rising as his body rocked back, slamming into the far wall of the cavern. He fell to the ground in a heap of dust and stone.

The Wizard turned back to him, surprised. His shoulder was bleeding, Felix's blade lay on the ground between them, useless.

"How brazen." The Wizard stared at his wound, clearly surprised that Felix's blade had penetrated. "That sword." He stared at it for a moment, unspeaking.

"You won't take Avidaura." Felix grunted, trying to pull himself up from beneath the stones.

"Nor will you." The Wizard snarled, the hatred rolling from him. Felix had made him angry.

The Wizard stepped from the room, raising his hand towards the ceiling as he stared at Felix, "This is your end." He snarled.

Power shot from his fingers, blasting the ceiling of the cavern.

All Felix could do was watch as the stone crumbled around him, trapping him in darkness while the Wizard walked away.

He felt the stone as it collapsed on him and the world went black.

ARMY

Gatlin had returned to the forest to talk to his herd, they had been working through the night preparing iron laced weapons for a war that had yet to be decided.

As Gatlin exited the Village, Mavera was the first to see him, the expression on his tired face carrying the news that things were changing.

Mavera trotted towards him, "What's the news?" He asked, keeping his voice to a whisper, though the others wouldn't hear him over the clatter of the swords being struck anyway.

Gatlin nodded his head, turning away from their new settlement to walk with Mavera to somewhere more private.

"That bad?" Mavera asked, following Gatlin along the wall away from the Centaurs and their loud noises.

Gatlin turned, "We march at dawn." He waited for Mavera to react before he told him why.

"That soon?" Mavera glanced over his shoulder, "We can't have all the weapons laced by then."

"I know, do your best, but they have to move quickly. King Felix has been taken." Gatlin stared at his companion, letting the statement sink in.

Mavera stared at Gatlin for a long while, then he began to pace, his expression blank, thinking. Finally he turned his head up, "Are you sure?" He asked.

Gatlin nodded, "He was taken, the girl, Piper, was with him when it happened."

"And the Clurichaun? Did they get to them?" Mavera was trying to get on the same page, he needed to know what had happened in the council meeting if he was expected to address the Centaur army.

"She returned with the Clurichaun. They seem... feisty." Gatlin tried to find the right word to describe their leader Murray. He had no doubts that the Clurichaun would fight.

"We still won't be able to lace all the weapons in time, and the arrows aren't ready." Mavera shook his head.

"Finish what you can, worry about the arrows for now, we must have ourselves prepared." Gatlin answered, worried more about his own kind than the thousands marching with them. He had to choose, and he chose the Centaurs.

"Yes." Mavera nodded in agreement, "I'll have them finish the swords that are prepared, and move on to arrows." He decided. "Is there anything else?" He seemed afraid to ask.

"Be prepared to move at dawn." Gatlin nodded, leaving Mavera to return to the herd and deliver the news.

Mavera nodded stoically, turning back towards the Centaur settlement, "We will be ready." He promised.

Gatlin stood outside of the wall for some time, debating his return into the Village. The council would be meeting again, and sleep was not an option for him. He trotted around the Village, coming to the entrance at the other side.

There was still someone he needed to talk to. He stared into the woods, the dark hues of the Forest of Night so close to the edge of the forest that it startled him.

It had been a long time since he had seen a Fairy, until that night. They were wiser than the Humans, had more history with the Centaurs. Though it had been centuries since the two species had a reason to meet.

Gatlin took a deep breath and began to trot towards the Forest of Night. He had to be sure that his ally was prepared for the war.

He entered the forest, not sure which way to go as he stepped through the veil and found himself in the darkness.

Eniki was waiting for him.

"It has been a long time." Eniki leaned against a tree, smirking at Gatlin.

"Longer than I care to admit." Gatlin answered.

There was something about Centaurs and Fairies that differed from their Human counterparts. Their lifespans were much longer, long enough that most of them had been in Avidaura since it first began. Though the Humans would never understand, they couldn't really, not when their lives passed so quickly.

"I was hopeful that you would come by." Eniki admitted, stepping towards Gatlin.

"I think we have some things to discuss." Gatlin admitted.

"If the Wizard wins the war…" Eniki nodded.

"So you think it's possible?" Gatlin was surprised, Eniki had seemed so sure at the council meeting.

"Anything is possible." He glanced back into the woods.

"Is there a way out?" Gatlin went straight to the point, he was concerned for his kind, for what would happen to them if the Wizard won and Avidaura was dismantled.

"I already conversed with the Elders." Eniki turned back to Gatlin, "Before the Human King found us."

"And…" Gatlin just wanted the answer.

"It's too late." Eniki shook his head, "If we lose the war, we go down with Avidaura."

"That's it then?" Gatlin had been hoping for a different answer, "There's no other way?"

Eniki was silent for a moment, his small dark face pensive as he considered his next words. "It's too late to leave." Eniki finally responded.

Gatlin stared at him, the impact of those words hitting him harder than any sword ever could.

"This is it then?" He whispered. The fear setting in as he realized the war was his only option.

"There is no other way. We fight." Eniki stared at him, the same fear reflecting in his eyes.

"Then I hope to see you on the other side." Gatlin reached his hand down clasping Eniki's in his. "For the sake of our land."

"And our lives." Eniki answered quietly.

Gatlin left the woods with a weight on his shoulder. A burden that he could not share with Mavera; they had waited too long. The only hope for their survival was to go through with the war, to stay until the end and see what happened next.

***

Evan and Ronan walked through the darkened streets, they had spread the word to their armies and were walking back to the meeting place. Word was spreading amongst their sleeping soldiers and the Village was waking to the news.

It was as though a wave of whispers had begun, and continued to grow louder as the word spread, though Ronan and Evan walked in silence.

By the time they reached the doors to the council meeting room, the whole Village was shouting, feet stomping, children crying. All they could do was cross the threshold and close the doors behind them, muffling the sounds as they waited for the council members to return, and the meeting to resume.

"Do you think they are ready?" Ronan asked, taking a seat across from Evan at the great table.

"I think they know what they are fighting for." Evan answered, letting his eyes fall on the table.

The door opened and Zarah entered. He had been dressed in armor, different than the garb the King's Knights used to wear, his helmet was tucked under his arm. He approached the table and set it on top, standing while he waited for the others.

"Are they ready?" Evan asked quietly. Zarah nodded.

Though it was unspoken, Zarah knew that Evan was asking about the sisters, Ash and Piper. Their success in the war hinged on the girls' ability to use the pearl. Without them it would be an utter failure.

The door swung open, "Has the meeting started?" Murray walked in, looking around the table as he realized they hadn't all arrived just yet. "Oh, good." He crossed the room and climbed into a chair.

A moment later, Ash and Piper entered, with Gatlin following behind them. As the door closed over and the chaos outside became a muffled mumble, the room stayed silent.

Ash walked to the head of the table taking her place next to Zarah.

"Are we ready?" She whispered, though her voice carried across the room.

"We are ready." Zarah answered, standing at her side.

"Then let us begin." Ash turned to the table. "It is time to discuss the war." She announced, and if the room was silent before, it was nothing compared to the silence that followed her words.

"You have all had a chance to discuss the inevitability of our marching sooner than later with your armies." Ash continued after a moment, "Are there any concerns moving forward?" She let the question hand in the air for a moment.

"How are the Centaurs coming along with the weapons?" Ronan asked, directing his question at Gatlin who stood at the far end of the table.

"We won't have time to finish all of the swords, though they have completed over half of the weapons that you sent to be laced." Gatlin answered.

"Half?" Evan seemed disappointed.

"That was all there was time for."

"And that is still quite a lot." Ronan nodded in appreciation. "How should we divide them?" He asked.

"Divide them?" Gatlin asked.

"The men who wield the laced weapons should know that they have them, they are the only swords that will work against the Dragons." Ronan continued.

"You are right." Zarah interjected, "Those that carry laced weapons must be prepared to face the Dragons."

"Should we take volunteers?" Evan asked, wondering who would willingly face a Dragon.

"I think it would be better if we made that decision here." Piper cut in, surprising most at the table. "This council is planning the war, we should know where the iron laced weapons are, in case we need them." She added.

The council seemed to agree with her, it was better to have a line of Knights prepared to face the Dragons than a few weapons scattered amongst the ranks.

The discussion about the laced weapons continued on for some time as they each chose those from their side who would stand against the Dragons. It was like drafting a team in Piper's experience, though what they were putting the Knights up against was something more dreadful than anything Piper had ever known.

Though the Dark Fairies had moved on to prepare themselves under the protection of the Forest of Night, the room was full, and the conversation loud as they discussed the final moves.

Gatlin felt that it would be unfair to leave the Fairies without the aid of the special swords; though there was no way to get them to the Fairies, as they had already moved their camp, and couldn't leave the Forest of Night during the day.

Murray had devised a plan that would keep the Fairies in the fight, and Gatlin had finally agreed. As the disbursement of swords finally came to an end as a discussion Ash took over again.

Ash stood at the head of the table, a weight had been lifted as she and Piper had finally found a way to use the pearl with the help of Lucinda. All the pieces were in place, Avidaura would be saved.

"With the aid of the Centaurs forged weapons, the Dragons will no longer be at the advantage." Ash concluded as they finalized their line of Dragon warriors, a list sitting on the table before Piper. The council seemed pleased with the new advance they would have.

Finnigan rushed through the front door of the meeting room, causing the council to take pause.

The room was washed in silence. All heads turned to stare at Finnigan, who appeared to be out of breath.

Finnigan slammed his fists on the table, catching his breath, though he already had all the attention.

"He's on the move." Finnigan finally breathed, falling into a chair as the room grew cold.

Ash stared at Finnigan, watching as he heaved, his breaths coming out ragged and uneven.

"What do you mean?" She and Piper both moved towards him, "The Wizard?" She whispered, though her question echoed in the quiet room.

Finnigan looked up into Ash's eyes, she already knew the answer was yes, there was fear in his eyes.

"The guards came back," Finnigan shook his head, "The Wizard is marching from the castle." He looked into Ash's eyes the fear growing as he continued, "His Knights, the Dragons, the whole bit…" The color drained from Finnigan's face, he lowered his head, unable to continue.

Ash turned back to the council, Zarah had stood from his seat, watching Ash talking to Finnigan. He nodded to Ash and turned to address the table.

"We are out of time." Zarah turned to the Chiefs, the table turning to regard him, the new news leaving them in a stoic silence. "Signal the army, we move *now*." Zarah concluded, nodding grimly at the council.

Without a word the Chiefs departed to prepare the army to move. Gatlin followed them out, though Murray stayed, his bold determination wavering as he looked to the two sisters with a sad expression.

Zarah sighed, "Ash, Piper, do you need Lucinda to join us?" He asked, unsure what their resolution was with the pearl. If the Mermaid was required to use the pearl then they would need a way to protect her on the battlefield.

Ash shook her head, "No, She should stay here where she will be safe. Evan's wife is protecting her." Ash turned to Murray, his expression hardening so she wouldn't see his weakness.

"Are your people ready?" Ash asked Murray, changing the subject as she prepared herself to leave the village.

Murray righted his shoulders and nodded, "Sober and feisty, nothin' will slow them down." Murray sounded sure of himself.

"How long?" Piper asked, she sounded nervous, her upbringing hadn't prepared her for what she was about to face.

"Soon, be prepared." Zarah answered. He turned to Finnigan, "Come with me, we will let them know."

Finnigan rose from his seat, his face chalky with nerves. He followed Zarah out the door, leaving Ash, Piper and Murray alone.

"Are ye going to be alright?" Murray's voice softened as he reached a hand out to Piper.

She nodded, steeling herself.

"This isn't going to be easy." Murray admitted, trying to prepare Piper for her first battle. "You stay with yer sister." He nodded to Ash.

"We'll be okay Murray." Ash rested a hand on his short shoulder, "Are your people prepared?" She asked again.

Murray nodded, his eyes blazing, "We took away the Ale last night..." He looked horrified, "There'll be no stopping them."

"Go and prepare them," Ash told Murray, "we will see you on the other side." She added as Murray turned away.

Murray nodded, his sad eyes turning away as he departed. For a moment Ash feared that that would be the last time she saw the Clurichaun.

Piper stared after him, "Are we really ready for this?" She whispered, turning to see Ash watching her.

Ash smiled, but Piper could see through it. "We couldn't be better prepared." She smiled, "Do we have everything?"

"I have the supplies here." Piper answered, her hand resting on the satchel at her side.

"Then we should begin the spell, before we depart." She turned to clear a space at the table.

Together the two sisters began the spell that would unite their powers with the pearl, once the spell was complete, they would be ready to march.

***

Zarah stepped from the meeting room into the bright morning sun. The chaos had already begun as the Chiefs had spread word to prepare the army to march.

Without Felix there to lead the army, Zarah had to step up and take his place. It felt unreal, leading an army against the castle that he had once called home.

The burden fell on him, though Ash had taken the title of High Wizard she was unable to lead the army. Her place was with Piper, and their secret weapon. The Wizard Sisters had enough to worry about without taking on the duty of commanding an army. And that left Zarah, once a simple adviser to the King, now the last survivor of the castle and what it once was.

The crowd parted for him without a word, Knights and villagers saying their final goodbyes. Zarah walked forward unseeing. There was no one left for him to say goodbye to. He had no family, no purpose other than the war. Behind him Finnigan struggled to keep up.

This was not how they had planned to save Avidaura, without a King, without a plan. But there was no other way.

Zarah wasn't sure what would happen if they won, no one had dared discuss how they would piece Avidaura back together without a King. There was also the possibility that they would lose, but Zarah pushed that thought from his mind and continued forward. There would be time to deal with the aftermath if they made it through. Nothing else mattered anymore, it was time to fight.

There was still a small hope that Felix was alive, though the doubt had already spread to Zarah's heart. He had lost too many in the battle already, and there was still so far to go.

Zarah took a deep breath. He had to be brave. For Felix, for the sisters for the Knights and the villagers that were fighting by his side. He had no choice but to march up to those doors and lead them to battle.

Zarah straightened his chain male, checking his sword in its scabbard at his hip. He carried his helmet under his arm, making his way through the crowd to the gates.

As he neared the post the crowd grew silent. Zarah took the three steps up to the lookout and turned to stare out at the waiting crowd.

Zarah waited as the crowd turned to stare at him, the silence washing back into the crowd as they waited for Zarah to address them before the departed.

He could feel the weight of the moment resting on his shoulders, some of the men standing before him would never return, of that he was sure. And as he watched their faces he wondered if there was another way, but it was already too late.

They were going to war.

"Today we stand for Avidaura." Zarah's voice boomed across the crowd, their silent face staring at him eagerly as they waited to march. "This land is our home, a place for all of the Kingdoms in this Universe. Today we stand united, as Avidaura was meant to, and together we fight for this land and our homes, our families, our futures." Zarah drew his sword slowly, raising it into the air above his head, "Today, we fight for Avidaura!" He bellowed.

Zarah stared out over the crowd, slowly their swords raising in a salute. Their voices calling "For Avidaura!", as they pledged to fight for their world.

In that moment as Zarah stared out at the army, he felt as though they were unstoppable. He stepped down from the lookout, holding onto that moment as he returned his sword to his side.

The gates opened, with Zarah taking the lead. He began to march, the footfalls behind him booming in his ears. The army was leaving the Village behind.

Zarah marched at the head of the army, not daring look back just yet. He led them onto the castle path, the time for hiding was finally behind them. Now it was time for them to be seen.

Finnigan was at his side, looking nervous as he instinctively checked the forest beside them for danger, which seemed strange, considering danger was what they were marching towards.

WAR

It was late in the afternoon when the army of the Fallen finally reached the place where the path from the Low Village met with the path that lead across the bridge towards the castle. Zarah stood at the front of the line, slowing to a stop as he saw that the Wizard had reached the peak of the bridge.

This was it.

This was the place where Avidaura would take its final stand. It all seemed so final as Zarah stared at their foe, so sullen and stoic on the arch of the bridge.

Behind him the army took their final steps, getting into position as a silence washed over the army. In that instant it was as though Avidaura itself had gone silent in anticipation of the battle that was about to begin.

The Wizard stopped, standing on the high arch of the bridge overlooking the path ahead of him. Behind him, an army sprawled out as far as the eye could see; Dragons perched on treetops, Trolls towered over the deserters, and Knights, wearing the True King's colors, stood with sneers on their faces.

If the Wizard was surprised to see an army waiting for him, he hid it well. His face belayed nothing more than annoyance at the crowd that stood in his way.

Zarah stared at him from the end of the bridge, searching for any glimmer of hope that Felix was among the Wizard and his followers. Behind him, the army of the Fallen waited for his command, their weapons drawn, unmoving.

It didn't take long for Zarah to realize that Felix wasn't amongst the Wizard's followers. Rage grew inside of him as he realized that they had lost their true King, the last of the bloodline; Felix had been like a son to him.

Avidaura had truly been brought to its knees, and there the Wizard stood.

It was all that Zarah could take.

"In arms." Zarah hissed, his hand was shaking with rage as he drew his sword. The army shifted, adjusting their positions as they prepared to move. The Wizard would not pass over the bridge, the mainland was theirs, and they would protect it with everything they had.

The Wizard laughed, throwing his head back as the sound escaped him, he waved to his army lazily. "Clear the way." His voice boomed, echoing across the water below him as he turned, his eyes bearing down on Zarah.

The silence lasted only a second after the words had escaped the Wizard's lips. Zarah stared at the Wizard, resolved to avenge Felix's death and save Avidaura. His hand stopped trembling as the Wizard's army began to charge across the bridge, swords drawn, feet thundering, stampeding towards Zarah who held the front of the line until the final moment.

Zarah stared them down, daring them to fight on the side of the usurper, daring them to defy their true King. A few faltered as they caught his eye, but soon the army was reaching the peak of the bridge, skirting around the Wizard as though they were afraid to get too near to their leader.

It was time.

Zarah raised his sword above his head, signaling his men to strike with a battle cry that boomed across the land as he dove into the fray ready to fight with everything he had left inside of him.

***

Finnigan rushed with the first wave, sword drawn as he took to the bridge, keeping the dark army at bay while swords clashed at his side. The noise was deafening, each strike echoing back from the moat beneath the bridge as through a second strike had followed.

Finnigan pressed forward, wasting no time as he parried through the masses, working his way through the dark army one strike at a time.

The bridge creaked beneath the weight of hundreds of armed men, each step Finnigan took was more perilous than the last. He could see the Wizard, standing so serene at the top of the arch, watching as his army rushed forward to clear the way for him.

The sight of the Wizard enraged Finnigan, to command an army and be unwilling to join them in battle was nothing more than cowardice. He didn't care about his people, he didn't see how anyone would be willing to side with such a cruel and uncaring leader.

There was no room on the bridge to move, Finnigan fought to make his way through, his shoulders pressed up against every Knight at his side. Though the Wizard's army was equipped with the armor of the True King, they fought like the cowards they were; men who had given up on their Kingdom, women who had chosen the path of least resistance.

As Finnigan pressed forward it occurred to him that the rest of Avidaura was counting on him. For the villagers it was just another day, kids would be playing, bread would be baking; and the entire fate of the Kingdom rested on the shoulders of their renegade army.

Finnigan wouldn't let them down. He pushed himself to the front of the surge, his sword striking the first foe he encountered. He turned as another blade bore down on him, blocking the strike just in time.

Finnigan turned to face his new foe, his eyes meeting those of Martin, one of the old guards from the Low Village, a deserter of the True King.

Martin had never been kind to Finnigan, to see him standing there fighting for the other side was not much of a surprise. Finnigan remembered his guard training and the wrath that he had faced at Martin's hands, it sent a wave of anger through him.

Finnigan struck again, their blades clashing as Martin parried his strike.

"Well if it isn't finnicky Finnigan." Martin snarled, taunting Finnigan as he tried to gain ground on the bridge.

Finnigan snarled, standing his ground as he struck again, this time gaining a full step forward.

"You couldn't best me in training, you might as well give up now." Martin huffed, pressing forward despite Finnigan's best efforts.

Finnigan stayed in his path, keeping Martin from crossing over the bridge to the mainland.

A Dragon fired, sending a wave of heat just over their heads. Martin used the distraction to strike at Finnigan's blade, kicking his foot out to press against the shield in his other hand.

Finnigan leaned towards the blow, seeing it coming before Martin had even struck. There was one good thing about Martin that he remembered from his guard training; he always used the same moves.

Finnigan smiled.

Without a second thought he turned his blade, knocking Martin up the side of his head, his helmet tumbled onto the bridge, forgotten.

Finnigan struck again, and the shield fell from Martin's hand.

Martin took a step back to regain control, but Finnigan was already waiting, anticipating Martin's moves.

"Not today." Finnigan growled, turning his blade on the back of Martin's leg. One swipe and he was teetering over the side of the bridge and into the murky waters below.

One down, Finnigan thought, looking up at the incoming army, prepared for his next opponent.

There would be many more to come.

***

Overhead the Gwin swooped from the skies, their screeching calls bringing the army to a stop for a brief moment as they tried to protect themselves from the incoming talons.

The Gwin were more fierce than Finnigan had ever imagined, claws ripped helmets from heads, gouging through the armor that the treasonous Knights wore. The Gwin lifted them from the bridge, dropping them into the waters below despite their screams and struggles.

Even without weapons they were armed to strike with more ferocity than most of the creatures that battled on the ground; Trolls were uprooted, Dragons were swarmed, it seemed that nothing would stop the Gwin.

And then came the second wave.

The sound came first, the screams of a thousand Gwin over the forest, the flock swooping from above the trees like a darkness that clouded the sun. They carried iron netting in their thick talons, a creation of the Centaurs that had been to impractical for the Knights to use.

The new wave of Gwin dove with a purpose, dropping the iron nets over the Dragons as their brethren swooped at the army of the Wizard.

One net after another, they trapped the Dragons, leaving them squirming and hissing beneath the iron nets that bound them.

The Fallen army rushed in, pegging the nets to the ground with enchanted spikes that Ash and Piper had made to keep the nets down and the Dragons from escaping. When they had run out of nets and pegs the Gwin continued on with their siege, striking anything that they could reach with their claws.

What was once a dozen Dragons protecting the Dark Wizard from the rebel army was soon contained to a mere four.

Four Dragons was still more than the army was prepared to face, they circled overhead, breathing fire atop the clearing and singeing anything that remained in their path. It was near impossible to fight a Dragon while it was in the air, though the archers were giving it their best from the back of the line.

If the Wizard was surprised at the loss of his allies, he hid it well. Still the Dark Wizard walked forward, slowly crossing the bridge, easily gliding through the battling army towards the path that would lead him through the Badlands.

No one dared bring their blade to strike him, any blade that came near was swiped away with a mild gesture, taking the wielder with it.

The Wizard clearly had a plan, and a destination, he seemed oblivious of the battle surging around him. His sights were set on something else, and the war would fail if they let him through their ranks.

Though some of the Dragons had been contained, their fires still raged on, blasting across the land in waves of heat as they tried to break free of the bonds that held them tethered to the earth.

With each blast the armies retreated away from the beasts, heat and smoke covered the battlefield. Soon the bridge had caught fire, Knights on both sides rushed to the mainland to continue their battle away from the flames.

Swords and arrows, fire and stone; not a single Knight was left to rest in the scrimmage that had taken over the path and into the woods.

***

Zarah held the line, keeping the Dark army from reaching the Centaurs behind him. His sword pressed against a shield, twisting his arm while he turned to strike the final blow.

A Gwin swooped down, lifting his opponent into the air high above the treetops, before he was released. His piercing scream stopped short as he struck the ground below.

Zarah had never seen a Gwin fight before, in fact he had never seen more than one in the same place at the same time. He was surprised, looking into the skies, to see just how many of them there were; and how fierce they truly were.

Perhaps when Avidaura was won, there would be another job better suited for them than just delivering messages. But there was no time to consider the future just then.

As the foe before him had been lifted away, another had taken his place, pressing towards Zarah with fire in his eyes.

The battle was not over yet.

***

Gatlin and his line of Centaurs stood at the woods, guarding the Fairies until they could join the battle.

Arrows arched from their bows over the army of the Rising, striking the Dark Knights as they landed with a deafening boom.

Mavera had equipped the Centaurs with arrowheads that detonated on impact for the first wave. Each wave of arrows plundered the Dark Knights, sending them diving to the ground.

The booming sounds of their explosives rattled the land, shaking the trees and sending men to their knees as they tried to outrun the blasts.

Mavera arched his bow, aiming for a crowd of the Dark Knights that had escaped the bridge intact. Releasing his arrow with a smile, he watched as the impact rattled them, swords falling from their hands and shields flying into the air.

"Take it easy Mavera," Gatlin grunted, letting loose another arrow, "we only have so many."

Mavera chuckled drawing his bow with another arrow, "Their army stands no chance." He smiled, knocking another arrow into the air.

He could see their army failing, one after another falling to the ground as they were defeated. Mavera's arrow struck and another three Knights fell.

The Centaurs wasted little time, launching wave after wave of arrows into the Dark army. When they had finally run out of explosives, they moved on to the their regular bows, lighting them with fire before they arched them into the air.

At the rate they were going, it wouldn't be long before they were reduced to hand to hand combat.

***

Guarding the pathway towards the Badlands, the Clurichaun had gone wild. For once they had allowed their savage nature to take over and were using it to fight for Avidaura. Without the ale to keep them docile and cheerful, they had changed into wild creatures that no army could contain.

Murray had anticipated the results of an ale-free army before they had ventured from the Village, ensuring that he and his men were kept away from the rest of the Fallen; for a sober Clurichaun would fight *anything* that crossed its path, and he couldn't risk his kind fighting with the wrong army.

Zarah and Piper had given their army clear instructions to stay away from the Clurichaun once they were in position, anything that happened after that was beyond Murray's control.

They ripped the chain male from each Knight that tried to pass them, swarming as they dispelled their weapons and shields into a pile by the border to the Forest of Night.

Soon the Fairy army would be well equipped to join the siege.

No one made it past the small fury that had taken over the path by the woods; each Knight that tried was disarmed, stripped of its armor and tied to a tree before they could raise a shield.

Murray and his clan, though savage, were not the kind to waste time taking lives, though it didn't stop them from taking out a dozen Knights in one go without breaking a sweat. Soon they had amassed a pile of squirming bodies, wrapped along the tree line, disarmed and stripped of their armor.

"Take em!" Murray shouted as another wave tried to pass them for the pathway.

With a surge of wild screams, his army complied.

***

Ash and Piper stood together, holding hands as they walked towards the Wizard. Piper could feel the power rushing through her, amplified as her power surged with her sister's. Ash held the pearl in her other hand, the energy radiating off of it protecting the two of them from the swords and arrows that careened around them.

They were the second wave, the end to the war. It was their powers that would stop the Wizard and save Avidaura from the reign of the Dark Wizard. His own nieces, his flesh and blood, they would put an end to him.

"Are you ready?" Ash whispered to her sister, giving her hand a light squeeze.

Piper breathed shakily, "As ready as I'll ever be." She answered, squeezing Ash's hand back.

Piper was terrified, she had never fought so hard for something in her life. The powers that she wielded were still new to her and she was relying on her sister to know what to do when they faced the Wizard.

He was easy to spot in the chaos, the Dark Wizard walked slowly and with purpose through the battlefield. His magics protected him from the blades and fires, much like his nieces who walked towards him.

For Piper and Ash it was as though they had stepped outside of the war; around them swords clanked and Knights shouted, but they sounded far away.

Piper stared at the Wizard, he hadn't noticed them yet, but her heart was racing and her hands were cold and clammy. This was the moment she had been having nightmares about.

Ash seemed to sense her hesitance, she stopped and squeezed Piper's hand again.

"We can do this." She promised, her eyes meeting Piper's for the first time on the battlefield.

There was a fierce look in Ash's eyes that reflected Piper's fear. Ash was handling her terror in a much more practical way, channeling an inner rage that set Piper on edge. Her fear washed away as she stared at her sister, remembering what they were fighting for, and what they had already lost.

"Let's do this." Piper hissed, gripping her sister's hand tighter as she turned back towards the Wizard.

The Dark Wizard spotted them in the crowd, slowly he turned towards them, a grim smile plastered on his face.

"Here we go." Ash whispered, gripping the pearl as she began the incantation.

Piper concentrated, letting her powers flow into her sister, letting go of her fear and focusing on their goal.

The Wizard walked closer, soon they were face to face. He smiled at them, like he hadn't a care in the world.

Together Ash and Piper raised their intertwined hands, the power bursting forth in a tidal wave that knocked the fighting armies back, leaving them and the Dark Wizard standing in a clearing amongst the chaos.

Piper felt the pull as the wave of magic struck the Wizard, and passed through him. He began to laugh, untouched by their show of power.

"Clever girls." He mused, staring at the pearl with fascination. "But not even *that* can stop me now…" He smiled.

Piper felt the color drain from her face, her heart beating in her ears as she dared glance at her sister who's mouth hung open in shock. Their magic combined with the pearl's power should have stopped him dead in his tracks. They had done everything right, Lucinda had told them it would work, Piper had *felt* it work.

And yet the Dark Wizard still stood before them, unmoved, unharmed, like their magic had been nothing to him.

He lifted his hand and his cloaks fell away, revealing a dagger in his hand. It was golden hued and gleamed in the fire around them as though it were alive.

Ash could feel the power radiating from the gem, she knew that they would only have one chance.

Without a second thought, both girls raised their hands again, power flowing through them like wildfire.

Still, the Dark Wizard seemed unaffected by their powers. He moved, the stone dagger in his hand glowing, light spread from the gem like a sun, illuminating the entire clearing and bringing it from dusk to midday with its brightness.

Ash could feel it happening, the pearl in her hand glowed brightly, slowly dimming until it had fallen flat. She turned to look at Piper, her face was grim, she was growing weak, as weak as Ash felt, the stone necklace at her collarbone glowed, slowly turning black.

"What's happening?" Piper whimpered, her stone draining.

"He's taking the magic." Ash gasped.

DEFEAT

Ash could *feel* the stone around her neck draining, though she knew that the magic inside of her had been untouched. Somehow the Dark Wizard had found a way to drain the magic from Avidaura, the land itself. Ash stared at him in horror as she realized what he was holding.

The carnelian crystal, the fabled gem that had brought life to Avidaura from another world. He had found it, and was using it to take back the magic that it had once bestowed on their Kingdom.

"Where did you find that?" Ash breathed, the question escaping her lips before she remembered who she was talking to.

The Wizard chuckled, "So you know what it is?" He seemed impressed. "And with the magic, and the crystal, I will start anew." He answered.

Ash understood, the end of Avidaura was within sight, her power wouldn't stop the Wizard from achieving his goal. She looked at the pearl in her hand, it had grown dull, lifeless; she worried how it would affect Lucinda back at the Village.

Their plan had been for nothing, it was too late, the Wizard had won.

"Ash." Piper hissed, she was staring at her necklace, holding it in her hand as it turned to a blackened stone, the power inside of it gone. "What's happening?" She asked, her eyes turning to Ash.

"He's taking the magic." Ash answered flatly, "There is nothing we can do now." She whispered, defeated. Ash let go of her sisters hand, tucking the pearl into her cloaks to protect it.

"That's it?" Piper sounded confused, "It's over?" Her voice was shaking.

Ash shook her head, "We did all we could." She answered, looking back to the Dark Wizard.

"No." Piper decided, reaching for Ash's hand again. "This is not how it ends."

Ash looked at her, the fear was still there, but her determination was bolder. She wasn't giving up.

Piper had turned back to face the Wizard, even without her power, she wasn't backing down.

"If you want Avidaura, you'll have to go through me first." Piper growled, squeezing Ash's hand tightly before she let go, facing the Wizard on her own.

The Dark Wizard stared at her for a moment, surprised at her gusto. He twisted the carnelian dagger in his hand, watching her as she stood her ground, unflinching.

"You should have joined me." He mused, stepping closer, the dagger poised in his hand, "I am unstoppable now, there is nothing left in Avidaura that will keep me from achieving greatness." He smirked.

"I can." Piper answered, still unwavering. Slowly she drew her sword.

Ash stared at her, Piper had no idea what she was saying, she was going to get herself killed. Ash stepped beside her, drawing her own sword, she wouldn't let her sister stand alone.

The battle had grown silent around them, Knights and Rogues watching with bated breaths as the two sisters stood before the Wizard.

"I would hate to spill the blood of my kin." The Wizard smiled, "Step aside, you have failed." He took another stride forward, offering them defeat as though he knew they would have no other choice but to bow down and do his bidding.

Piper raised her sword, aiming it at the Wizard. "For Avidaura!" She shouted, lunging forward.

Though the Wizard sidestepped her strike, the battle erupted anew, pressing in on all sides.

Piper darted into the fray, her sword swinging as she tried to turn herself back to face the Wizard. The blade in her hand was heavy, she had only just learned to hold a sword, it was clear to her that she was ill prepared to wield a sword in a battle.

She swung her blade, parrying the sword that was coming for her face while she kicked out her foot, making contact with the offending Knight's knee. There was one thing to be said about a Wizard who had never been trained in combat, her opponents had no idea what they were up against.

Piper channeled every action movie she had ever seen, spinning wildly through the battle with her sword swinging and her feet kicking. She struck at anything that came near her, even managing to kick a few of her Knights in her attempt to stay alive.

Her heart was beating at a speed that she couldn't control, her ears were ringing, drowning out all the sounds around her as she battled frantically, afraid for her life.

Piper had lost sight of Ash somewhere in the chaos, now she was only trying to stay alive, kicking and screaming as she worked her way through the battle.

Without armor, Piper was unprotected from the blades around her. Her wild battle screams seemed to draw more attention to her than she would have preferred. A blade struck her arm and she howled, not sure where the guttural sound had come from. She turned, striking the offending sword bearer with everything she had in her, her screams unfiltered as she let loose a wave of fury.

She didn't have time to check her wound, her arm was still able to hold a sword, so it couldn't be *that* bad. She knew if she looked at it it would only make the pain worse, so she pushed the thought from her mind and carried on into the battle.

It was harder than she had expected, being in the thick of it, sweat and blood dripped down her face, and she wasn't sure if it was all hers. All she knew was that she had to keep fighting.

They seemed to be everywhere, the Knights, and it was hard to tell which were on her side and which were fighting for the Wizard. The armor all looked the same to her.

She didn't recognize any of the faces, not that she could see them very well behind the helmets. Still, it made it harder to fight, worrying if she was wounding her own.

A sword swooped past her shoulder, grazing her, but missing her skin. She turned to strike, whipping her sword through the air without planning ahead. Her sword struck a Knight in the side, ringing out as it made contact with his metal armor. She stared at her opponent, unsure what to do next.

He had drawn his sword against her, his shield blocking his body as the blade came down towards her. She lifted her sword, not sure how to counter the strike, her instinct telling her to move.

She sidestepped the blow, it missed her by mere inches as she turned back to her opponent, trying to find a weak spot in his armor before he struck again.

***

Ash hadn't been prepared to draw her sword. She had expected that the war would have been won when she and Piper had confronted the Dark Wizard with the pearl. To be reduced to a mere sword was harder than she had imagined.

She had been trained to wield a sword, she had been practicing since before she was the Wizard's apprentice. So when the scourge took over and she found herself faced with the Dark army, she could handle herself against the blades that stuck at her.

Though without her magic amplified, she was having less luck with her accuracy than she could have anticipated. She hadn't realized just how much she had relied on the stone around her neck until it had been drained. It was the little things that were throwing her off, like foreseeing an attack, that left her feeling anxious as she battled against the Dark army. Usually she knew just when and where she was about to be struck, though her only experience with a sword was in training. She had never been in a war before, and without her magic working, she felt more vulnerable than she had in her entire life.

Each strike came as a surprise, and her reflexes, normally quickened by her powers, were struggling to keep up with the frantic fury that surrounded her. She was slower than normal, even her own strikes seemed easily dodged.

To make matters worse, the Rogue Knights kept stepping in her place, not giving her a chance to fight through on her own. They had been told to protect the sisters at all costs, and were taking it very seriously. Which left Ash, beginning one battle after another, unable to finish.

It was infuriating.

Ash couldn't seem to get away, she couldn't fight, and her mind was so distracted by what was happening, versus what should have happened. She was losing hope that the war would ever end, or that anyone would be left standing when it was over.

She couldn't imagine that there were so many willing to fight for the Dark Wizard. He had made his mission clear; Avidaura was going to be destroyed so he could make way for something new, something he could control. To think that so many were willing to fight for that was insanity. Had he offered them a place in his new universe? Did they expect to live when it was all done and over? Ash couldn't wrap her head around it.

She couldn't let them win.

Finally she managed to get away from the Rogue Knights long enough to find herself alone on the battlefield. It wasn't long before she found an opponent.

A dagger was his weapon of choice, and with her longsword, he didn't stand a chance in getting close enough to use it.

She knocked him upside his arm, the dagger nearly tumbling from his hand as his armor vibrated with the impact.

"What are you fighting for?" She demanded, wanting an answer.

He turned, trying to get around her sword to strike.

"What has he promised you?" Ash yelled, still waiting for an answer.

The Dark Knight paused for a minute, and Ash held back her sword. He seemed confused that she was asking so many questions.

"What are you fighting for?" She asked again, waiting for him to respond.

"For Avidaura." He shouted, his eyes glaring at her like she was the enemy.

"If he wins, Avidaura won't exist." Ash shouted, she couldn't believe that someone could be so stupid, to run into a war without knowing what was at stake.

"What?" He was still poised to fight, but Ash could see him falter.

"The Wizard is leaving, and Avidaura won't exist if he wins." Ash shouted over the battle, she couldn't believe that she was still trying to explain it to him. He should have known.

"No." He shouted, raising his dagger, "We are fighting for Avidaura, the new Avidaura."

" Oh, you're an idiot." Ash huffed, swinging her sword at him. She struck him upside the head, his helmet ringing out as her blade struck. While he was distracted she disarmed him and left him on the ground, "You're on the wrong side." She hissed as she stepped over him to fight someone with a brain.

Ash could hear Piper in the battle, her screams echoing loudly across the battlefield. At least she knew that her sister was still alive, somewhere out there, fighting for her life.

As she battled through the scourge, Ash couldn't help but notice that Avidaura felt different. The magic was still draining from the land, she could feel it pulsing beneath her feet as the Wizard absorbed it, leaving the land barren. It was worse than the disturbance at the Field of Mirrors, the magic was dissipating so quickly that she could *see* the difference. The soil was dryer, more lifeless as she walked across it. It gave her an eerie feeling, like she was in another world, like Avidaura didn't exist anymore.

Even if they won the battle, even if they stopped the Wizard, Avidaura was changed. Still, she pushed forward, because giving up wasn't an option, because it would never get better if she didn't try, because her sister was still out there fighting for her life.

***

Finnigan was still fighting, he had paused for only a moment, long enough to know that the battle wasn't going to be won by the sisters. Their plan had failed, the Wizard had even seemed amused at their attempt to thwart him. And the battle had surged forth anew, his hopes of a quick siege put to rest as a sword had knocked his helmet askew.

He wasn't sure what exactly he was fighting for anymore, if there was much point to continuing on. But as he stared out at the path and saw his comrades with their swords engaged, he knew that he couldn't back down.

STRUGGLE

Dragons had reached the mainland. They were suffering without magic in the land, it was quite apparent in the way that they landed, and failed to fly. They shook the earth as they climbed from the moat, stomping to their master's side to protect him from the siege.

Even without magic their fires still managed to burn. With each breath, they blasted heat out across the battlefield, charring everything in their path as they tried to clear the way for the Dark Wizard.

He stood behind them, patiently waiting for the way to be ready, watching as the smoke curled from the burning bodies, armor flashing red as it heated to the point of melting on the path ahead of him. Though it wasn't safe for him to travel yet, he seemed pleased with the Dragon's work.

There was only one thing standing in the way.

A wall of Clurichauns waited at the ready, their savage faces staring down the beasts as they moved towards them. They were the last defense, the last thing standing in the Dark Wizard's path; and they were ready.

Murray led the charge, waiting for the last blast of heat to escape the Dragon standing before him, then he made the call.

"Get em." He shouted, his sword raised. He was ready to defeat the giant beast before it had time to regenerate its inner fire.

The angry screams of a thousand Clurichauns followed Murray as they rushed forward to dismantle the Dragon.

Armed with weapons that had been laced with iron, the Clurichaun clamored atop the beast, taking it apart, one scale at a time.

They made quick work of the first Dragon, descaling it enough for another Knight to step in and finish it off. There was already another Dragon coming towards them, and they had to be ready.

The next Dragon was more cautious, steaming from the nose as it approached, saving its fire so it could blast them clear with its flames.

Murray was smarter.

"Loop around." He screamed, and his army was quick to move.

They took to the trees, the Dragon following them with its snout while a second wave of Clurichaun snuck up behind it. Before it had a chance to blast them, they had struck it through the heart. It seemed to burn up from the inside as it collapsed, igniting and bursting into flames in the middle of the path.

It was enough to slow the Dark Wizard's progress, he wouldn't be able to get through the Badlands until the Dragon had burned out, unless he tried to go around.

And they were ready for him.

***

Finnigan was losing speed, his breaths had grown ragged and he had nearly been throttled by Piper twice as she twisted through the crowd in her strange battle dance.

He had begun to follow her in an effort to keep her from falling peril to the swords that she wasn't watching for, but somewhere in the fray she had disappeared again, and he had found himself face to face with a Troll.

It was taller than him, but not by much, and it carried weapons that Finnigan hadn't been trained to block; axes and hammers. It seemed to have a never ending supply on its belt, just waiting to be used.

The Troll was ambidextrous, something that Finnigan had never faced before, it was able to wield two weapons at once without difficulty, and he was having trouble keeping himself from being throttled as a hammer and ax swung at him with ferocity.

Finnigan twisted to the side, the tip of an ax just missing him, he could feel the breeze from the swing as he turned and focused on the Troll. It smelled ripe, like it hadn't bathed ever, though it was refreshing in comparison to the blood and dirt that had taken his senses over on the battlefield.

He heaved himself forward, timing his strike as he twisted and sliced the Troll in the arm, knocking the ax from its hand.

The Troll grunted, reaching for another ax as his other arm swung a hammer towards him. Finnigan ducked, but the side of the hammer cracked against his shoulder, the Troll had anticipated his recoil and had been prepared. Already there was another ax swinging towards him. It seemed like it would never end.

Finnigan was winded, but he didn't have time to think twice, the Troll was still coming. Its eyes were locked on Finnigan as both arms started swinging towards him again.

It was all he could do to block the blows and step back, the arms kept swinging and he hadn't a chance to strike himself as he blocked blow after blow, losing ground as the Troll cornered him. Soon there would be nowhere left for Finnigan to retreat to, he was almost in the moat and the steep incline was causing him to slip farther and farther away, giving him less room to block the attack.

Something struck the Troll from behind, and for one moment Finnigan was sure that it had finally stopped. Surprise crossed the creature's face, and then it began to fall towards him, arms still swinging, unable to get its feet under its body. It landed on the ground beside Finnigan, still swinging, but somehow unable to get back on its feet.

Finnigan looked up, and there stood Piper. She looked quite proud of herself, her sword was drawn, blood smeared her face, and her cloaks were ripped and ragged. She reached a hand down to Finnigan, helping him back to his feet.

"How did you do that?" He asked, stepping away from the Troll as it pulled itself towards him, still not getting back up.

"Go for their ankles," She smiled, "it'll slow them down." Without another word she disappeared back into the crowd swinging.

Finnigan looked down at the Troll, it was still swinging, but it couldn't seem to get back up, Piper had taken the legs out from beneath it.

Finnigan smiled, and raised his sword.

***

Zarah weaved through the crowd, he could see Murray across the battlefield, standing atop the head of a fallen Dragon with his sword swinging wildly. Arrows arched overhead and Zarah ducked, barely escaping the latest barrage of fire tipped strikes from the Centaurs behind him.

The army was losing speed, but the battlefield was growing sparse for another reason. Some of the Dark Wizard's followers had taken to the woods in retreat. He could hear their screams as the Dark Fairies defended their boarders, not quite able to join in the siege just yet.

Despite the deserters doing what they did best, the Wizard still had numbers on his side. Dragons and Trolls were still maintaining their line, keeping the rising from reaching their leader, keeping the army from ending the fight.

Fires raged, spreading as far as the trees, soon they would grow wild, taking what was left of Avidaura down in a wave of flame. But there wasn't time to worry about that just yet, they could stop the fires when they had a world left to save, when Avidaura was safe from the Wizard and his plans of utter destruction.

Zarah wasn't sure how much the girls knew, how much Felix had known before his disappearance, but he remembered how it had all begun. Unlike the Centaurs, the Fairies and the Gwin, his knowledge had been passed down, it wasn't a firsthand account, but it was enough to set him on edge.

If the Wizard left and took the carnelian crystal with him, Avidaura would cease to exist. It had been created from nothing, and if the crystal left, it would return to nothing.

The Wizard's ambitions to start anew, to create a new center of the universe would first begin with the destruction of the world that they lived in.

Somewhere in the masses of Knights, Trolls and warriors, Zarah spotted the Wizard. He seemed impatient, waiting for his way to be cleared, no one dared step up to him, but they had at least stopped him from moving forward with any ease.

He blocked a sword with his shield and turned to address his attacker, though his mind was still elsewhere.

The plan had failed, the pearl hadn't worked against the Wizard, and Zarah was hard pressed to think of another solution. He had been so sure that it would work that he hadn't even considered another option. And now there was no time to think, one wrong move and he was as dead as the mounds of soldiers at his feet.

Zarah pressed forward, keeping the Dark army at bay while he tried to consider another plan, though he knew that it was only a matter of time before the Wizard had his way cleared and left them, and Avidaura, in ruins.

It was too late to think of something clever. And there was no easy way to stop a Wizard with unlimited power. Their only hope was to take him by surprise, and it wouldn't end well.

Zarah had already made up his mind, he worked his way through the siege towards the Wizard, ready to strike the moment he was distracted.

Someone had to do something before it was too late, and he was the only one left to take a stand.

***

"We're out of arrows." Gatlin knocked the last of his into the battle, the bow resting uselessly on his arm as he reached to his quiver and found it empty.

He tossed the bow to the ground and reached for the sword at his hip. Beside him Mavera knocked another arrow at the army, finding his quiver to be depleted as well.

"Already?" Mavera sighed, tossing his bow to the ground beside Gatlin's, "Blades." He shouted, alerting the rest of the Centaurs to their change in tactics.

The arrows should have lasted them until the end, but something had gone wrong with the sisters' plan. The battle had continued and Gatlin had watched as the sisters had joined in, drawing their swords.

It was supposed to have been perfect, the pearl that they had obtained should have stopped the war before it had even begun. Instead the Centaurs were left with little choice but to join the fray.

Mavera raised his sword, signaling the Centaurs to rush in. They obliged with a roar, their hooves trampling against the ground as they raced off into the crowd, swords drawn, prepared to fight until the bitter end. There was one thing that the Centaurs would not do, and that was retreat, they would stay and fight until the last of their kind was gone, or until the opposing army had fallen, whichever came first.

"So you think they have another plan?" Mavera asked, he had waited back with Gatlin as the other Centaurs had charged.

"I have no idea." Gatlin responded, glancing out across the sea of swords, "Only time will tell." He nodded to his companion, turning to charge into the battle himself.

Mavera watched him go, holding the line at the forest's edge, he would stand guard until the sky darkened and the

202

Fairies were free to join them. He drew his sword, facing the siege, waiting.

***

Her sword was bloody and getting harder to hold by the minute, but Piper wasn't ready to give up just yet.

It had hit her all at once, the Wizard had won, and she wasn't going home. She was stuck now and Avidaura was all she had left. Though the tears streamed down her face she couldn't let them deter her, she had one last thing left to fight for, her life; and she wasn't giving up.

She screamed, slicing through the air and missing her opponent as she startled him with her cry. She kicked dirt up into his face, and reached for his hair, his helmet fallen and forgotten.

She had caught him off guard. She had caught them all off guard, because she had no idea what she was doing.

She tugged at his hair pulling his head down as she raised her knee to strike him in the nose. It hurt her more than she had expected, but she had finally knocked the sword from his hand with her maneuver.

"You suck." She screamed, tossing him aside for another Rogue Knight to finish off, there was already a new foe waiting in his place. "You all suck." Piper screamed, diving forward for the next attack.

FELIX

Felix awoke in the dark, the blackness a faint reminder that he was still in the underground tunnels beneath the castle, and how he had gotten there.

"What have I done." He whispered. Silence answered.

He had failed, again, but this time he had ruined everything. He had given the Wizard the one thing that could destroy everything, he had practically handed him the Universe. How could he have been so foolish?

The Wizard had left and there was nothing anyone could do to stop him, though he knew that Zarah and the army wouldn't give up. They just had no idea how dangerous the Wizard had become.

Felix had to warn them, before it was too late. It was bad enough that he had given the Wizard the carnelian crystal, he didn't need everyone he loved dying in a battle they couldn't win.

He needed to warn them that it was too late.

He had to admit that it was over.

But first, he had to get out.

He was stuck in the underground, rocks collapsed around him, he could barely move, and the darkness was absolute. It was so dark that he couldn't see his hands before his own eyes in the blackness. But determination had set in, and he wasn't letting that hold him back.

Closing his eyes, so he wouldn't keep trying to rely on his sight, Felix pounded his fists into the stone around him, releasing some of the frustration that had built up inside of him. There was no time to waste feeling sorry for himself, no reason to second guess why he had followed his dead father into the tunnels, what was done was done.

The stone pinned him to the ground, he could still feel his legs, but the pressure atop them was unbearable, he began to shift the stones, eyes still closed, moving the rocks off of him, one shove at a time.

Dust and debris showered him from above, it wouldn't be long before the rest of the cavern collapsed, and his shifting wasn't making matters any better. He had to rely on his other senses to get himself out of there, he could feel the cool tunnel breeze from the other side, and knew that as he pushed the last fallen rock off of himself he was going to have to move fast.

He crawled over the debris, following the cool air, behind him the stones tumbled, more of the ceiling caving in. He had just barely made it past the threshold when the dust started to waft towards him, he turned, trying to close the door over, pressing his back into it, as he struggled to close it before the stone began to cascade out into the tunnels beyond.

The door clicked, and Felix felt the pressure ease, the room had been lost, but at least the rest of the tunnels were fine, still dangerous, but he would deal with that in his own time, at least he had escaped being stoned to death.

He was far enough into the underground catacombs that it would only waste time returning to the castle proper, his only option was to go out the other way and come out beneath the bridge. It wouldn't be an easy task without Ash and Piper to help him across the moat, but it was still faster than returning to the castle and leaving through the front gates. He couldn't risk being seen, so the secret entrance served his purpose much better.

Felix tried to catch his bearings, he vaguely remembered where he was in the underground. Though during his descent with the Wizard he had been under a spell and the memories were hazy, he knew how far down he had gone, and roughly what dangers he was about to face to escape.

It wasn't going to be easy by any means, there was no light, he was alone in the darkness, and the section of the underground he was trapped in was the most heavily guarded of them all.

It would be a miracle if he made it out alive at all, let alone in time to warn the others.

Felix didn't know how long he had been down there, but he was sure that the Wizard had already made his plans and set them in motion. For all Felix knew it was already too late. But he couldn't just stay there, he had to get out one way or another.

He pressed his hand against the cold stone wall beside him, trying to see down the tunnel ahead, but it was no use. With a sigh he began forward.

It was eerie being in the tunnels alone, each step he took echoed through the winding darkness, there were drips and cracks and hisses off in the distance that distracted him and made him nervous. He had lost his sword in the cavern, and there was no going back for it. Without his weapon he was vulnerable to the creatures that lurked in the underground, and he was keenly aware that they had no trouble seeing in the dark.

Felix was sure that they were watching him, an odd skitter here and a hiss there, the Hobgoblins were aware that he was in the tunnels, and he was sure that he wasn't alone anymore.

He tried to hurry, but the winding tunnels slowed his progress more than once, finding the path markers in the dark was near impossible, trying to decipher them even more so. He was losing precious time, his frustration growing by the minute.

The ghostly memory of his father, the one that he had followed into the underground, floated into his mind. He should have known that it wasn't the King, he should have seen through it, and yet he had wanted to see him so badly that he had let the Wizard get the better of him.

Another memory drifted into his mind, from the day he had wandered too far as a child. He and his father had been walking out of the tunnels, from the very cavern where Felix had been trapped.

Felix had asked his father how he knew his way around the tunnel, that was the day that his father had shown him the path markers. But there was something else his father had said to him that he had never understood.

"There are other ways out of the tunnels, Felix, you just have to ask."

Felix felt the path marker in front of him, turning towards the next tunnel as he repeated those words in his head, *ask who?* He wondered, but he had never asked his father what he had meant, he had pretended to understand so his father would think he was clever. There was no one left to ask, he was alone. But the words remained, on a loop as he walked through the dark tunnels, searching for a way out.

His foot landed on a trigger, Felix paused as he felt the stone sink beneath the sole of his boot. He couldn't see the tunnel ahead of him, so he paused, foot pressed into the stone, listening to the sounds of the tunnel ahead of him to try and determine what he was up against.

He didn't have time to wait, taking a deep breath, Felix steeled himself for what was coming. Wounds would heal, but if he lost Avidaura it would be forever.

Felix took a deep breath and lifted his foot from the trigger, sprinting forward to meet whatever fate was in store for him. The ping of arrows arching from the walls and striking stone echoed out behind him, but he didn't slow down until he hit the wall on the other side.

"I made it." Felix breathed, his voice louder than he had expected, he ran his hands over himself, half expecting to find an arrow sticking out of his side. But he had made it through unscathed.

He heard the skittering again, the Hobgoblins were still close, soon they would make their presence known. Felix didn't have time to wait and celebrate his small victory, he had to keep moving forward.

Felix turned, deciding which way he would continue down the path. A light thud in the tunnel ahead of him indicated that the Hobgoblins were done watching.

The hiss filled the tunnel, mere inches from Felix as he stared into the darkness, the hairs on the back of his neck standing on edge. He was weaponless, blind, and in a hurry.

"No." Was all he could manage to say, his steely voice echoing back to him as it passed against the stone, "I do not have time for this." Felix marched forward, unafraid of the creature that waited in his path.

The Hobgoblin stood in his way, Felix stepped right into him, feeling his sickly cold skin against the tops of his boots. He tried to step around it, but the Hobgoblin moved with him.

"Get out of my way." Felix hissed.

The Hobgoblin hissed back, unmoving.

Felix tried to push forward, taking the creature with him, but it hissed at him and wrapped its thin fingers around his ankle, holding him in place. He could hear the others, waiting in the dark, watching.

"Let go of me, I need to get out of here." Felix tried to shake it off, but the creature was surprisingly strong for its size.

It hissed at him again, tugging him back the other way.

Felix kicked his leg out, shaking it off, but it stayed in his way, still blocking him from escaping through the tunnel.

"Don't you get it?" Felix grumbled, "I need to get out of here, or Avidaura is *gone*." Felix shouted, his voice echoing across the tunnels and back to him.

He heard the words as they returned and a chill rolled down his spine. There was more at stake than just Avidaura. The Wizard had plans that even Felix couldn't understand. The other realms, the places where the inhabitants of Avidaura had come from, he was going to destroy them all. He was going to lay waste to the whole Avidauran Universe if he wasn't stopped.

The Hobgoblin had stopped hissing, it had taken Felix's cloak by a corner and begun tugging him in the other direction again.

"I need to get out of here." Felix whispered.

The Hobgoblin tugged harder in response.

Felix stared into the dark, curious. The Hobgoblin hadn't attacked him, it hadn't even tried, yet it refused to let him go down the path in the direction he had chosen.

"Are you trying to help me?" He asked, not expecting a response.

The Hobgoblin hissed, tugging harder, Felix could hear the others, climbing slowly on the walls around him.

"Fine, I'll follow you." Felix sighed, starting down the path as the Hobgoblin pulled him by his cloaks.

The creature had no trouble seeing in the dark, Felix followed as it skittered ahead, guiding him by the tails of his cloaks, around bend after bend, through the underground at a speed that Felix couldn't have managed even with a light to guide the way.

They were still winding through the tunnel when the pulse hit. A wave so strong that Felix was nearly knocked from his feet. Around him the Hobgoblins began screaming, their painful cries drowning him in the dark.

Something was happening to Avidaura.

Felix could feel it, like a wave of nausea, something was wrong. The screaming subsided, and the Hobgoblins stood still, waiting for some sort of command.

"We need to hurry." Felix spoke to the darkness, "And I'm going to need my sword." He added, feeling the empty sheath at his side.

He felt his cloak tug him forward, the creature in the dark dragging him forward again.

There seemed to be more urgency as the Hobgoblin pulled him through the tunnels, several of the other creatures had taken off in the darkness, perhaps to clear the way so Felix could get out quicker.

It still seemed strange that the evil creatures from the underground were helping him, there was still a thought in the back of his mind that they were leading him to certain death. But he couldn't navigate through the tunnels as fast as them, and if they were helping, then they were saving him a tremendous effort by getting him out.

He could smell the brine, the salty air that told him that they were nearing the end of the tunnel. He could also smell the smoke.

Felix couldn't be sure where it was coming from, the castle atop them could have been on fire for all he knew, but as the scent filled the tunnel, the Hobgoblin began to race faster. Felix could barely manage to keep up without tripping on his cloak as it pulled him forward and around another bend.

The tunnel was getting lighter, Felix could tell that they were nearing the opening under the bridge. It was like a weight had been lifted off of his shoulder. The Hobgoblins *were* helping him, he was going to get out.

DARKNESS

Sweat was dripping from Zarah's forehead under his helmet, but he didn't have time to wipe it away. The sword in his hand was covered in the slick blood of a thousand blows that he had taken since the battle had begun.

They had started out strong, no chance at all that the Dark Wizard would be able to defeat their army, and then the magic had been drained from Ash and Piper. Zarah had felt it too, rising from the very soil beneath his feet, the magic was leaving the land one small bit at a time. It was powering their dark foe as he made his march across the land, leaving them in ruins.

Their only hope was to keep the battle going as long as they possibly could, until they found another way to defeat the Wizard and stop his siege on the land. Though Zarah was sure as he pulled his blade from another faceless foe, that they had reached the end of the fight.

He was out of energy, and out of hope. Zarah had lost his reason to keep the fight alive. The Wizard was winning, he could see the effects of the magic being drained from the land growing stronger. The trees wilted, the Dragons' scales gleamed less, the world was ending and all he had left was the sword in his hand.

***

Murray shouted, his wild cry echoing across the desolate land as another Dragon managed to get past his line, slowly pushing them back towards the path that lead to the Badlands. They were losing ground, slowly, just as they were losing men.

The swarm of Clurichauns ambled towards the newest foe. Their sluggish movements a sign that they were running low on energy. It had taken everything they had to stop the last Dragon, they wouldn't be able to hold this one off for long.

They were going to need reinforcements.

They were going to need ale.

Murray sighed, thinking longingly of the fountain of ale, running freely in their Village, just a ways off the path. But he couldn't abandon his post. Avidaura was counting on him, and he was needed where he was.

There would be time for ale later, when the Dragons were defeated and the war was over.

Murray ducked and rolled as the Dragon heaved a breath of steam. As the magic drained from the land the Dragons were finding it harder and harder to maintain their inner flame, but that didn't make the steam coming from the beasts nostrils any less dangerous.

The iron nets weren't holding them anymore either, there was a loud ping that echoed across the field as a Dragon broke one of the pegs from the net across the battlefield.

Murray sighed, there would be more Dragons to face soon enough.

He stared into the eyes of the beast before him as he drove his sword through its neck.

***

Finnigan pressed forward, his sword had been lost amongst the battleground and its victims, the carnage spanned out as far as his eye could see. He had taken to hand to hand combat until he found a suitable sword replacement. His iron clad fist shot forward to strike a Dragon in the snout.

Murray shouted at him and he stepped back allowing the Clurichaun to take over as they swarmed the beast, there was already another Dragon waiting.

It had taken only a moment for the Dragons to break free, once they had realized the magic was draining enough to escape they had tossed their shackles, their massive wings catapulting the iron chains into the skies as the prisoners beneath regained their freedom.

Their fires were low, but their fury remained.

The sky was growing dimmer by the moment, Finnigan glanced back at the forest, knowing that they already needed the next wave, but it wasn't safe for the Fairies to join just yet.

Finnigan blocked Murray from the next Dragon, finding a sword in the ground that he could use to knock the beast up the side of its head, turning its snout at the last second before a stream of steam escaped its nostrils.

Murray glanced towards Finnigan, he hadn't seen it coming, and had just barely missed the blast,

"Thanks mate." He huffed, tugging his dripping sword from the skull of the Dragon beneath him, "Let's get em." He jumped down, joining Finnigan as they began their next battle.

***

Piper and Ash had found one another again, backs pressed together they turned slowly, keeping themselves from being maimed, but otherwise failing to keep the Dark army at bay.

The battle had turned in an instant, it was as though the hope had been drained from their army at the same time that the magic was taken. Piper could feel the desperation around her, the hopelessness that echoed in every battle cry.

They were losing the war.

The light was leaving the land as though it was being pulled away with the magic. As the last ray of sunlight escaped over the horizon Piper felt like the world had ended.

Sure, she could still see the battle raging on, fire and stars lit the scene around her. But the hope was gone, the spark that had kept them going had died.

She felt a tear slip down her cheek as she kicked out at a Dark Knight, screaming at him in the night.

It wouldn't be long before they were all dead.

***

The sound started slowly, at first it was just a shout that echoed across the battle. Then came a scream that pierced through the night like a banshee calling its prey.

Soon a bellowing thunderous cry, the sound of a thousand rage filled voices, echoed across the battle field shaking the clearing.

The army stopped as a wash of violet light came cascading from the woods, surging onto the battle field like a new dawn had broken.

The Dark Fairies had arrived.

They swarmed out of the woods with their staffs aglow, casting their magics at the opposing army and slowly pushing them back up towards the castle and the bridge that was still burning with Dragon fire.

Wave after wave, the Fairies took over, allowing the Fallen army a moment of rest as they took up the rear, allowing the Fairies with their fresh energy a turn at the battle.

For a brief moment it seemed that they would win, that the tides had turned and the rebellion would be able to take Avidaura back and stop the Wizard.

Until one by one, the violet lights on the Fairies staffs began to brighten, bursting as the magic was drained away from them and into the Wizard's stone.

It was the brightest thing on the battlefield, the golden dagger that was draining the Fairies of their power, the whole land seemed to be cast in its amber aura.

Piper stared in horror as one by one the Fairies lights went out, their magics no longer at their disposal. The bright violet glow that had brought hope back into a futile battle drained, and soon they were back beneath the stars. Only it seemed so much darker after that moment of light.

The Fairies had been prepared, not to have their magic drained, but rather to battle with the weapons that the Clurichaun had stockpiled for them.

It only took them a moment to change course, abandoning their staffs for their iron blades as they shouted with a battle cry that rattled Piper to her very core.

***

Eniki tossed his staff to the ground, the amethyst had gone still, its magic sucked away. He could see the amber glow across the battle field, the carnelian dagger in the hands of their foe. He hadn't expected the Dark Wizard to go to such great lengths. Though the Elders had warned of the possibility of something dire, Eniki had expected the Fallen army's plan to work.

If the girls had managed to use the pearl before the Wizard had procured the carnelian dagger, the war would have been over before it ever started, and the Fairies wouldn't have needed to step out of the Forest of Night at all.

Eniki hadn't expected that the Wizard would have found the carnelian dagger, in the short moment while his magic had lasted he had been sure that the battle would have been a short one. The Wizard's army, though consisting of larger creatures, was smaller in numbers... and brains.

The Trolls had abandoned the battle and begun fighting amongst themselves, the Knights, deserters of the true Human King, were weak with their weapons, but the Dragons were formidable.

Eniki had watched from the forest, safe in the darkness, while the battle had raged on. His hands had been itching to join the siege, but the sun had kept him from crossing the barrier from the Forest of Night onto the battle field. Now that he was in the thick of it, he could test out the weapons that the army had left him. The blade was longer than he had expected, meant for a Knight of the Human variety. It didn't take long for him to adjust to the weight, he was the head Knight of the Dark Fairies, training with strange and new weapons was his specialty.

He may have been shorter than the Human Knights in stature, but Eniki fought with more finesse than even the boldest of the King's guard.

He spun the sword through the air at Finnigan's side, striking a Knight of the Wizard's army with a blow to the chest that rattled through the blade in his hand. The opposing Knight recoiled, another taking its place as Finnigan stepped in for his turn at the battle.

Finnigan parried the Knights sword, leaving Eniki an opening to strike the Dark Knight down while he was still unsuspecting.

A blaze of fire lit up the land, just barely missing Eniki as he ducked to save himself from the blast. The fire was quickly followed by the thunderous sound of a Dragon landing in the clearing before him.

Clearly they had not all lost their fire, not yet at least.

Eniki took a deep breath, facing the beast head on, his heart racing. Its dark eyes gleamed with fire, but it would be a while before it could spout another burst of flame.

Finnigan and Zarah were at his side instantly, their swords flying as they tried to tackle the beast. In that moment's hesitation, Eniki knew that it was time to face his fear.

He had to fight a Dragon.

He tossed his sword aside, taking a sword from the ground, one of the iron laced creations that the Centaurs had prepared. He finally stood a fighting chance against the creature, though its sheer size was still daunting to him with his small stature.

Eniki had encountered Dragons before, they were predators to the Fairies in the Forest of Night, and he had found himself cowering in their presence more than once in his lifetime.

This was not the case.

Eniki stepped forward beside Zarah and Finnigan, his blade poised to strike as he stared the beast down.

It was so large that even the stars in the sky seemed to disappear as Eniki dove towards it.

"Aim for the eyes." Zarah shouted, his words muffled by the sound of a thousand swords.

Eniki turned his blade at the last second, striking the beast in the eye before quickly recoiling to stay as far from its monstrous teeth as he could manage.

A piercing shriek filled the sky, chilling Eniki to the bone as he watched the gaping mouth of the Dragon inches from his face, its teeth larger than even he.

Spittle rained down on him as the Dragon howled in agony, turning its head as it tried to protect its face from another strike.

Eniki was frozen with fear, so terrified that he didn't see the Dragon's tail as it came swinging towards him, striking against him and rocketing him into the air.

He landed with a sickening crunch, his arm bent beneath his body, the sword that it had gripped, twisted into his leg.

Eniki stifled a scream, as he turned his head to see where he had landed the terror washed through him. He had landed near the mouth of the beast, his blood pooling around him, his arm unable to hoist his body from the ground.

But still he tried, with heaving motions, Eniki pulled himself from the ground, using his other hand to yank the tip of his sword from his leg.

The blood was pooling at his feet, it was a wound that he would not survive. But he wasn't about to give up his fight with the Dragon just yet. If he was going to die, then he was taking the beast with him.

***

Finnigan launched himself forward, his sword aimed at the Dragons other eye. The beast was already moving its long neck and extending its massive jaw as it reached towards Eniki with its sharp teeth.

There was nowhere for him to run, nowhere to hide.

Finnigan could see that he was injured, his sword held in a weaker hand, his small determined face set as he stared down the beast. But he didn't stand a chance.

Finnigan lunged, driving his blade through the beast's good eye, but it was already too late.

Eniki had fallen at the jaws of the great beast.

The Dragon twitched as a sword struck through its neck from the inside. Eniki had made his final move.

The beast collapsed with a deafening thud as it went limp, taking Eniki with it.

HOBGOBLINS

Felix had made it to the end of the tunnels and found himself standing at the edge of the rocks, staring out at the scene before him. So close and still so far away.

He was tucked under the bridge to the castle, a bridge that had caught fire and had nearly all disintegrated into the moat below him.

It dripped with fire, smoke curling up into the darkened sky, he could barely breath as he stared at it. The bridge was falling into the moat in smoldering chunks, hissing as it hit the water and smoke curled up to greet him.

Fire lit the skies, he could hear the swords, the shouts, the cries. The war had begun while he had been trapped in the dark, it was too late to warn them of the crystal the Wizard possessed. He had probably already used it, and there was nothing any of them would be able to do to stop him.

Ash and Piper were at the most risk, their powers, the only weapon they had, would be stripped away, and he didn't know how they would manage without.

Felix could feel that the air was different, he had felt it in the tunnels, but now that he was out in the open Avidauran air, it was more noticeable. Beneath the smoke and sulfur, the air was lighter, there was something missing that Felix couldn't quite place, but he knew what it was. Avidaura was being stripped, one piece at a time.

Avidaura was dying, and with it the inhabitants were falling, one after another in a battle that they could not win.

His heart fell, he hadn't even been there to lead his army into battle. His friends, his people, were fighting for their lives and he wasn't even there. He looked down at the moat, there were bodies floating in the smoking water, and the bridge was still collapsing one fiery piece at a time into its depths.

Across on the mainland, there were Dragons on the shore, one of them was caught in a net, but it didn't seem like it would hold for long.

He was stuck, he couldn't go back through the castle, the bridge was gone, and beneath him the moat was so filled with squirming bodies and fire that he didn't stand a chance getting across. He was trapped, on an island, watching as the world around him fell apart.

He couldn't just stand there and watch the war, he needed to find a way to help, a way across, anything that would make him more than a useless gawker watching the world burn.

Felix rummaged through his cloaks, searched his trousers, there had to be something on him that could help, some way that he could get across to join his people. Finally his fingers landed on something small, metallic, he drew his hand out of his cloaks and looked at his palm. All he had left was the coin Eniki had given him.

He held it in his hand, turning it over as it slowly began to turn blue. Even outside of the Forest of Night it began to glow, Felix had never seen it change outside of the dark woods before, a sure sign that the magics in Avidaura had gone awry.

Behind him, the Hobgoblins hissed, backing away from the glow, like the small light hurt their eyes. Felix turned away from them, closing his palm over so the blue light wouldn't escape. It wouldn't help him get to the war, it wouldn't save him, the coin would be a mere trinket in a matter of minutes if the war continued and the Wizard finished draining the land.

An idea struck Felix as the light disappeared, contained in his hand. The hissing had stopped, but he was thinking of the Hobgoblins and their ability to guide him through the tunnels. He turned to face them, their dark orb eyes reflecting the fire on the mainland, they stared back at him like they were waiting.

"Any chance you know a way across the moat?" He asked, sure that they wouldn't answer, they couldn't really.

In the darkness one of the Hobgoblins stepped forward, the others moving to make it a path.

Felix could see the glint of his sword from the fire behind him, the small creature carrying it towards him raised above its head like it was a relic.

"My sword!" Felix gasped, accepting the offering, "How did you get to it, that chamber collapsed?"

He looked down, the Hobgoblin before him slowly turning its eyes to meet Felix's. It was a quiet moment, the look on the creatures eyes sent a chill through Felix. He stared past the small Hobgoblin at the others behind him.

They were all staring at him, like he was their only hope left. They hadn't hurt him in the tunnels, they had found him a way out.

They expected him to save them.

Felix didn't know what to say, there was still no way across the moat, but they eyes of the Hobgoblins were still staring at him, expectant and pleading.

Felix bowed his head, "I will do my best." He whispered, taking one last glance at them before he turned back to the moat to find a way across.

His sword wouldn't help him get across the expanse, but it still felt good to have it at his side again. The sword had come from his father, Zarah had saved it for him. It was a remnant of a time when the world was normal, before the quests, before the chaos. He tucked it into his side and stared out at the world, wondering what he would have to do to get to the other side.

Something flew past him, smaller than a Dragon, but still as ferocious. It carried a Dark Knight, dropping him into the moat with a swift dive that brought it into Felix's view.

A Gwin.

Felix had forgotten that they had joined the war. He smiled, staring out at the skies as he realized that there were more of them, so many that they seemed to block the stars.

If only he could find a way to catch their attention, they might be able to find him a way across.

Gwin were clever creatures, but more than that they could carry a message. He could get help, he could find a way across the moat. He just needed to get their attention.

"Gwin!" Felix shouted across the water, but the Gwin had already departed, off to find more prey, busy with the war. Too busy to notice someone shouting in the night over the screams and clatter of the war.

He had to find another way.

His palm was hot, the coin still in his hand seemed to pulse with energy, like it was trying to keep its magic despite the drain that was pulling Avidaura to pieces.

Felix opened his hand, staring down at the blue light, an idea forming.

The coin wasn't as bright as it had been when he had first retrieved it from his cloak, but he hoped that it would be enough to catch the attention of one of the Gwin. He waved it over his head, shouting into the night, waiting for the next Gwin to notice him, standing there on the ledge beneath the moat.

It seemed to take forever, waiting for the Gwin to come back with their next victim, his arm was growing tired, his voice hoarse. And just when he was ready to give up and find another way, a Gwin flew towards him.

It circled the moat once, it had seen Felix and was assessing the situation for danger. Another lap around the moat and it came in for a landing, hopping across the stone outcropping until it was standing before Felix, a strange expression on its beaky face.

"King Felix, you're alive!" He gasped, looking at the man before him on the ledge.

"I need a way across. Can you carry me?"

"Not alone." The Gwin turned, releasing a piercing shriek into the air.

The sound echoed through the tunnels, ringing in Felix's ears. It wasn't long before the call was answered, a hundred shrieks sounded across the battle field as the Gwin took to the air.

Felix held his coin up, showing them the way, but there wasn't room for them all to land.

They circled the moat, their dark silhouettes flickering against the fires that had consumed the land.

Felix felt a tug on his cloaks, he looked down. A Hobgoblin stood there, his eyes narrowed, he hissed at Felix and pointed out across the moat.

"You want to join us?" Felix asked, surprised.

The Hobgoblin nodded.

"They'll be needing a way across too." Felix turned to the Gwin, who looked at him with surprise.

"The Hobgoblins?" He asked, to be sure.

Felix nodded.

"One at a time then." The Gwin nodded, leading the first Hobgoblin to the edge of the rocks.

A Gwin swooped in from overhead, taking the Hobgoblin by the shoulders and carrying him across the moat to the battle on the other side.

One by one the tunnel emptied as the Hobgoblins joined in the siege. Soon it was only Felix left.

A second Gwin landed, regarding the King with a low bow. "Are you ready?" He asked.

Felix nodded, kneeling so the two Gwin could mount his shoulders.

"You're going to have to jump." One of the Gwin whispered in his ear.

Felix stepped to the edge of the rocks, looking at the steep drop before him, he closed his eyes and leapt into the dark.

He could feel the wind whipping against his face, his arms stretched out beside him, one Gwin on each shoulder. It felt like he was falling forever. And then there was a tug, and he began to rise, the Gwin catching the breeze on their wings and lifting Felix into the air.

He opened his eyes, watching as the moat floated beneath him, fires and battles drifting beneath his feet as they carried him towards the battlefield and the Wizard that he needed to face.

The ground rushed towards him as the Gwin descended, releasing his shoulders a few feet above the ground and letting him drop, Felix landed on his feet.

Quickly he drew his sword, turning quickly to assess the field around him.

The soldiers closest to him had paused, watching him as he had landed on the field. Their whispers and shouts echoing through the night.

"The King has returned," and "King Felix lives." It wouldn't take long for the rest of his army to hear the news.

Felix didn't have time to waste with formalities, he marched across the field, his target in sight on the other side of a Dragon that had been swarmed with Clurichaun.

The Dark Wizard.

He was staring at Felix through the battle, aware that his adversary had survived the tunnels. Felix held his sword at the ready, not sure how formidable the Wizard had become in his absence.

He could see the carnelian crystal in the Dark Wizard's hand, it glowed a brilliant amber, casting light like a beacon onto his target.

He had to get the crystal away from the Wizard. He had to end it while he still could.

***

Piper watched as a strange shape swooped overhead, landing in the clearing on the other side. "What was that?" She shouted over her shoulder to Ash.

The answer came quicker than she expected, the roar of Knights shouting of the return of the King filled the battle around them and Piper felt her heart racing.

"Felix is alive?" She turned, facing Ash.

Ash had the same surprised look on her face. "We have to go." Ash grabbed Piper by the shoulder and began to sprint towards the place where the shape had landed.

Knights moved out of their way as they sprinted across the field. Finally they stopped, watching as Felix drew his sword and walked towards the Wizard.

"He *is* alive." Ash breathed.

"He's going to get himself killed." Piper pointed, Felix was marching towards the Dark Wizard.

The Wizard was watching him, the carnelian crystal glowing in his outstretched hand. It wouldn't be long before the Wizard cast a spell and stopped Felix short in his tracks.

"Take my hand." Ash demanded, holding her other arm out towards Felix.

"But our magic is gone." Piper protested as Ash squeezed her hand.

"Just the stones, as long as we are alive it will course through our veins." Ash whispered, concentrating.

Piper could see the shimmer, it was faint, and it wouldn't stop much, but Felix would be protected long enough to retreat.

Ash pulled Piper forward, following Felix forward through the battle, keeping her eyes trained on him while Piper watched the surrounding battle, trying to keep them safe from any oncoming attacks.

It was hard to believe that Felix was still alive, Piper's heart was racing at the thought that the Dark Wizard had left him alive. Where had the Wizard taken Felix? What had he wanted from him? Piper had been sure that Felix was gone forever when he had been carried away on the claws of a Dragon. She had no idea what he had been through while they had been preparing to rush to war, but he had returned.

And he was determined.

***

Gatlin had given up on protecting the forest when the Fairies had rushed out to join the battle. He had galloped into the fray with his sword drawn, ready to stand at their side while they fought.

The Fairies had run in with gusto, Gatlin had barely been able to keep up despite the fact that his strides were twice that of a Fairy.

They had been pent up, waiting to rush into battle, stuck in the forest for so long watching that when they were finally let loose, they seemed unstoppable.

For one brief moment, Gatlin had been sure that their magic would have lasted. He had been so sure that they would be impervious to the crystal that the Wizard carried, he had even allowed himself to become excited.

Their Fairy Magic *should* have been untouchable, it was older than Avidaura, it had existed before the crystal had brought life to the land. And yet it had only lasted moments, just long enough to light the clearing with their glow. As the light drained from their staffs, the likelihood that they would survive the war had disappeared.

Gatlin knew that it was too late. He had known as much since he had met with Eniki in the woods. He just hadn't admitted it to Mavera yet, to the other Centaurs. They were still counting on him for a way out, for a chance to survive.

And he had no answers for them.

Mavera trotted towards him, "I think it's time for the other plan." He gestured behind him, the Centaurs were waiting. They expected Gatlin to have a way out, a plan, a way to escape the war.

Gatlin shook his head, "It is too late, there is no other way."

"What?" Mavera gasped, it was as though the air had been sucked from his lungs, he looked out across the fires, the war, the battle. And then he looked back at their Centaurs. "You cannot... this cannot..." He turned back to Gatlin, tears in his eyes, "This is it?" He asked, to be sure.

"This is." Gatlin confirmed, his heart aching as he knew that he had betrayed his herd, they would never trust him again.

Mavera turned his hindquarters on Gatlin, without another word to him. He was about to reveal his betrayal. Gatlin would be banished, not that he would survive long enough for it to happen.

He still felt it.

Before Mavera had a chance to speak of his betrayal the whispers had begun. A swarm of Gwin had arrived, dropping Hobgoblins on the field and soon, another had arrived in their midst.

The Human King had returned.

Gatlin turned, catching Mavera's eye. Mavera nodded once, giving Gatlin the benefit of a few moments, the chance for the King to end the war before he outed Gatlin for the betrayal he had confessed to committing.

Word spread quickly of Felix's return, to both the Fallen and the Dark. Soon the Wizard's army had become fearful, the return of the true King striking terror in their treacherous hearts.

They began to rush to the woods, searching for a way out, leaving their dark leader behind. Gatlin found himself chasing deserters as they raced towards the forest, abandoning the Dark Wizard as the tables turned and the Rogue army had their hope returned.

He wasn't sure what they expected a Human King to do that would thwart the Dark Wizard, especially while he was in the possession of the crystal. He carried the powers of the Universe in his hands, and King Felix only had a sword.

Still, Gatlin and Mavera had taken back to the woods, rounding up the deserters, tying them up so they could face their King if the war was won. It was still a long shot, but at least they had given up fighting, though across the field the battle still continued.

"We're running out of rope." Gatlin grunted, tying another deserter to a tree. Beside him Mavera was having less luck.

"Cut off their feet?" He suggested, blood smeared across his chest from a slight wound.

"Too much work." Gatlin finished his knot and turned away, leave it to Mavera to find the worst solution.

"Come on, there are more of them. The Fairies won't be too happy if they get to their Kingdom." He trotted towards another Knight, wrapping the last of his rope around his waist as he lassoed the offending rogue.

"Are the Fairies stuck too?" Mavera asked, keeping his voice down as he leaned towards Gatlin, helping with a knot.

Gatlin nodded, "It was too late to leave, I tried." He promised, though Mavera still seemed cold to him.

"Isn't their Kingdom protected." Mavera sighed, helping Gatlin drag the Knight towards the tree line.

"Only if the magic is working." Gatlin answered, though he wasn't sure of his answer, he wasn't sure of anything anymore.

RIFT

The Hobgoblins had descended upon the war as though they were a final disaster. Murray watched as they fell from the sky, delivered by the Gwin like a plague. It was hard to tell which side they were fighting for as they fell to the ground, ripping through anything that crossed their path or dared go near them. Their quick reflexes and keen eyesight made anything that moved a target for their thick claws and sharp teeth.

Murray had never seen anything like it before, he had never seen a Hobgoblin in his life, and he hadn't imagined that they could be so dangerous. If the Clurichaun were considered savage without their ale, then there were no words for what the Hobgoblins had become. Screams from their victims rang out across the night air. Horrifying sounds, hisses, screams, it was the most terrifying thing that Murray had ever seen.

He had nearly lost a chunk of his beard to one of them as he had tried to sidestep the tail of a fallen Dragon. And he was on high alert for the small furious creatures after that.

They were hard to spot, they moved so quickly, their pale sickly skin blending with the soil as they darted from one target to the next.

Murray was in the midst of disarming one of the Dark Knights when a Hobgoblin landed on his opponent's shoulders.

He could see the terror in the Knight's eyes before the creature began to rip him limb from limb. Then it turned to regard Murray, blood spattered its ghastly body and its eyes seemed to see right through him. If Murray had ever felt fear, it was nothing compared to the terror that gripped him in that moment.

He had never seen a Hobgoblin up close before, the eyes were as dark as night itself. Murray backed away, searching for a way out. He knew that he couldn't fight a creature like that, he could see that it was feral. If the Dark Wizard commanded the Hobgoblins, then they were in for some carnage.

Murray turned, and instantly there was another one there blocking his escape. It stared at him, those dark beady eyes reflecting his own face as a fire flickered in the distance. It was one thing to be afraid, another to see the look on his own face as he knew his death was coming. He felt his heart skip a beat, he was surrounded.

The Hobgoblin stared at him for another moment, as though he were sizing Murray up before an attack. Then it nodded to him, as though in greeting, and continued on as though it had determined Murray to be an ally.

And then Murray understood. He had heard the whispers, but he hadn't dared believe them. The Hobgoblins had come from the castle, and they hadn't come alone.

Murray turned, scanning the battlefield, the fighting was sparse and it didn't take him long to find what he was looking for, the one who had brought the demonic creatures of the night to battle, the one they served.

The King.

Through the darkness, Murray could see him, walking towards the Dark Wizard. His sword was drawn, his face set, he was going to try to end the war.

And he was all alone.

Murray whistled three sharp ringing notes and waited for the Clurichaun to hear his call.

If anyone needed them now it was Felix. And Murray had made that boy a promise that he would be there if Felix ever needed him; when he had still been a Prince, when he had still been naive and new.

Murray wouldn't let him down.

***

Felix marched forward, closing the gap between himself and the Dark Wizard. He could see the look on the Wizard's face, waiting for Felix to walk towards him, making no effort to greet his foe.

Felix raised his blade and locked his eyes with the Wizard, taking the final step as he drove his blade towards the Wizard's heart.

It happened quickly, the blade was about to make contact when the Wizard flicked his wrist. It was as though a hurricane blasted past Felix, though it didn't reach him, he seemed caught in the storm, untouched.

He could see the surprise on the Wizard's face, a flicker as he looked over Felix's shoulder. Something behind Felix was troubling to him, but the distraction lasted only a moment. And then his eyes were back on Felix, his amusement gone.

"I wasn't expecting you to make it." He admitted, his eyes narrowing as he sized Felix up, "You have more in you than I thought."

"It's over." Felix decided, watching the Wizard's face, trying to determine the best method of attack to catch his foe off guard so his powers wouldn't be able to thwart him again.

The Wizard looks around at the chaos surrounding them, "You couldn't be more right Felix, Avidaura is going out with quite a stand."

Felix snarled, the Wizard had twisted his words, but he wasn't wrong. Felix could smell the fire, the blood, the sweat. Avidaura was falling apart, and the Wizard hadn't had to do any more than take the magic and stand back to watch as it imploded.

"You can't stop me." He shook his head, holding the crystal out for Felix to see, "I already warned you." He seemed shocked that Felix was still trying to fight him, he seemed to believe that he had already won.

"I won't give up on Avidaura." Felix growled, poising his sword to strike again. But the Wizard was ready for him, and whatever had protected Felix from the last spell wouldn't last forever.

The Wizard smirked, "Have it your way." He hissed, holding the crystal out, his hand twitching as he prepared to send something awful to strike.

The energy was coursing through him, as his eyes bore down on Felix, neither of them saw it coming.

Zarah appeared as if a shadow, just as Felix's sword moved to strike and the Wizard released his magic.

The world seemed to move in slow motion for Felix as he watched in horror, twisting his blade away at the last second, but it wasn't enough.

Zarah's blade hit its mark, slicing through the Wizard's arm, separating the crystal from the rest of his body as it began to fall.

But the Wizard's magic had already been cast, Zarah had taken Felix's place as his target, and there was no one protecting him.

The magic hit, and for a moment the world went dark as Zarah turned bright. It was as though he had absorbed the sun, if only for a moment.

He hadn't even begun to fall when the crystal struck the earth, shattering into a million shards of glowing amber.

The blast that followed sent a wave of power surging from the place of impact. The surge was so strong that it knocked Felix back and left a crater in the earth.

The magic had returned, but something had gone wrong.

A rift had opened, a shimmer in the darkness, there was something on the other side. It reminded Felix of the Mirrors in the field on End Key, the light reaching to the heavens.

He could feel it pulling, trying to suck a piece of Avidaura towards whatever was on the other side.

Zarah's body had landed, too close to the rift, too close to being taken away.

Felix rushed forward, pulling Zarah away, he could feel the power surging through his body, and knew that it was already too late for him, but he couldn't let him go, he couldn't let him be gone.

His skin was like stone, as Felix turned Zarah over, resting his head against his shoulder he could see the pain in his eyes.

"Zarah." He whispered, ignoring the chaos that had erupted around him. He could see Ash and Piper racing towards the rift, busy with something that didn't matter to him anymore.

"Zarah?" He stared into his eyes, seeing the pain as they rolled back.

"Felix…finish it." His voice cracked, "You earned the crown, your father would be proud." It seemed like he was turning to stone, his body was growing stiff and cold, his eyes growing dark, "*I'm* proud of you…" His voice faded, his lips drying as the skin turned black. The spell had done its work, Zarah had taken what was meant for Felix.

"Zarah?" Felix whispered his name, though he knew that there would be no answer.

He didn't say another word, though Felix held him there, unmoving, ignoring the world around him; pretending that he hadn't just lost Zarah as the stone form in his hands began to crack, and piece by piece he had to let him go.

END

As the carnelian crystal struck the ground and shattered, it sent out a wave of power that knocked everyone in its path. Ash felt it rip through her as she fell to the ground landing in a heap. The soil beneath her fingers surged beneath her palm as the magic returned to Avidaura. Her necklace began to glow, it was hot on her chest, and for a moment she was sure that it would shatter from the energy surging through it.

She could feel it coursing through her veins, the magic that she had lost, amplified again as it was restored to her.

"Piper!" She shouted, turning to find her sister on the ground beside her, "It's back." She breathed, though the look on her sisters face told her that Piper already knew.

"Ash, look!" Piper shouted, leaping back to her feet as she stared at the place where the crystal had fallen, Ash followed her stare, rising from the ground to follow her.

The crystal had created a rift, a tear in the fabric of time itself. It was as though a mirror had opened, though there was nothing to contain it. The Wizard stood beside the opening, and Ash knew that they would have to hurry, or he would take the easy way out of Avidaura.

It was dark on the other side of the portal, there was no way of knowing where it led, and Ash wasn't wanting to follow the Wizard through to the other side, Piper's world had been enough for her for one lifetime.

"Now!" Ash shouted to Piper, through the ringing in her ears. The two charged forward, past Felix who seemed frozen. He was on the ground, the last of their weak magic had saved him from the crystal's blast, but he seemed preoccupied with something so Ash rushed past him without stopping.

The rift seemed to be sucking Avidaura through, a Hobgoblin struggled near the edge of the portal, finally losing its battle as it was sucked to the other side. The Wizard's robes seemed to be pulling him towards the opening, though he stood still, staring at the rift as he considered what might be on the other side, eying it as though he planned on using it as an escape route.

Finnigan reached him first, he came out of the darkness, leaping onto the Wizard's back before he could take the easy way out, and disappear to whatever was on the other side.

The Wizard was bleeding from the stump where his hand had once been, but his powers were not gone. He flicked his arm to the sky and Finnigan was tossed aside, barely missing the rift as he landed in a heap on the ground.

Ash grabbed Piper's hand, reaching for the pearl in her cloaks. The Wizard didn't have time to move before Ash had cast her powers at him, trapping him as she allowed the pearl to drain his power.

He had been all powerful only minutes earlier, the look on his face as the last of his natural magic drained from him was pathetic. Ash felt a twinge of guilt at what she was about to do, but then she remembered why she was doing it, and what he had done to deserve it.

Her father had been his first victim.

The Wizard was contained, but it wouldn't last. Finnigan had already gotten back to his feet, taking the Wizard's arms behind his back and pushing him forward through Ash and Piper.

"You will kneel before the True King, and he will decide your fate." Finnigan grunted, taking the Wizard past the sisters towards Felix.

King Felix was on his knees, his face turned downward, his hands held before him, shaking, and empty. He turned as he heard Finnigan approach, his eyes flashing as he saw the Wizard.

In one swift movement, Felix rose from his feet, his sword slicing through the air as he drove it through the chest of the Dark Wizard.

"It's over!" Felix shouted into the night. His blade forgotten in the chest of the Wizard, who had already slumped over at Finnigan's feet.

There was no cheering, no moment of joy. The swords dropped to the ground on the battlefield. The Dragons, those that were left, lifted into the air to return to the Badlands.

The army gathered, slowly moving towards Felix as he stood before the Wizard. It was a silence like nothing Felix had ever heard, it could be felt like the a chill in the air.

"You did it." Piper appeared from the crowd, her arm was bleeding, her face covered in mud. But she was smiling like nothing Felix had ever seen before.

"What?" He wasn't sure that it was really over, he looked around, realizing that indeed, the battle had finished, and they had come out victorious.

"You did it." Piper repeated, Ash appeared at her side, "You saved Avidaura."

"Now what?" Ash asked, staring past Felix at the still burning fires, the portal resting on the path, the chaos that had finally ended.

"Now we have to put it back together." Felix stared into the sea of tired faces, the injured, the maimed, they had survived.

He looked to his feet, the remnants of Zarah long gone in the soil beneath him.

Nothing would ever be the same.

ABOUT THE AUTHOR

Katlin Murray lives in Cambridge Ontario, where she spends her days working as a Production Manager and Author. When she isn't in her office typing or on a film set, she likes to spend time outside on adventures with her two boys.

For more about Katlin Murray and the Avidaura universe visit:
KatlinMurray.com
Or
Avidaura.com

Made in the USA
Middletown, DE
14 October 2021